THEY CALL ME GOMER...

by

JC Miller

ISBN: 978-1-7339386-4-8

Library of Congress Control Number: 2020918264

This is a work of fiction. Any references to historical events, real people, or real places are used fictitiously. Names, characters, and places are products of the author's imagination or used in a fictitious manner.

The Holy Bible, New International Version®, NIV® Copyright © 1973, 1978, 1984, 2011 by Biblica, Inc. ™ Used by permission. All rights reserved worldwide.
The World English Bible is in the Public Domain.
"Joy to the World" written by Isaac Watts 1719.
"Rock of Ages" written by Rev. Augustus M. Toplady 1763.
"His Eye is on the Sparrow" Civilla D. Martin and Charles H. Gabriel 1905.
"O Child of God, Wait Patiently!" written by Frances Jane Crosby and Ira D. Sankey 1886.
"Cinderella Dressed in Yellow" Jump Rope Rhyme
"Quote on Love" by Oscar Wilde

Front cover art: @llartismylifell
Book graphic design: Chanel Smith, WPD Media LLC
Editing: Tee Marshall, Marshall Editing and Consulting

Printed in the United States of America.
First printing edition 2020.

Jess, Mo' Books LLC
P.O. Bx. 1808
Albrightsville, PA. 18210
www.jessmobooks.com

Dedicated to homegirls everywhere. You rock!

Table of Contents

INTRODUCTION

They call me Gomer, but who is she?
Another brown-skinned girl in this overpopulated world withdrawn in her own skin?
Invisible to men?
Uncounted?
Overlooked?
Misplaced amongst the nation...like a worthless thing.
A beast came and swallowed me whole.
I'm on the inside looking outside.
I hear with its ears.
I speak with its voice. A language, not mine.
I'm in a beast, or is the beast my mentality?
These were my invisible years.

Dear Diary: *December 12, 1994*

My dream guy drives a midnight blue Lexus GS, pimped out in a full body kit with chrome BBS rims, and a sleek black leather interior. He cruises the streets in a gangsta lean, with tinted windows deliberately rolled down so that everyone can see him with me.

My dream guy is a smooth chocolate brother, a Nubian king, who smells as good as he looks. From the crown of his S-Curl parted box fade to the sole of his Jordan Steel kicks, his gear is always tight. The gold and diamond-encrusted Jesus piece he wears around his neck cost more than the average yearly salary in the hood. Everyone gives him props. He earns respect, and you dare not cross him. He'll shoot anyone who gets out of line and not think twice about it.

My dream guy and me, we eat expensive seafood dinners at fancy restaurants. We sit at the VIP tables in the clubs and sip on bottles of Cristal while losers straight-up jock us hard. I can't blame them though; we do look good together.

At night, my dream guy lays me back in our king size bed, in our leather decorated penthouse apartment overlooking the city, and he makes...my...mind...and body...feel...free.

You ever know a dream guy and wanted him so bad you'd do just about anything to be with him? I know mine, and his boo ain't me.

Damn shame,
Go-Go

PROLOGUE - MY DREAM GUY

"What the—?" Jeri spontaneously yelps, reaching for the gun strapped under his jacket as he enters his penthouse apartment. He's startled, but I dare not move an inch. I continue to seductively pose, standing in his hallway, buck-naked and awaiting him, glistening in my sister's oils. You would think that I would feel self-conscious, but nope, I don't have any shame. I'm nowhere near being fit, but my curves are all in the right places.

"Why don't we stop playing games?" I coyly smile and strike another sensuous position against the wall.

"How the heck did you get in here?" He grills me, regaining his cool and lustfully staring like I'm a surf-and-turf meal that he's about to indulge. He removes his mink-trimmed leather coat and tosses it to the floor. I inhale deeply.

The smell of expensive stuff does something to me. A brisk chill runs down my spine. *This could all be mine. Whoa.* I exhale, attempting to play it cool but the excitement has already reached my breasts. I reveal the spare key that Rah, my sister, and his boo, made in case of emergencies, dangling from a rabbit-foot keyring hooked around my pointer finger. I bite down on my bottom lip. *Eeeooowww, it's about to be on.*

"Pfft! I should've known that key was a mistake." Jeri removes his pagers and then loosens his tie. There's no doubt he's referring to giving Rah the key to his world when he should have given it to me.

Earlier, at Jeri's strip club, *Vixens*, I witnessed him in what seemed like a vengeful ranting, pimp Rah out in an auction to the highest bidder. He was acting like she wasn't the girl he'd been boasting about being his ride or die for the past six years. Sensing a break-up, I quickly made my move and jumped on the chance to become my sister's replacement. I didn't stop to think of the consequences. From the moment I met Jeri, I craved him like chocolate. So when the opportunity arose, I tossed caution to the wind and left the club early with a plan of seduction in mind.

Strutting down the hall boldly, wearing only a pair of black patent leather stilettos, I stop to allow Jeri to absorb all my lushness, then I toss him the spare key. He catches it mid-air with one hand without taking his eyes off me. I swallow hard. *Hmm, a multi-tasker. That's what I'm talkin' bout.*

"So, what you wanna do?" I pop my fingers and roll my neck.

Jeri takes a step toward me. I can feel the rhythm of Jamaica beating in sync with his diddy-bop. He licks his lips and moves in fast. *Oh, snap!* I brace myself. *This is really happening.* His favorite rap group is *Wu-Tang Clan.* As he approaches, I swear I can hear the chorus to "*Shimmy Shimmy Ya,*" by *Ol' Dirty Bastard*, playing from the back of his mind. Raw isn't what I was expecting. Naively, I anticipated something smoother like *Denzel Washington's* character *Bleek Gilliam*, with his sexy self, playing the trumpet. Some rose petals and candles scattered about, and Jeri lifting my big butt off the ground, but he doesn't. He rips off his shirt—the buttons and all. He's built like Adonis. I melt.

"Oh, damn!" I say out loud, mentally scanning his god-like image for future reference.

Jeri's eagerness is making me nervous. I lead him into his bedroom, hoping the change of atmosphere can conjure up a more romantic and gentle side of him. I want this dream to play out in high-definition slow motion and not fast forward. The bedroom setting only excites him more. He doesn't give me a chance to become a part of the moment. Before I know it, Jeri is kneading my body like dough, but no shivers run up my spine. His strong clammy hands grab me but don't hold me in an embrace. His juicy lips are sweet but not as sweet as I imagined. His mouth is cold, and his kisses lack the transformative ability to carry me away. I'm still not where I'm supposed to be. Instantly guilt and remorse set in, but it was too late for that. Jeri is grunting, humping, and speaking in tongues on top of me. I try to psych myself into enjoying the moment that I dreamt of all these years, but I can't. *This negro is high, and he smells of too much tequila.* My eyes are on my chocolate dream, but his eyes are not on me. *Yo, don't you realize that this is us...or maybe it was only my dream?* Jeri roars in prematurely released pleasure. *Damn, I really should have had a V8...I mean like really.*

I'm just about to curse him out when Rah, who wasn't invited, but not altogether unexpected, hysterically yells from the bedroom door.

"Go-Go! What are you doing?" Her eyes frantically dot over the forbidden scene. Still, from her expression, I can tell that she hasn't fully registered what she witnessed.

Jeri and I scramble in shock. I shield my naked body with my arms, while he instinctively jumps for his pistol on the nightstand.

"Damn," he mumbles under his breath, placing the pistol down and picking up a cigar instead. "Well, isn't this a blip," he teases with impish laughter, leaning back on the plush white pillows that Rah decorated their bed with. He lights the stogie, laughing harder. Payback is written all over his face, and that's why I love him. We're the same kind of evil.

"How could you? Why would you?" Rah asks, mainly toward me. The betrayal is tearing her delicate heart apart, and I'm embarrassed but gloating nevertheless in my achievement.

I lean back into Jeri's outstretched arm. All these years, I waited for Rah to familiarize herself with the pain of defeat. *Yup, I'm taking this front-row seat.* An arrogant mien smears across my brazen face, but at the same time, I can't help but wonder, *what am I doing?* Our eyes lock. Suddenly, I feel like I'm 8-years-old again, and it's September 3, 1982. Two things happened on that day that I'll never forget: I acquired an older sister, and I fell in real love.

PART 1: 1982

Rahab, the Older Sister

I never wanted or needed an older sister, so I don't know why Puah, well, we call her Poo, that's my mother; brought one home. Daddy nicknamed me Princess Go-Go for obvious reasons. Whatever mistakes Poo made in her past, she should have left them where they were. The speech she nervously practiced on the ride home from the funeral she attended in Louisiana didn't go over well. We were all emotional wrecks, and Senior, my daddy, wasn't helping either.

"I promise you're going to love her!" Poo declared, wiping me and Sy's wet eyes and runny noses to hush our crying.

I didn't know why I was crying; hearing my older brother cry made me cry as well. Silas was a tough kid. Our parents didn't baby us...well, maybe they babied me...just a little. But if Sy was crying, it was serious. Poo just sprung the news that we had an older sister named Rahab Auguste. *What kinda butt-ugly name is that?* I remember thinking. I was a rude kid too.

"But...what about us?" Sy asked in between the sniffling that followed his hard cry. I nodded in agreement, sniffling myself.

"What about you?" Poo asked, catching the harshness in her tone. She was rough around the edges. In the most motherly tone she could conjure up, she rephrased, "Sy, I'm always going to love you and Go-Go." She knelt on her knees and drew us near. She was even more beautiful up close. Sy pulled away from her.

Are we supposed to be mad, too? How could I be? Poo smelled and looked like a goddess. I rubbed her worried face and she attempted a smile.

"Including Rah into our family isn't going to change how much I love you, Sy." Although Poo's cliché response was comforting, he was undoubtedly worried about our security.

Would Poo abandon us? I thought about it and I know my brother did too.

When Rah was a few months old, Poo left her in Louisiana under her mother's supervision and ran away to New York City in search of a new life. Our grandmother, Big Mama, whom I never knew, raised Rah for nearly twelve years then suddenly died. Poo was returning home from laying the dead to rest and collecting her tarnished past from the Bayou. Embarrassed, she explained to us that Rah was the unfortunate result of her being raped at a young age. The experience was too much for her to deal with, so she ran.

"I was young and afraid," Poo insisted, dotting her eyes between me and Sy. "But I want you both to know, and accept, that despite everything, I love her." She squeezed us tightly, looking to Senior for support. Annoyed, Daddy turned up his nose and twisted his mouth; we could tell that he wasn't pleased with the situation either.

Senior was jealous-hearted when it came to Poo. He watched over her like a hawk, so much so, it got in the way of their relationship.

"Leaving Rah behind the way that I did was a mistake," Poo continued, trying to coax us into seeing things her way. "I'm sorry for keeping her a secret. Can you guys please forgive me, and let's try to start over?"

"Okay," we sniffled in unison, nuzzled under our mother's arms, but we both still felt the fear permeating in our hearts of the changes to come.

Sy was eleven-years-old at the time. He sort of understood. A neighborhood girl was raped on the roof of a building during Christmas break. Her disappearance was all the gossip that summer. Some rumored she had a baby and gave it up for adoption; others said that she was forced to move far away. Whatever the case, Sy was afraid. I, on the other hand, at eight and a half-years-old hardly understood what Poo was rambling about, but I read the disgust on Senior's face, and Sy's tears commenced me to cry.

After twenty minutes of us whining and asking too many questions, Poo announced that she was seconds away from telling everyone where they could stick their drama and how far to shove it. She was nervous, and our lack of compassion was making her angry. *Things are going to change around here.* I pulled my act together. After all, we were already dysfunctional; how much worse could things get? Adding another kid only meant more company for me and Sy. Our parents were barely home. They worked hard and played even harder. *The O'Jays* must have been singing about Senior and Poo when they wrote, *"Livin' For the Weekend."*

Latchkey Kids

Poo was a registered nurse. She worked night shifts and slept through the day. Senior owned two dry cleaning businesses. But on Friday nights, come what may, they punched in their timecards, laid their burdens down, and partied the weekends away.

Sy and I were latchkey kids. When we arrived home from school, usually, Poo was running out to make a double shift. Some days we came back to an empty house. Senior stumbled in around six or seven o'clock at night with take-out dinners, but he quickly disappeared into his bedroom carrying a six-pack of *Coors* under his arm, and a bottle of *MD 20/20* tucked away in his coat pocket. Most nights, he laid in bed drinking and cussing. Sometimes he got up and disappeared for a few hours, but by morning he was always home, sobered up, and ready for work.

On the weekends, Sy and I occasionally stayed with friends, but mostly we slept over at our grandparents, Paw-Paw and Tante Maw-Maw's house. They were a different type of dysfunctional. Their crazy was seasoned well throughout the years, and they didn't run amok like Poo and Senior. When they were going through their drama, we weren't permitted to visit at all. Tante Maw-Maw enjoyed her liquor, but when she was babysitting, she preferred to be focused. She enforced stern rules and kept a strict eye on us. I wasn't even allowed to be alone with my own grandfather. Tante Maw-Maw insisted, "Young ladies should never play with grown mens and 'em. They should never be alone with 'em...and don't you ever let me catch you sittin' on no man's lap, ya hear!" That was a big no-no. Despite her many odd rules, we loved going to their house. They spoiled us rotten. But when Tante Maw-Maw got to drinking, no one could visit, nor would anyone want to. Tante Maw-Maw, who is, in reality, our great-aunt, mastered binge drinking. Only in periods of what she called her *moods* did she drink excessively. What Tante Maw-Maw was, was bipolar, and, at times, psychotic.

Paw-Paw is Poo's biological father, Big Mama is her mother. Paw-Paw married Tante Maw-Maw who is Big Mama's younger sister. The dysfunction doesn't fall that far from the tree. In their youth, Paw-Paw and Tante Maw-Maw performed with a cabaret act. She danced and sang, and he played the saxophone. By 1982, when Rah entered our lives, Tante Maw-Maw and Paw-Paw were well established as proud owners of a jazz nightclub and a neighborhood bar. They lived in a beautiful brownstone in Harlem and owned a beach house in Sag Harbor.

The Green-Eyed Monster

Poo kept a watchful eye on the front window of our house, waiting for Tante Maw-Maw and Paw-Paw to arrive with Rah. Tante Maw-Maw and Poo traveled to Louisiana together for Big Mama's funeral. They brought Rah back with them. Paw-Paw and Tante Maw-Maw took Rah to City Island for dinner while Poo came home to break the news about her to us. It was also Rah's 12th birthday that day, and they all felt that they should try to do a little something for her despite all the drama that was taking place. It wasn't Rah's fault, she was a child.

Poo almost jumped out of her skin when Paw-Paw pulled up in front of the house in his fancy pimped-out *1981 Lincoln Mark VI*. In anticipation to greet them, she swung open the front door and nervously watched as he struggled to park his baby, *Burgundy Mama* is what he called her, into a tight spot. Paw-Paw was attempting not to hit a yellow moving truck that he was going to be blocking in.

"They're here!" Poo announced, anxiously fixing herself in a gaudy oval-shaped mirror adorning the wall of our small but functional foyer. Sy and I ran by her side to catch a glimpse of the new sister that no one wanted. We stood under Poo's arms and wrapped ourselves around her body, feeling both apprehensive and territorial.

Paw-Paw walked around the car to open the doors for the ladies. He smiled and waved at us.

"Y'all ready to meet your big sister?"

Sy ran back into the house as soon as he saw Rah's foot hit the pavement, but I took a deep breath and edged out from the doorway. My heart raced. *How will she look?*

A thin, high-yellow leg wrapped in faded denim was attached to the foot that sent Sy running. Paw-Paw spoke softly to her, trying to persuade her that everything would be alright.

"Come on now, sweetheart, let's meet the rest of the family. Come on now—they ain't gonna bite." He took her hand like she was the Queen of England and helped her out of the car.

Just great—she's pretty! I remember thinking. Pretty girls get what they want, and I had our house under wraps. *But why is she dressed like a boy?* I moved in closer for a better look at the wolf in sheep's clothing but quickly glanced back at Poo for approval.

Poo's face was reddened with pride. Her hands were clasped together by her mouth, and her eyes sparkled in a teary delight. She hadn't given me a second thought. "*Don't you dare go out of that gate,*" she usually warned when I tried to leave the house without her permission. That's when it happened. The green-eyed monster reared its ugly head. Poo squealed, and she's not a squealer, then she ran right past me to greet Rah.

I was baffled. This wasn't the usual protocol. I watched as everyone kissed, embraced, and oohed and ahhed over Rah, forgetting that I existed. The merriment only stopped when the angry driver of the yellow moving truck loudly beeped his horn for Paw-Paw to move his car. *Burgundy Mama* was blocking him in on our one-way street, he couldn't pull out. After cursing out the impatient driver for honking his horn at him, and for his truck being, "Too doggone long for this tight behind block in the first place," Paw-Paw grudgingly moved his car. That's when I caught first sight of our new neighbor.

Hosea Felix stood behind the yellow moving truck holding his father's hand. He looked like the widow *Prissy's* son, *Eggbert,* from *Looney Tunes Foghorn Leghorn* cartoons. Hosea's circular glasses, too big for his round face, sat low on his flat nose. He waved shyly toward me, and I forgot about my abandonment. I waved back at him with enthusiasm and instantly fell in love.

Lavender in Summer Breeze

Sy lingered under Senior for the remainder of that evening, which wasn't usual for him. That night, they shared a unified disliking of Rah and found comfort in each other's misery. They pretended to watch television while covertly eyeing her acclimating herself to the house. I tagged along behind her and Poo. Rah seemed sad or lost, and for me, that softened her appeal. She also had a head full of sandy-brown hair that I couldn't wait to play in. *My Make Me Pretty, Barbie* styling head suddenly lost its playtime.

Poo situated Rah in my room and promised to buy us new bed sets. We both agreed on bunk beds. However, I cried when Poo and Rah began talking about new color patterns and changing things around. I was growing tired of the girly *Pepto Bismol* pink colored walls, but I didn't want anyone changing my room without my permission. Hanging out with Senior and Sy, watching television, suddenly became more interesting.

By the evening's end, as family programming turned into late-night shows and Poo and Daddy started carrying-on over each other, we were sent to our rooms for bed. Poo straightened the matching *Pepto Bismol* colored ruffled satin sheets on my canopy bed, then placed pillows on either end.

"Y'all try and make do until we can go furniture shopping." She kissed our foreheads before leaving the room. "Don't stay up too much longer," she added, then closed the door.

Rah was still settling in. A big cumbersome wooden trunk that she appeared fond of sat opened in the middle of the bedroom floor. It was full of different things, but not much clothing, and I was glad of that. My walk-in closets were full to their capacity, and Poo was already talking about putting my things into storage to make room. My inner princess was not happy about that.

"What's that?" I asked, curious about the wooden trunk Rah was busying over.

"Muy Big Mama's chest," she answered in a quick Creole drawl that took me and Sy some time to get accustomed to. "You wanna see what's in it?"

I jumped off the bed and took a seat on the floor near the mysterious trunk filled with all types of pretty colored jars, bags of dried flowers and herbs, ribbons, sachets, tools, handwritten notes, fabric, and doo-dads. It smelled delightful, and Rah had fascinating stories for each item.

"Here, tie a few bushels of dis here lavender together." She handed me some white ribbon and stems of dried flowers. I dared not ask why. At the time, I was particularly curious and just wanted to be a part of whatever she was doing. "Ya tink Poo will let me plant some seeds in de backyard?"

"Probably," I answered, focused on my task. *Poo will probably let you do whatever you want.* We were all acutely aware of the guilt that she was feeling.

"Ah can't imagine living without lavender or sweet rosemary," Rah was worried about what she was going to do when her stock of Big Mama's homemade oils, soaps, and elixirs ran out. It was all she was accustomed to and explained her sweet scent and radiant glow.

Rah dug through her treasures and pulled a plastic *Winn-Dixie* bag out from the trunk. She patiently began to untie the knot holding it together. Once done, she inhaled its contents and smiled brightly. She quickly unlatched her overalls and pulled the faded orange Houston Astros tee-shirt she wore over her head. Without any hesitation or embarrassment, on her part, she removed her flesh-toned bra. Her bosom was as big as Poos. I tried not to stare, but I was impressed. *...and I'm supposed to believe this girl is twelve?* She continued, pulling from the bag a brightly patterned silk fabric then fanned it open, revealing an oversized Muumuu. She tugged it on over her head, inhaled its scent, and smiled her enchanted smile again; then, she slipped out of her dingy overalls and tennis sneakers. Rah pranced across the floor and admired herself in the dresser mirror.

"Dis here is Big Mama's house gown...still smells lak her—see."

She allowed me to sniff the scent of our grandmother still trapped in the fabric. I turned up my nose. *Vicks!* It smelled like menthol, on top of the same floral scent that Rah smelled like. I half-smiled and rubbed the silky fabric between my fingertips. I never met Big Mama; I didn't even know she existed. Smelling the material again, I wondered how she looked, probably like Poo in her heavily creamed caramel-colored skin. I admired Rah in the flowing gown. *Now she looks like a girl.* I wondered if I had anything silky to wear. Intrigued, I jumped up and rummaged through my bureau drawers until I found a *Care Bear* gown that was of a similar fabric. I sucked my teeth. *Why don't I have silky things?* Embarrassed, I changed clothes while hiding in the corner, my breasts didn't meet the big girl cut—they hadn't even come out of the dug-out yet. Rah didn't notice, at least, she pretended not to. She proceeded to hang the dried lavender tied to white ribbons from the window frame.

"Dis here will keep de skeetas out and freshen de room up fuh sho." She busied herself, rearranging things. I followed behind her, placing items that we hadn't previously agreed on relocating back in their original positions.

"Thank ya, fuh sharing ya room." She noticed my agitation. I wasn't the average little sister, but I could tell that Rah liked me. We were both feisty. How could we not be with a mother like Poo?

After fussing around with the room, Rah sat in my rocking chair near the opened window and began writing a letter to a friend back home; a boy. I wondered if Poo knew about him, but I decided not to tell—yet. Since Rah was in my chair, I took the opportunity to play in her hair. I loosened the thick messy braid and released bundles of sandy-colored curls and twirls. I brushed the bush that looked like it hadn't been tamed in a minute. Rah sighed in relief. She rested her shoulders and laid her head back with her eyes closed. Tears unexpectedly rolled from her eyes and she quickly wiped them away. I think I reminded her of her Big

Mama, and she needed remembering. The late-night lavender-scented summer breeze blew through the opened window as we quietly talked about things we didn't know about each other. All the while, Hosea Felix watched from his neighboring bedroom window and esteemed me in his heart.

Break, For Love

Dear Diary: June 4, 1992

There is no one like Hosea. Where I fall short, he fills in my spaces. Besides Daddy, he's my first love and best friend. He genuinely wants to be with my crazy behind self, and I promise you—there was no bullying, bribery, or blackmail involved on my part. Hosea came along willingly and by his own contentment. I can't keep a friend to save my life, but Hosea Felix has stuck like glue. He doesn't care that I'm ratchet, common, and unworthy; being Christ-like, he covers me. We've loved each other from day one...but sometimes I wonder, what's love got to do with it...you know? I put Hosea through hell, and as a dog returns to its own puke, he keeps coming back. A tragic romance. I don't deserve him...and I often wonder, how did I make a friend like Zee? Lucky, I guess.

Go-Go

An Oasis

Hosea Felix moved to Charlotte Street from Brooklyn the summer that I lost my way. Before then, I was accustomed to being pampered. Hosea caught me at a time when my life took a horrible spin. Sister became like a mother. Brother was like a father and life as we knew it forever changed.

Hosea wasn't shy, but he was little for words. He wasn't fresh, dope, or debonair, but he had an aura about himself that drew people near. Me, on the other hand, I'm always seeking attention, and I'm not shy about conversation either. I went straight to Hosea's house that following morning after breakfast to introduce myself. Rah had captivated our household, and I needed an out. When Senior discovered that she could cook, he and Sy took turns running to the supermarket and bringing back all types of ingredients for her to cook their favorite dishes. My parents couldn't boil water. Having a live-in chef was big news. When I left that morning, Rah was busying around the kitchen like the Cajun chef on *PBS*. Although the eggs and bacon they spoke of sounded delicious, I had other plans in mind. I gobbled down two bowls of *Cookie Crisp*, mixed with *Smurf Berry Crunch*, and got out of the house before Senior returned with the groceries. I asked Poo if I could go meet the new kid next door; she agreed, and Sy walked me over.

Charlotte Street was a beautiful yet unusual place to live compared to the areas surrounding it in the South Bronx. It was like an oasis in the middle of dry land. Some wise guys downtown decided to build prefabricated houses on an abandoned stretch of land for middle-class brown folk. The South Bronx in the early 1980s was indeed a burnt down borough; every hoodlum, vagabond, and reject lived there. Poo and Senior knew the struggle, and they did their best to protect us from outside corruption. That's what the prefabricated house was for—our protection. But when the streets call your name as loudly as they called mine, usually you come running. I guess that's why I was escorted everywhere.

"Can your little boy come outside to play?" I asked the tall, dark-skinned man with the well-trimmed mustache that I saw the day before holding the little boy's hand. With one hand on my hip and the other holding a jump rope, I rolled my neck when I spoke, not with an attitude but being fo'ward as Tante Maw-Maw called it. Sy nudged my arm, reminding me of my manners. I looked up at him and rolled my eyes then gave the man answering the door a half-smile.

"Can my likkle boy come outside to play with you?" The man repeated in a proper Trinidadian English accent loud enough for his wife and son to hear. I thought that he was correcting me because kids used to make fun of my raspy voice.

"Yeah! That's what I said, Mistah." I curled-up my nose in disapproval. The man was beside himself. He looked at me like he was thinking, *who the heck is this little girl.*

Hosea and his family were *Seventh-day Adventists.* I would learn not to call on him from sundown Friday to sundown Saturday in observation of their Sabbath. Hosea's dad, Barry, answered the door that morning, expecting *Ma Bell.* They had a service connection appointment between the hours of 8 am and noon. Flabbergasted, Barry looked like he started to tell me something like, *we're in prayer. Maybe Hosea can come out later,* but his son walked past him with a marble notepad tucked under his arm.

"Dad, ah believe ah ready. De harvest is plentiful," Hosea uttered, winking, referring to a bible text his father once quoted him in trying to get him more involved with other kids. "*If you going to layba for Christ, Hosea, you must first be willing to harvest de field. Doh merely hear de Word, be a doer as well.*"

Hosea was ten-years-old, going on forty when I met him. As an only child to older parents, he didn't play much. He had an old soul. He preferred reading books, playing the drums at church, and spending time with his family over playing with children his own age. When I showed up at his front door, every ounce of his being said, **"Get up and move."** Hosea breezed past his father and stopped in front of me. He pushed his glasses up on his nose and smiled.

"Come on, then!" I grabbed him by the arm and pulled him through the doorway.

Still shocked, Barry reached for his son, but his wife, Anna, had come to the door and firmly rested her hand on his shoulder.

"Leh em play, Beeri," she whispered, slightly teary-eyed.

Sy offered to come back and pick me up in an hour or so, which ticked me off, but Anna insisted on letting me stay as long as I wanted. *Humph!*

"Leh her be, man, dey limin'," she joked, impressed that her son was having fun. "Yuh de neighba live here, right?" She pointed to our house.

"Yes, ma'am," Sy responded, ready to leave. He had some errands to run and didn't want to miss any of his Saturday afternoon Kung-Fu flicks.

"We'll make sure dat...wha' she name?"

"Elizabeth," Sy answered, using my first name. He knew I hated it. Looking concerned, he watched as I ran Hosea around their front yard. When our eyes met, he mouthed, "*STOP IT*," feeling I was being too rough on the new kid. Sy wanted me to be able to stay, not because he cared about my happiness, but because he wanted the television to himself. Back then, there was only one TV per household, not counting the big one that the little one sat on top of—that never worked, it was strictly for show.

"We'll bring she home shortly," Barry added, smiling to himself at how quickly Hosea and I connected. His son was laughing, and it seemed odd to him.

Anna, as I would learn, wasn't keen on entertaining company outside of family members. She made an exception for me. Had Anna known earlier of the mischief and misery I'd bring the family, I bet she would have reconsidered Hosea and me spending so much time together. Anna is the Felix household representative, and she doesn't hold her tongue.

Barry, on the other hand, is a Trinidadian gentleman. He's a school teacher by trade, but he moved his family to the South Bronx to accept a Vice-Principal position at our local elementary school. He and his wife heard of the rebuilding and formalization plans happening on Charlotte Street and decided to also invest in one of the newly fabricated affordable homes.

Jump In

"What's that," I asked, noticing Hosea's marble notepad. He had already lost his stamina from running and sat on his stoop to rest. I jumped rope in front of him.

"It's like a journal," Hosea stated, patting the notepad and inquisitively observing me from over the top of his glasses. I was a slightly overweight but agile brown girl who could keep up with the rhythm of a jump-rope. He seemed impressed and cleaned his smudged glasses for a better look. I must have looked angelic because his head tilted as he stared in a trance.

"What do you write about?" I was curious. I kept a diary myself.

"Huh?" He shook his head and cleared his throat, coming from the trance.

"What do you write about...in the book?" I repeated, shaking my head and giggling. *This one is strange,* but I was as captivated as he was with me.

"Oh!" he snickered. "It's a prayer book. Whenever I pray for something, I write it down. When the prayer is answered, I write that down too." He opened the book and turned into its crinkled pages. "It helps me to remain grateful. Look! See here?" He turned the notepad toward me.

I stopped jumping rope and leaned over the book, squinting my eyes. I didn't have on my glasses. I hated wearing the designer frames that

Tante Maw-Maw bought me. They made me look nerdy, and nobody was going to be calling me four-eyes. Thank God, I grew out of them.

"I can't read in cursive yet," I fibbed, but was still curious about what it said. The only people I knew who prayed were on television.

"Let's see...about one year ago, I asked God to send me a best friend." Hosea approvingly smiled, then checked off a box near the prayer request and noted the date and time. I couldn't help but smile too; he was both weird and charming.

"What's your name?" He asked, finally getting around to formalities. As an efficient note-taker, he needed it for input.

I proudly said, wanting to make sure that my name was clearly stated as 'the best friend,' "Elizabeth Gomer Williams, but you can call me Go-Go, or Go like everybody else. I hate Elizabeth—it's a white girl's name." I watched, squinting over his shoulder to make sure he entered it correctly.

"I'm Hosea Felix," he announced since I hadn't asked.

"Ho-zee-ah?" I squinched up my nose. I never heard that name before. It sounded like José, and I didn't like a boy named José. He was a fat, dirty-faced bully I went to school with. He was a ten-year-old with a mustache, or most likely, a dirt stache. José Rivera used to purposely trip me up and tease me about my weight like he wasn't chubby himself. We fought every day, and I wasn't one to be played with. I wish this were all I had to say about José; unfortunately, he has a more prominent role in my life than he should. "I'm calling you Zee." I spontaneously decided, being that Hosea emphasized on the 's' and 'e' in his name, as Zee. "Yup...that's fresh," I went back to jumping rope directly in front of him.

Zee smiled. He tilted his rock head and nodded in approval—like *hmm, this chick is dope.* At least that's what I thought of myself. He told me that his name had never accompanied the slang word fresh before. He put his notebook down and stood up, ready to play some more. I was jumping rope in a slow up and down fashion, and I guess Zee felt it looked simple enough for him to try. After all, he was now—fresh. I hopped backward to give him some room, swinging the rope wide enough to accompany him. Zee turned red and bashfully stepped away.

What's wrong with this kid? Everybody knows how to jump rope. Sy jumped Double Dutch better than any girl on the block. Girls asked him to play rope with them before asking me. Just because my glands were swollen didn't mean I couldn't jump. Big girls are light on their feet. That's why I played by myself—I didn't mess with anybody! But I was curious about my new friend, Zee. It might seem strange, or maybe strange to me, but I wanted to know about the prayer book. I slowed my jumping down a little. *Come on, bro, a kindergartener can get with this.* Zee looked like he was counting in his head—mapping out the pattern. I shook my head in disappointment. *Up...down...up...down. Cinderella, dressed in yella. Went upstairs to kiss her fella.* Easy. "Do you go to church?"

"Yes, usually on Saturdays."

Made a mistake and kissed a snake. How many doctors did it take? 1, 2, 3...

Zee was focused. He pushed his sliding glasses back up on his nose, took a step backward, and began rocking in the jump-in motion that he'd seen other kids do. At least he had rhythm.

4, 5, 6... "What did you do wrong?" I blurted, replaying old television reruns in my mind, like *The Waltons*. To me, God was the man in the sky that television characters, especially *Laura Ingalls* from *Little House on the Prairie*, prayed to when they required something or did something wrong.

"What do you mean by that?" Sensing his timing, Zee successfully jumped in. I turned the telephone cable that I used as a jump-rope faster as we got into a groove.

"My mother says that people go to church and pray and stuff like that because...they did something wrong and want to feel better about it." I lied. I didn't want the sparkling light brown-eyed young man smiling hard as he jumped along with me to think that I knew absolutely nothing about church and God and all that. It wasn't a topic of conversation at home.

Zee steadied his focus on me. His big smile slowly turned into a half-smirk. I could tell that he liked me. He was satisfied with the best friend that his prayers earned him. He looked comfortable, but he carefully chose his words in answering me. He didn't want to insult me, or my mother for that matter.

"Well...the bible says that *all have sinned*, so I guess that statement is partly true. As for me doing anything wrong, or having sinned recently, I can't think of anything offhand. But when I do mess up, I know I'm in the right place." His smirk brightened into a broad smile again.

We played until the streetlights came on, and we were forced to go indoors to separate homes. But from that day forward, we have been the best of friends. Zee was like a breath of fresh air to me, and well into adulthood, he became my conscience. For Zee, I believe that I was the extension of his being—his rambunctious side. I said the things that he may have thought, and I did the things he dared not do. Zee was a good boy. He still strives to be upright. I challenge his integrity and test his patience every chance I get. There's a complexity to me that's bewitching to him. When he thinks that he's finally figured me out, his feelings get run over. *Humph*—like in *Frogger*. I am unlike anyone he's ever known...and I like it that way.

Zee & Solo

Even though he's an only child, Zee comes from a sizable Trinidadian family brimming with uncles, aunts, and cousins. They all treat him like the savior returned. Zee was a child prodigy, preaching, and teaching the bible from the age of five. I was his interruption. I treated him like a regular kid. To me, he was just a boy who enjoyed comic books, scary movies, and sci-fi. The preaching thing was a hiccup. *It'll go away*, I thought, but I wasn't bothered by it. All that mattered was that we made each other laugh.

Zee's favorite superheroes are *Superman* and *Luke Skywalker*. When we played together, he always tried to convince me to be the damsel in distress. He begged me to play *Princess Leia* or *Lois Lane*, but I'm not an underdog. I preferred to be *Darth Vader*.

Zee used to get so frustrated. He sucked his teeth hard like his mother saying, "Yuh makin' joke? What kinda gyul wants to be *Darth Vader*?"

I rolled my neck and eyes like my mother and disputed him.

"*Superman* is wack—flying around in his underwear. And everybody knows that *Luke Skywalker* is a punk. I like *Darth Vader*."

"Whaaa yuh say?" he sang. Zee gets so upset. He's a passionate person. When I mocked his heroes, he grabbed his head, pacing, and mumbling under his breath. Once, okay, maybe more than once, I made him so angry that we almost stopped speaking. "Yuh bol' face, yuh know!

You insist on being difficult!" He goes in and out of a Trini dialect.

"No!" I answered, with an attitude. "I calls 'em like I sees 'em. You...you believe whatever people tell you...like your *moomi*, and daddy, and your church," I whined in a baby voice to get under his skin. "How do you even know if there's a God, anyway?" I was deliberately provoking him. I wanted to see his temper. I didn't know why, but I did that a lot. I can't help it. Zee was angry. I insulted all that he found near and dear, including the pretend heroes.

"I was born of muy muddah and fuddah; why wouldn't I trust them? My muddah birth me, just like her muddah birth her...and her muddah her, and so on." He stated, instinctively entering a creation speech. "Everyone on dis earth come...from...someone. Haven't you ever wondered who the firstborn?" He knew that I had questions by the simpleton look on my face. "How else would that person have gotten here...had it not been fuh...a creator?"

Now, I was mad. Although the topic of creation was something I wondered about, what I wanted then was anger from Zee, not a history lesson. His speech calmed his temper. Even in a debate, he knows his purpose.

"Go-Go, I don't believe in God because my parents or the church told me to. Yeah, they introduced us, but I've always known God. My spirit...that *Jedi force* inside of me," He used terminology that I could understand. "It knew and sought out its creator. I cannot look up at the trees, into the sky, or at the ocean and not know inside of myself that there is a God. And you're right, it is something that you have to seek and find and know for yourself."

I stood there in Zee's backyard, the pretend *Millennium Falcon*, flush-faced in silence. I was accustomed to anger and unintentionally thrived on it. This turnabout threw me. I wanted to counteract, but my inner yearnings caused me to engage him. I looked up at the sky that held these mysteries. "I think...that I would...maybe want to meet Him one day."

As anger faded, and a deeper understanding grew, we smiled at each other.

"Hey, why don't you go ahead and play *Darth Vader*. He is pretty cool." Zee stretched out his arms and pulled out a plastic bat *lightsaber* in defense against his arch-rival. "The patio can be the *Star Destroyer* and—"

"No," I shook my head, causing more confusion. "I'm *Han Solo*. I wanna stand by your side and fight the Galactic Empire with you." I proudly pulled out my *Blaster Pistol* (aka Sy's *Nintendo Zapper* gun). He would have killed me if he knew I was rough housing with it outdoors. A huge smile crept up along Zee's face, and together we took on *Darth Vader* and his army of *Stormtroopers*. That's how I got the nickname Solo.

Playing with Zee felt like a refuge. I was safe with him. As the years progressed, his house became a real refuge.

PART 2: 1984

Dear Diary: May 15, 1995

   I miss Senior so much that at times I can't breathe. How many years can a person live without a heartbeat? I'm present but merely surviving.

   The song "Loving You" by Minnie Riperton brings tears to my eyes. No matter where I am, I cry. Our favorite snacks don't taste the same without him. I can't eat pickled eggs, smoked herring, Ding Dongs, or sardines with hot sauce on saltine crackers without feeling down. The smell of Old Spice does something to my spirit.

   Every night, I dream of him. Every Sunday morning, I wake up expecting to see him sitting in his favorite chair watching westerns with his long legs crossed and wrapped around each other, at least twice.

   "Mornin', Pud," he used to greet me with a crooked grin on his handsome face.

   I can still remember Senior dozing off during commercials, and me wondering how long it would take for the ash growing on the cigarette stuck in between his dry lips to fall off and burn his chest. I used to get worried and place an ashtray under it. Senior would wake up snarling, then grab me around the waist and tickle me. I would scream and laugh as the ashes fell all over, then I would jump into his lap like Tante Maw-Maw said young ladies shouldn't, and we snuggled and watched the cowboy shoot-out at the O.K. Corral.

   Dang, I can't even write this. It hurts too much. I thought journaling was supposed to be therapeutic. Senior, why did you have to leave? R.I.P., Daddy. I'm numb.

   Your Princess, Go-Go

An Opened Window

By the end of 1982, Senior was using heroin. The once handsome Louisiana bred hard-body rapidly declined into a dope fiend. Not able to keep up with his work, he sold one of his dry-cleaning businesses to a fellow employee and was unintentionally working on losing the other. At home, he grew violent, even more so than before. Instead of locking himself in his bedroom, and cursing the world, he took his feelings out on Poo, Sy, and especially Rah. To Daddy, Rah was the reason behind his rapid downfall. If the sun didn't shine, it was her fault, and Senior spent most of his day trying to figure out how to make her pay for it.

Every day, he acted more like a different person and less like my beloved father. He allowed his anger to morph him into the man that he strived not to become. The duplicate of his father. When Senior was a young man away at college, his drunken father fell asleep one night while smoking a cigar and accidentally killed himself and his wife in a house fire. Senior carried the pain and resentment for years. His anger led him down the same generationally cursed path of drugs and alcohol that his father took, and, ultimately, he too lost everything.

Bill collectors and drug dealers hunted Senior down for money. Eventually, Daddy surrendered his second business in a desperate trade-off for his life and quickly learned that a user should never sell drugs. By May 1984, things were so bad that Poo lost her job at the hospital because she was stealing meds for him. The family had no money, the house was in foreclosure, and Poo was running out of patience. She loved Daddy with an incurable love, but his habit was running the family into the ground, and Poo was forced to make some tough decisions.

I was the only member of the household safe from Senior's random torment. I was his princess; he named me after his precious mother. I could do no wrong in his sight, but when Daddy took to terrorizing everyone, even I was liable to get hurt in the crossfire.

One night when Senior barged into me and Rah's room ranting and raving, I was accidentally hurt. He swore he saw Rah at Crotona Park earlier that day, getting fresh with some old dude. Daddy didn't allow himself to hear the truth; Rah was with me all day. In a violent lashing, he beat her with a wire hanger, and accidentally cut my arm. I screamed bloody murder and cowered in a corner. That was my first wound acquired at the hands of a man, and the first to keloid my delicate skin. Senior's wire hanger ricocheted and cut his face, so he advanced to using his fist. He raised his voice in anger and slapped Rah around as she laid in a fetal position on the floor. Even through the lashing, she noticed me crying in the corner and screamed, "RUN!" She pointed toward the opened window. This time, I listened to her and scattered across the floor.

By then, we were aware that Zee's bedroom window was adjacent to ours. Embarrassed by his peeking, he warned us to shut the blinds at night, but we never did. Zee would have to close his. Every night, and every morning, Zee and I spoke across our yards through our opened windows. When Zee heard the tapping of pebbles against his pane, he knew it was me. That night, I escaped the violent room and climbed the fence that separated our yards. Zee was awakened by the rapping of my knuckles against his window. On my body, I wore a new silk nightgown, but my face wore fear. Zee hurried to let me in. He momentarily froze, catching an unexpected glimpse of Rah being beaten. She had drawn Daddy's attention away from the window so I could sneak out.

"Zee!" I whispered, not wanting to alert his parents nor Senior. Frantic, he came to himself and helped me to climb through. I fell into his arms. Zee shut the blinds and led me to his bed.

"Leh me get meh muddah," he said, noticing my bloody arm, but I wouldn't let him. No way was my daddy going to jail. I just needed a place to lay until the ordeal was over.

Unfortunately, the beatings would get so frequent that Zee set up a tent in his bedroom just for me to secretly hide and sleep peacefully through the night. As that year progressed, his parents would find out.

The Neighbors

A lot changed over those two years that Rah was with us on Charlotte Street. As a family, we went from being well-to-do to hardly-doing. On a personal level, I went from an innocent but spoiled, chubby brown girl with a bad attitude to straight wildin' out. Of course, I was showing out, but it was more than that—I wanted to feel something other than fear. I wanted to sit on men's laps and play doctor with curious teenage boys. I became increasingly aware of my sexuality. It started innocently, with me looking through Sy's trashy magazines that he left lying around his room. Then, there was the time during a sleepover that one of Sy's friends put his roaming hand up my nightgown. We all laid sprawled across the living room floor in the dark, watching *Blacula*. Sy's friend, also in the peculiarity of his wonder years, inadvertently aroused something in me that at the time should have remained dormant. My inquisitiveness peaked watching the sexual innuendos of popular 80s television like *The Benny Hill Show* and rated-R movies on *WHT*. My parents didn't hide their attraction toward each other either. I made it my business to sneak and listen in on them when they retreated into their bedroom. I wasn't a bad girl. I'm not a bad woman—I'm flawed.

During one of Senior's violent nights of chaos, I crept out of my bedroom window and into bed with Zee. Not as I had done times before seeking comfort, but in curiosity.

"Let me see yours, and I'll let you see mine," I bribed him as he gathered his bedsheets around himself. He was twelve, and I was a very grown ten-year-old. I had seen them before in magazines, but I wanted to see one in person.

"Noooo, Go-Go, stop! I don't want to," Zee insisted. He only called me Go-Go, or Gomer when he was being serious. He pushed my reaching hands off him. I bet he thought to himself, what kind of behavior is this for *Han Solo?*

"Fine, I'll let you see mine first," I announced, anxious for anyone to notice my maturing breasts. I used to prance topless, back and forth in front of our bedroom window, hoping Zee would take notice, but he never did or pretended not to. He closed his blinds. But that night, I begged to be seen. I cried needing somebody, *anyone*, to SEE me. He opened his eyes and looked into mine. They were wet with tears. "Look at me, Zee."

Zee swallowed hard. He was too young to be tempted by lustful wiles. He knew he shouldn't look, but I cried out to him.

"My son, keep my words and store up my commands within you…" He told me he heard these words in his heart. **"Guard my teachings as the apple of your eye…They will keep you from the wayward woman…"**

Without looking below my eyes, Zee forcefully pulled my gown down taut. I counteracted by quickly grabbing his face and kissing him on the lips just as his mother opened the door. Anna was stunned as to be expected. She stood at his doorway dumbfounded, with her mouth open, likely imagining the worst. She had heard Zee's pleading and came to check on him.

"Mum, before you get upset, leh meh explain," Zee said in his usual calm manner, extending his slender arms in a 'wait a minute' fashion. He got down from the bed. I remained there. I didn't know why at the time, but I coyly smiled. I secretly longed for the 'perfect family' to display some sort of anger, but instead, Anna gave her Hosea the benefit of the doubt. She went and got her husband, and they listened as Zee explained how I ended up in his bed at midnight on a school night. They gathered the information and questioned me about my safety. I crossed my fingers behind my back and swore that Senior wasn't hurting anyone. Zee knew that I was lying.

"Senior gets mad sometimes and messes up the house when Poo's at work." It was somewhat true. "But I'm scared when he does that," I confessed.

Zee respected my wishes and didn't tell. Anna agreed to allow me to sleep in the guestroom once she spoke with Poo, and, of course, I had to promise that there would be no more monkeying around.

Barry and Anna knew about Senior's battle with drugs. By then, it was being rumored around the neighborhood, and Daddy's boisterous warfare every other night was an indication of his decline. The Felix family used to attend the elaborate red-light basement parties that Senior threw when his habit was still young. The parties were stocked with alcohol, and later, cocaine was passed around. We were all there. The Felix family excused themselves early in the parties and went home after a few dances and dining on the southern cuisine that they couldn't believe Rah prepared. Even at my age, I could see that some of the activities at the parties were discomforting to them. The evenings would start off fine with Tante Maw-Maw and Paw-Paw, co-workers, and a few neighbors, but as the night progressed, so did the riff-raff. Poo wasn't even looking happy anymore.

Poo and Anna Felix have similar ways. Neither is keen on unexpected guests or being bothered with people in general for that matter. They were, however, hospitable toward each other for Zee's and my sake. Here's a little surprise, I attended bible studies with the Felix family every Wednesday night, so I guess Poo felt she had to speak to them. Senior and Barry were always neighborly. They talked about their yards, sports, cars, and community affairs. Before Senior's lifestyle change, he was an outstanding citizen. He gave to different charities and was very generous toward friends in need. He made a lot of acquaintances, but as the saying goes, *fake friends follow you in the sun but leave you in the dark*. The Felix family stuck around. After Poo and Anna's conversation about me sneaking into their house at night, the women built a working relationship.

The morning after Anna caught me kissing Zee, she woke up early and firmly waited by her kitchen window for Poo to get in from work. I waited with her. That woman was not going to get me in trouble. I would call her a lie to her face.

"Aye, Mrs. Willi-ams," Anna yelped when she saw Poo's usual taxicab pull up. I ran over to the window and peeked along the side—hiding. We both ignored witnessing Poo, playfully whispering something into her driver, Mr. Jenkin's, ear and then giving him a lingering kiss on his cheek. Anna cleared her throat, looking down at me with distress showing in the wrinkles on her forehead. She sighed, knowing there was nothing that she could do and then ran to the screen door, opening it to yell, "Mornin', neighba."

"Morning," Poo dryly responded. Knowing my mother, she was thinking, *dang, why you on me so early,* and she probably wondered if Anna had seen her kiss Mr. Jenkins too? Poo unlatched our squeaky gate door, which was our alarm for intruders, and walked into the yard.

"Aye, Mrs. Willi-ams, ah know it's early, but can we talk privately?" Anna asked, quickly jumping over her blooming daffodils as she ran toward the fence that divided the yards as Poo was walking by.

Poo stopped and held her head back as if to say, *what the heck.* "It's Ms. Auguste, for the one hundredth time...and can this wait?" she responded, struggling not to make a stinky face. She looked frustrated, and that scared me.

This is not the time, lady. I thought, still peeking from behind the curtain.

"Oh, kooosh!" Anna sang, holding her chest in astonishment.

Poo was fired from her job that morning, and knowing her, all she wanted to do was crawl into bed with a spliff as her only companion and sleep the day away. She began to walk away from the fence.

"Wait nuh, ah have ya daughter," Anna revealed, capturing her attention.

Poo stopped dead in her tracks with a sobering look on her face that hid fear behind it. I know she worried about us being alone with Senior. It was her worst nightmare to come home to someone hurt or dead at his hands.

"Please, come over," Anna asked, not wanting to air their business in the streets.

I exited from behind the curtains with my head bowed in shame. My mother must have leaped over the fence because within seconds, I was in her arms.

Poo sat at the Felix family kitchen table, embracing and rocking me in

43

her lap as Anna revealed to her what Zee and I were doing for the past few months. Anna made sure to clarify that she and Barry were unaware. I was too afraid to look up at Poo, so I held her tightly and hid my face in her bosom. The bluish-gray uniform that she wore smelled like the hospital.

"I'm sorry, I wasn't aware of it either," Poo responded, shocked but trying not to appear emotional. She was. The family was going through a lot, and she was dealing with it alone. Paw-Paw had suffered a heart attack and some mild strokes at the beginning of that year. He was showing signs of dementia and Tante Maw-Maw wasn't handling it well. She started drinking heavily, and no one could get through to her.

"Ah know, love," Anna said, aware of the tears hiding in Poo's eyes. "Meh husband, Beeri, and I talk with Go-Go, and it's fine if she stays overnight. We have a guest room for she," Anna continued, talking past the tears rolling down Poo's face.

My mother is very strong-willed, prideful, and extremely private. It was hard for her to accept Anna's generosity.

Anna extended a hand on Poo's shoulder, not making the situation uncomfortable with an unwanted hug. "I know, meh sister is going tru with her eldest son. Eh easy, but yuh must kick dis ting in de butt fuh it goes too far, and somebody bash up."

Poo nodded in agreement, covering her mouth. *Too late for that*, we both thought.

"Come now, take ya baby gyul home and love on she," Anna suggested, in an accent that switched between Trinidadian and American diction. She held the news of my forwardness with Zee to herself. I guess she thought that Poo already had too much on her plate.

That night, Senior didn't come home. He showed up three days later, looking sickly, wearing a hospital ID bracelet. Whatever happened to him was enough to make him decide to get his life in order. He and Poo sat down and discussed getting help. A few days later, he entered a private rehabilitation facility and was gone for nearly three months. Poo pawned some jewelry, and a few designer purses that she hid at Tante Maw-Maw's house to make ends meet while Daddy was gone. Mr. Jenkins, the cab driver, was properly introduced to us during that time.

A Crooked Crown

"Kids, this is Mr. Jenkins," Poo announced, entering the living room where Rah, Sy, Rah's best friend, Le-Le, and I were goofing around and watching *New York Hot Tracks*. We all fell awkwardly silent. Rah was frozen in mid-dance. She loved to dance, and we loved watching her. When no one answered, Poo unwaveringly repeated, "I said, this is Mr. Jenkins!

"Hi," Rah, Le-Le, and I answered as though startled. Sy rolled his eyes and stood up with his arms aggressively folded and his legs firmly parted.

I guess Poo felt that Mr. Jenkins was going to be around for a while. "This is the wonderful man who made sure that I got to work and back home safely every day." She flirtatiously smiled at Mr. Jenkins and rested her hand on his broad shoulder. He returned her smile, lightly rubbing her back.

"And what did YOU do for him?" Sy boldly asked in a condescending tone that sounded a lot like Daddy's. He crossed his arms tighter and leaned his head back to the side with a twisted mouth.

"Excuse you?" Poo warned, seconds away from his behind.

Mr. Jenkins chuckled, unbothered by the question. He walked further into the living room, removed his hat, and nonchalantly planted himself in Senior's favorite chair. We all gaped at each other, believing Sy would lose it.

"It's okay, sweetheart. Let the young man express himself." Mr. Jenkins shifted in Daddy's seat, getting rather comfortable.

I looked at Poo as if to say, *"You gonna do something about this?"* She nervously crossed her arms and scratched her head, uneasily smiling.

Mr. Jenkins was a tall, handsome, hefty, older man who smelled incredible. I'm big on scents. He had a neatly trimmed salt and pepper beard that complimented his round honey-colored face, and he always wore a brown pageboy hat cocked to the side on his head. Like Paw-Paw, he was as smooth as the jazz music they both listened to.

"Silas," he continued, looking Sy directly into his eyes. "I ask for nothing from your mother in return. I consider myself a gentleman, and she—a lady," he expressed, winking toward Poo, who was blushing. Sy sucked his teeth and left the room.

Mr. Jenkins really liked Poo. He preferred more from her than the sexual favors she, no doubt, offered as payment for his kindness. If it weren't for him, we probably wouldn't have made it through that period. But at that moment—Sy and I hated him. Rah smiled and continued her dancing. For her, anybody was better than Senior.

I was a daddy's girl; I didn't take well to his leaving me. No one asked me for my opinion. Senior left at night to avoid a confrontation. The only information that Poo offered was that he was getting himself some help. She said it like his leaving was a burden off her shoulders. I knew that Daddy was on drugs. The few neighborhood kids bold enough to tease me brought it to my attention. After beating them up, I asked Sy about it. Sy and Daddy hadn't been getting along for a while. Whenever Senior entered a room, Sy left. When I asked him about Daddy being on drugs, he answered, "Yeah, he's strung-out, and that ain't all, either" sarcastically, like he hid a secret. Whatever it was, I could tell that it pained him. I loved Daddy, no matter what. I believed that he could have fought his addiction at home if it weren't for Rah being there. Senior blamed everything on her, and in his absence, I blamed everything on her too. No matter how much of a wonderful sister she was.

Daddy returned from drug rehabilitation at the beginning of September 1984 looking better than he had in a long time. But everything at home had changed. The house on Charlotte Street that he worked hard to move his young family into was gone into foreclosure. Poo still hadn't found a job, and supposedly the family was moving to Harlem to live with Tante Maw-Maw and Paw-Paw until she could figure things out. Senior tried to start up where he left off with Poo, but she wouldn't have it. She acted like she didn't want to be bothered with him. She wasn't rude, but she was not kind to him either. It tore my heart apart, watching her disregard my father even though we all knew that he was feeding us pipe dreams. Poo explained that we needed to move in with our grandparents to save money, but Senior claimed, "I would rather live in a shelter receiving food stamps than ever live under Mag's roof again." Tante Maw-Maw often threatened that she had a bullet with Daddy's name on it. I didn't want him living with her either. They could say what they wanted about my father. Still, the fact remains that when he had his act together, we never wanted for anything nor lived in no nasty crackhead infested buildings. We always owned our own. From the house on Charlotte Street to the two-bedroom apartment over top of the dry-cleaning business where we lived when I was much younger, Senior owned them all. Our fate would soon change.

It was the night of Rah's 14th birthday. In usual Williams/Auguste family fashion, we were in the midst of a party. The modest home on Charlotte Street was full of soulful music, comfort foods, drinks, and familiar people. Little did I know that when I kissed Daddy goodnight and left with the Felix family to spend the night, that my life would change. When I left, Senior and Poo were slow dragging to *Luther Vandross* and I was happy to see them trying to get along. When I returned the next day, Poo, Le-Le, Sy, and Rah were packing to move, and Senior was gone. Just like that, everything that I was became nothing. The imaginary crown my parents placed on my head tilted like it no longer fit. Everything in me knew that it was Rah's fault.

What did she do? "I want my daddy! Where's Senior?" I screamed loudly into the universe.

No one could comfort me, and none of my cries mattered. The family packed and left Charlotte Street. We left Zee and all our memories behind.

The Break Down

One day, I overheard Poo telling Tante Maw-Maw, "Only dead men disappear from the face of the earth." Eventually, it was so in our hearts and in our minds. Senior was dead. But Poo's conscience bothered her. Even though they had said their goodbyes, she knew that Senior would never leave her without disclosing his whereabouts. After all, they came to New York City from Gonzales, Louisiana, together. Poo diligently searched for Daddy whenever she and Mr. Jenkins dropped me off at Zee's house to play. No one heard of a Minton Silas Williams—no hospitals, no shelters, no drug dealers, no nothing. Senior was most likely another claimless corpse at the city morgue, buried in Potter's Field—a paupers' grave.

Life was like a horrific melodrama playing around me. I was there to witness everything going on, but I had no place in any of it. I was a kid to be seen and not heard. We moved in with our grandparents. Tante Maw-Maw eased-up on her drinking to help Poo where she could, but her sole focus was on her own husband. Paw-Paw had developed Alzheimer's disease, and it was quickly debilitating him. He was no longer the sleek and sharp grandfather that we were all accustomed to. He was an aging, silver-haired man who roamed the house wearing expensive silk pajamas and plush monogrammed robes. He had forgotten everyone's name but Tante Maw-Maw's, who insisted that he wanted for nothing. She sold their night club, the house in Sag Harbor, and rented their neighborhood bar to the bartender so that she could be with Paw-Paw every hour of the day, treating him with the caviar taste he was accustomed to.

After months of endless job searching, Poo finally found a night position as a home attendant for some rich old man downtown. We barely ever saw her. When we left for school, she was coming in from work. I think she preferred it that way. She didn't have to face us or deal with any of my questions concerning Daddy. Mr. Jenkins hung around. He continued as Poo's personal driver, taking her back and forth to work as well as driving me to the Bronx to visit with Zee. Who, by the way, was the only person who saw me hiding inside the beast that I had become. He spoke directly to me like I still existed.

As for Sy, things were different. He acted as if nothing mattered, but, everything did. Senior was his hero. Sy started carelessly running the streets. He sold and smoked pot and stopped going to school altogether. Instead, he religiously went back to Charlotte Street every morning, getting into mischief and secretly searching for Senior. The streets granted Sy the firm hand that he lacked at home. He would end up a teenage father locked away in juvie. Somewhere between Charlotte Street and our grandparent's house, Rah's best friend Le-Le and Sy hooked up, and she got pregnant. I missed that one. I missed the entire ending of 1984.

Rah meant nothing to me. I didn't care what she was going through, and she didn't bother to see me either. She met some guy named Jayson at her birthday party and he was always hanging around. She and I were supposed to be roommates, yet I preferred sleeping in Poo's bed while she worked. I didn't want to be in the same room with Rah, but Jayson spent a lot of time there. Although I was no longer interested in the lustful sounds that lovers make, I could hear what he and Rah were doing through the vents. I could have told, but the way things were, Poo hardly cared about what we were going through. She strenuously worked like money was the only answer to our problems and allowed Rah to modify our lives once again. Rah was a hex on the family, and her coming to live with us was an omen. She single-handedly ruined us.

***

"Ma! Maaa," I screamed. It was the first time that I could remember calling Poo that, and she didn't even hear me.

I was sitting in the back of Mr. Jenkins' cab banging on the car window. We were coming back from the hospital. It was Christmas Eve and I had the flu. Mr. Jenkins sat in the front seat of the car wringing his hat, and every so often, he'd bang the dashboard while shouting obscenities. Poo was out there. The blank night sky was lit with flashing red lights and the piercing sound of sirens. Something horrible had happened, and Poo ordered Mr. Jenkins to stay in the car with me and lock the doors. I was feverish, my body hurt, and my head pounded, but Poo was out there, and I wanted her back. All I could see was her frantically running from one ambulance where EMT workers were attempting to strap Tante Maw-Maw down, to another area where technicians rolled a gurney containing a body bag laid on top of white sheets into an ambulance. I saw bloodstains.

Poo, visibly crying, ran back to Tante Maw-Maw, who was screaming and reaching for her. They wouldn't allow Poo into the ambulance to comfort her. A cop held her back. I could hear Poo pleading with him and yelling to Tante Maw-Maw, "It's gonna be alright. I'll be there, I promise. It's gonna be okay!" When the driver closed the door, Poo ran back to the other van containing the body before they whisked it away. The cops had to pull Poo away from that ambulance.

"Daddy," she hauntingly yelled in distress. Up until that moment, I hadn't realized she had one. I had never seen her cry and scream so hard. I mimicked her and Mr. Jenkins cursed and banged the dashboard some more. Poo paused in the middle of the street, doubling over and clenching her chest. She took several deep breaths, then collected herself and ran to the stoop of the brownstone where Rah, Sy, and Le-Le were. They were surrounded by cops. Rah had blood on her gown and face. Sy was shielding her from the men with their notepads. Poo fainted.

"Maaaa!"

In 1984, we lost Senior, Paw-Paw, and Tante Maw-Maw. I woke up on Christmas morning to a mournful house. Poo laid crying beside me, curled up in Mr. Jenkins's arms. He must have thought we had a jacked-up family, yet he chose to stay. At least he knew the truth. They covered it from me, and I was a person too. I was a family member deserving of the facts. Maybe I would have been kinder to Rah had I known the truth, but they gave me no choice other than to draw my own conclusions. All I was told was Paw-Paw was dead, and Tante-Maw-Maw lost her mind and was admitted into the 'crazy house'. That's all I got. I knew it had something to do with Rah. Everyone was walking on eggshells around her and treating her special. "Leave Rah alone," is what I was told. I heard things, I saw things, and I knew that something had happened between Paw-Paw and Rah. Something that made Tante Maw-Maw mad enough to kill. I remember thinking that Rah probably sat in his lap, and there is no way that Tante Maw-Maw was having that. Bad things happen to little girls who sit in men's laps.

Not too long after that incident, we were padlocked out of Paw-Paw and Tante Maw-Maw's brownstone on Strivers' Row. It had something to do with tax evasion. We moved back to the Bronx into Mr. Jenkins' two-bedroom apartment in Soundview. He and Poo got married. Le-Le moved in with us, something about her running from an abusive home—like ours wasn't. She and Sy had a baby girl and named her, Krystal Skyy Williams. And if that all wasn't enough drama, Mr. Jenkins was held-up at gunpoint one night in his cab and was shot. He ended up unemployed and wheelchair-bound, as a paraplegic. Sy started selling hard drugs and was arrested a few times before getting locked away in juvie. Mr. Jenkins couldn't afford his rent, the medical bills, and the cost of living for five additional people on his Veteran's benefits, so we moved into a welfare hotel downtown—further away from Zee.

That's the breakdown. Sucks, yes?

I stopped going to those Wednesday night bible study classes with the Felix family. God didn't hear the ghetto. I was right all along, He only heard people like *Laura Ingalls*, with her pigtails and her white freckled face. That sure 'nuff ain't me. *Poor Zee. The sooner he learns, the better.*

PART 3: 1988

Dear Diary,   September 6, 1988

    I met my baby daddy yesterday. Besides Senior, he's the most gorgeous man I've ever seen. And can you believe that Rah brought him home? I don't know what he's doing with her but we soon will see. He looks about as big-time as big-time can get. He must be a drug dealer. All I know is that he's my ticket out of here. He moved us into his building last night. A fully furnished three-bedroom apartment! I have my own room and everything.

    Something must be done about my weight so that I can get this chocolate dream. There has to be a way to get Ding Dongs out of my life. The family is struggling, yet I'm getting fatter every day—how is that even possible? I don't know what's wrong with Poo, Rah, and Le-Le. Them chicks is hungry! Poo is depressed. Rah's an undercover ho. And Le-Le—she's just glad that Sy is out of jail. Maybe now she'll eat some of that arroz con pollo she cooks and be a mother to Baby Girl instead of thinking I'm a babysitter every ding-dong moment. I'm mean too. I'm mean to everybody. I don't know how they deal with me. I'm the devil's daughter. I gave my soul away when Senior died.

    That tasty treat that Rah brought home, he's soulless too. I was born on Halloween—so I can tell. Evil knows evil. You have to be callous to make it out here. What's it that Zee says? You can gain the whole world but forfeit your soul. Well, that brother must own the world because his soul is Audi 5000! That's how I know he and Rah ain't gonna make it. She cares too much. I don't care about anybody but me, and I barely care about myself. I hate everyone and everybody sucks. Life sucks. Zee doesn't suck, though. He's about the only thing that doesn't suck in my life. He still makes me laugh even though I'm mean to him too. Speaking of, we 'bout to go peep this Nightmare on Elm Street 4 movie, so peace out.

Ya girl, Big Meanie

My Dark Chocolate Addiction

It was like he fell from heaven; he was so fine—but dark. Oh, yeah, he was a silky smooth, dark-skinned brother, but I'm not talking about his complexion. His spirit was dark. When I first gazed into his cold deep-set brown eyes, I knew right away that he was straight from Hell, but I loved him anyway. I was fourteen about to be fifteen-years-old when we first met Jeri in that broken down, one-bedroom welfare hotel room appropriately placed in Hell's Kitchen.

Rah was missing. She went to work on Saturday and didn't return. It was Sunday morning when Poo discovered her absence. Sy was the last person to see her, and he was trying his best to relieve Poo's nerves about her disappearance, but I could tell that he was slightly nervous himself. Rah was in the company of a man that she had just met. She and Sy worked at a strip club on 42nd Street. I wasn't supposed to know that either. Rah danced, Le-Le made her costumes, and Sy was her manager and bodyguard. I guess he didn't do his job right that night, but he did feel confident enough when he came home in the wee hours of the morning without her to go straight to bed. Around eight in the morning, Poo woke the entire house, questioning, "Where's Rah? Sy, where's Rah?"

I already knew she was missing. I stayed up that night to keep from sleeping. I hated Rah but at night I needed her. We slept together in one of the two queen-sized beds. Sy, Le-Le, and Baby Girl slept in the other, while Poo and Mr. Jenkins were on the pull-out in the living room. After

Paw-Paw's death, I had nightmares, crazy dreams that subsequently always ended with me screaming and falling through a dark hole. Every night, Rah was there to catch me. She patiently massaged my head, gently rubbed my back, and quietly soothed me, "shhh," until my breathing came back to normal. She would then wrap her arms around me, and we slept. I pretended not to remember the dreams. I couldn't have her thinking that I owed her.

"Ay, Papí, come on...how could you leave her like dat, Sy?" Le-Le whined in her annoying nasally voice, rocking their water-head daughter. She needed to put Baby Girl down and finish making breakfast.

Sy ignored everyone, turning the volume up on the television show that he and I were watching, and sinking deeper into the raggedy old hotel couch. He had already explained at least ten times.

"Your job, Minton Silas Williams, Jr., is to protect your sister. You don't hand her off to the first person that comes through the door shining. That's not what we do. What the heck were you thinking, boy?" Poo yelled, pouring herself yet another shot glass of Smirnoff. It was only nine o'clock in the morning.

Mr. Jenkins, sitting near her at the kitchen table, whispered, "Don't you think that's enough?"

"No! And why don't you go get you some business... I'm not in the mood, James." She caught herself before she said something else that she would regret.

"Sweety, you are my business, and I'm not gonna sit here and—"

"Then don't! Don't sit here...stressing me out." Angry, Poo looked piercingly into his eyes. She was dead serious. "Why don't you take Baby Girl and go put her to sleep in the back. That crying is gonna make me snap." She shifted in her seat, fanning him away. Mr. Jenkins looked perplexed. Nobody told him to marry her, the signs were always there. I snickered and shook my head as he rolled over in his wheelchair to take Baby Girl from Le-Le.

"You need to chill with that, Poo," Sy added, mumbling something ill-mannered under his breath. He grew to respect and appreciate Mr. Jenkins. He was doing his best to teach Sy how to be a responsible young man. I liked him well enough, but he wasn't Daddy. I probably called him Mr. Jenkins for longer than I should have.

"Ooh!" Poo sang, picking up the Smirnoff bottle. "I need to chill, huh? I'ma chill, alright. I'ma come chill right upside ya head with this damn bottle!" She shook the bottle toward Sy. He sucked his teeth. "You a pimp now? You selling your sister for rent?"

With that, Sy got up and left the room with Mr. Jenkins.

Isn't that what y'all doing anyway? Selling Rah for rent. I shook my head and placed a pillow over it. I was feeling tired from being up all night. Poo and Le-Le continued venting up until noon when Rah finally found the decency to call.

Sy had met Jeri a week prior to that day. Jeri pulled Sy aside at the strip club where he and Rah worked inquiring about her. Rah was apparently drawing lots of attention to the obscure club. Jeri gave Sy a business card and told him to visit his swanky spot uptown where he felt Rah would fit in better. Still on probation at the time, Sy wasn't supposed to be doing anything illegal. He and Rah were both under-age, and they shouldn't have been in establishments that sold alcohol. Not new to hustling the streets, Jeri knew Sy's story without even asking. He offered Sy a legit job that he could list with his probation officer as a maintenance person in one of his buildings but actually gave him a more suitable job, off the books, as a bouncer at his other club in Brooklyn. Sy got comfortable with Jeri and told him all that the family was going through. Jeri, feeling confident in his visions for Rah as a professional dancer, also offered a job to Mr. Jenkins as the superintendent of his condo building in the Bronx, where he promised to move us. It all sounded too good to be true.

Sy said that Rah and Jeri hit it off right away. It was Rah's 18th birthday that day. Jeri took them to dinner and then went clubbing afterward. Sy said that the two of them were getting cozy with each other and he could sense that they wanted some time alone, so he left. That's the part where Poo went off. Supposedly, Rah hadn't had a boyfriend in four years since she broke up with Jayson. Le-Le swore to it too. After the thing with Paw-Paw, Rah didn't do too many leisure activities. All she did was work, go to school, and come home. I don't know, though. It's the quiet ones that you gotta worry about. I was a fast little girl, but I was also the one who was still a virgin. Rah danced at strip clubs, and we were supposed to believe that she was nun-like. Hysterical. My family was hilarious.

I'll never forget. It wasn't until seven o'clock Monday morning when Rah came walking through the door with this sexy specimen of a man following behind her. Suddenly, everything made sense to me. I wouldn't have come home either. I was sitting on the couch trying to read *The Odyssey of Homer*, the last book on my summer reading list, when they walked in. When I saw him, I used the book to cover my face and tried to appear small. I was fat as hell. I moved from a reclined position to sitting straight. Think skinny thoughts, I told myself, peeking from behind the book. I wanted to blend in with the old-fashioned floral print that adorned the raggedy autumnal-colored velour couch where I sat.

Rah called the night before saying she would be home early in the morning, and for us to be packed, dressed, and ready to go. Jeri had a surprise for us. He wanted to take the family on an outing. She said, "Don't worry about your stuff, Poo. Jeri has a moving van coming late tomorrow night when there's no traffic and no nosy neighbors around. Don't worry. Trust me." Poo didn't know how to feel, and I can't say that I blamed her. It all sounded terrific yet extremely shady. Rah was now of age to do as she pleased. I guess Poo figured either we go with her or risk breaking the family apart. Either way, Rah was excited. She swore that we had our own place, with no strings attached. She said that she and Jeri were doing business together. He was going to help her become a professional dancer in videos just like she always dreamed. They were going to run the clubs together, and Rah was going to help in grooming the dancers. Whatever that meant. It sounded iffy to me, but anything was better than the roach-infested slum we were in.

"Poo, this is Jeri...Jeremy Cole. We're moving into his co-op building in Pelham Bay." Rah was glowing and practically jumping in her skin. She had been saving the money she made from dancing to buy the family an apartment in Co-op City, and then, just like that, one fell into her lap. She latched onto Jeri's arm and smiled uncontrollably like he was a superstar. He could have been. Something that good looking should have been in pictures, and he knew it too. He devilishly grinned and removed the licorice-flavored chewing stick from his mouth and kissed Poo's hand.

Man, I wish I was that chewing stick!

"Mr. Cole," Poo repeated and nodded her head in approval, but her mouth was twisted in suspicion.

Jeri and Rah must have practiced this approach. Poo was a southern belle. She was a sucker for proper manners and curtseys and all that crap.

"Rah, you didn't tell me that ya moms was this fine...then again I should have known." Poo blushed, and Rah swooned over him.

Rah looked different, not as she looked days before. She looked like she had been with a man and it was good. She continued introducing Jeri to the rest of the family as he complimented each of us. I could detect a slight West Indian cadence mixed with his Brooklyn accent, and I definitely saw it in his swagger. As Jeri's presence filled the room, Poo walked over to Mr. Jenkins and leaned on his wheelchair. They whispered from the sides of their mouths in private, probably sizing him up.

"Rah, can we talk?" Poo eventually requested, holding the bedroom door open.

Rah excused herself and left Jeri with Sy. He and Sy spoke briefly in a quiet tone that neither Le-Le nor I could hear what they were saying. Jeri then handed Sy a Dr. Jays shopping bag that he came in with, and Sy headed to the bathroom. As I peeked from behind my book, Jeri smiled and focused his attention on me. *Oh, my Goodness. I could have died.*

"Whassup, cutie?" He vocalized in a homeboy type manner, walking over. "Wah mek yuh hiding dat pretty face?" He sat down beside me, reading a page that just came through on his beeper. I was embarrassed and couldn't speak. I took hold of the vocal cords belonging to the beast that swallowed me and refused to allow her to insult my new boo. Jeri slumped onto the sofa and leaned against my arm, put his head on my shoulder, and peeked into my book; he smelled like...*Joy to the world, the Lord has come!* Chile, I heard a choir singing, he smelled so good.

"Oh! Old *Homer,* my dude." He smiled, taking the book from me.

I had nowhere to hide. I wished that I could jump into the pages and hide on the island of Ithaca with *Odysseus.* Instead, I smirked and quickly slid my hand across my bushy head. *Oh, no!* I tried not to appear shocked. I looked like a pickaninny. One side of my head was braided, and the other was standing up in a tangled mess. I was still a tomboy then. I preferred cornrows over perms. *That Rah!* She was supposed to be rebraiding my hair. *That's why I hate her. She wants to sabotage my life.*

"What page you up to? *Odysseus* escapes the war at Troy yet?" he thumbed through the book.

Hmm, he's smart too. I shook my head even though I was practically done with the book. Jeri looked down at another page on his beeper. *Money never sleeps.* I was excited by the life he must have lived.

"Yo, babe, come on. We gotta go!" he yelled, getting up and throwing my book on the couch. "Blu is downstairs with the whip." He turned back and extended his hand. "Come on."

Jeri met me at my worst, but he still said that I was pretty. I had willfully given up on myself and was trying to eat my way out of this wretched blood clot of a world, this placenta called life. I wanted to break free, but a mass was covering me. I couldn't breathe. Jeri was the interruption that I thought I needed. I felt like I was drowning in a light-skinned household. I was being flooded by light-skinned thoughts and light-skinned ways. I'm a cinnamon brown-colored girl with red undertones. My daddy's twin. Daddy and I were the same, not privileged thinking like those redbones. Well, not Sy. He's handsomely caught somewhere between Poo and Senior's complexions and attitudes. But during the winter months, when he too can use a good tan, he acts funny. Until Jeri came along, I was the black sheep of the family. The emptiness in me was attracted to the darkness that he eluded. Jeri walked into that hotel room like he owned the building. He didn't really care about how attractive Poo was, or that Mr. Jenkins was in a wheelchair, and Baby Girl wouldn't shut up. He looked at me and owned my heart without knowing that it skipped to a different rhythm for him. I slipped a black applejack hat on over my messed-up hair, rolled on some of Rah's oils, and slid on Poo's red lipstick. I was ready for Jeri.

The Parkway

Jeri pulled out all the stops trying to impress us and gain Poo's trust. When we got downstairs, two matching white BMWs were awaiting us in front of the building. Jeri drove one and his head henchman, Blu, drove the other. Everyone on the block took notice as we purposely strutted into the cars. Jeri and Blu were dressed in crisp white attire and wearing the latest *Air Jordans*. Sy came out from the bathroom, dressed in black and wearing the same *Air Jordans*. A day in Brooklyn that we would never forget was planned for the family. We were going to Eastern Parkway for the West Indian-American Day Carnival.

When we reached the parkway, Rah was given an elaborate costume from Jeri's trunk. Then, we all followed them into a local restaurant for her to change. There were a lot of women dressed in similar costumes there. Beautiful women of all shapes and sizes smiled and flaunted around Jeri as he interacted with each of them—hugging, kissing, and smacking them on their behinds. They all spoke in a swift Caribbean dialect that sounded like music. My heart fluttered. I felt like I belonged. Jeri owned the restaurant, and the women were there to dance with his float in the parade. Poo, Le-Le, and I stood back, amazed by everything. It was right up Poo's alley too, being Louisiana Creole and all, and I was sure that Le-Le's mind was buzzing with new designs.

Hmm, maybe Jeri isn't just a drug dealer?

"So, yuh ready to git dress?" Jeri asked Poo, finally getting back around to us. He was with his people; his vibe had changed. He wasn't hood anymore; he was home.

"Whaat!" Poo laughed, but her eyes twinkled. "Please, these girls don't want me out there."

No, Poo, don't do it. I lowered my head. Some older woman had set Baby Girl and me up at a nearby table. We were served ackee and saltfish with dumplings. I was in heaven.

"Ooh, it too much fi yuh?" Jeri coyly played with Poo, whining his waist to the music coming in from the J'ouvert, a popular day-break festival that preceded the Carnival.

"Please!" Poo exclaimed, blushing. "We Creole, this is nothing. Back home, I used to dance in Mardi Gras all the time. No offense, but I'll put these girls to shame." Rah and Poo were excellent dancers. Tante Maw-Maw used to say they took it from her.

"Alright then! So, yuh want to dance wid dees girls in di streets, or yuh want to be di queen madda on top of di float with dees girls here...," he asked, pointing to a new set of girls filing out of the bathroom. They were dressed in brilliant white and black two-piece leather bikinis studded with glistening diamonds. Strippers. Their headpieces were gorgeous. They were Jeri's Video Vixens.

Poo's mouth dropped. Le-Le frantically rummaged through her bag for a pen and paper to start sketching; she settled on using napkins. The strippers sparkled. Their skin glowed. Jeri handed Poo a similar white and black feathered headpiece from a table and a simple white unitard that accented her tall curvy body nicely.

"I'm going up top!" Poo proclaimed, slapping Jeri a five and taking the outfit. She kissed Mr. Jenkins on his forehead and ran toward the bathroom. Jeri winked at me and quickly continued dishing orders.

When Rah exited the bathroom, the room fell silent. Of course, her costume was more exquisite than them all. It was a beautiful mix between the street dancer's feathered costumes and the stripper's leather and diamond-studded ones. She held a platinum-coated scepter, and her long wavy hair that she dyed black a year ago shined with diamond beads. All the Caribbean dialects that filled the room previously turned into whispers, clicking of tongues, and sucking hard of the teeth. Jeri jumped up on a table, calling attention.

"We goin' change up a few tings, mon. Dis is Miss Voodoo Doll. She goin' lead di parade. She di new leader."

Rah stood, brightly smiling with her shoulders held back, and her chest propped forward. A long sheer white cape shimmering in mica flakes and trimmed in white fur hung from her shoulders.

Oh, this is going too far. I stood and walked over toward Rah mad because I had to abandon my breakfast, but I could feel the energy changing in the room. Poo, and Le-Le must have felt it too because they followed me. The previous leader sucked her teeth and quickly snapped a statement about how they practiced a routine.

"Listen, teach her di steps...or forget di routine. Voodoo Doll is the new leader...PERIOD!" The hood resurfaced in Jeri's dialect, and he jumped off the table.

The uptight women gave Rah nasty looks. I parted my feet and cracked my knuckles, capturing their attention. There wasn't going to be any of that. The only one allowed to treat Rah any kind of way was me. I cracked my neck on both sides to make the message clear. Rah gave a twisted smirk and crossed her arms. She knows how we do. The island women sucked their teeth, eyeing Rah with jealousy in their hearts. They pretended to teach her the drill, but she didn't need their sloppy routine. When the parade started, and the steel bands played, my sister stepped into her position, whipped that cape from around her shoulders, and danced like Jesus Christ himself had returned. The feathers on the rear of her costume took on life, rotating with her butt's gravitation. She didn't need any routine. Rah was the whole parade. Everyone wanted to dance with her; police officers danced with her, women, children, and even politicians. She carried the rhythm of Mother Africa in her hips, the iridescence of pearls in her smile, thunder in her thighs, and an earthquake in her butt. She was beautiful to watch, but the way that she lost herself in dance was mesmerizing. Eventually, those island girls gave in to her, smiled, and danced with her instead of against her. Jeri knew precisely what he was doing when he made Rah the new leader. Voodoo Doll was on the cover of three major newspapers the next morning.

I watched the parade from Jeri's car. I sat near him the entire time, making all the girls jealous. They had every right to be, he was the full package. He had the looks...check; a dope body...check, check; and tons of money...check, check, check! Women flocked around his motorcade. That's what Sy and the other guys in black were for, they kept Jeri safe. My brother looked so handsome, marching with the bouncers. They all wore matching Air Jordans and Nubian styled beaded chains around their necks with hanging leather medallions shaped and colored like the Jamaican flag. Jeri had everything so nice. He did the Carnival parade every year, and every year his motorcade got bigger and bigger.

Jeri and I drove alongside his float with his street dancers in front of us. His Video Vixens danced on poles built into the Island Boy Promotions float, which was dedicated *'In Loving Memory'* to his mother. But Poo was the queen mother of the float that day. She stood up top, acting like royalty, waving, and blowing kisses. She danced for Mr. Jenkins as he sat nearby, enjoying the view. Jeri made sure to keep her drinks coming. Le-Le and Baby Girl were up there too. Le-Le was told to study the costumes. Jeri said, "If you can create anything better than what I see here today, I want you to come work for me." He knew that she made Rah's outfits and was impressed by her work, especially the functionality of the pieces. Apparently, they came off in the blink of an eye.

Whenever Jeri felt like dancing, he stopped the motorcade, and his crew circled him along with his choice of a dance partner. They danced like no one was watching while women tried to break through the circle wanting a chance to be discovered. If Rah wasn't marching in front of the motorcade, I'm sure she would have been pissed. Jeri knew I wouldn't tell. He got back in the Beemer, swearing and laughing, "Dees girls bashy today, eeh, Go-Go?" He wrote secret notes on the pieces of paper that the women passed him then stuck them into the glove department.

On another stop, I spotted Zee in the crowd. "Yo! Jeri, can we stop here? I see somebody I know." Jeri stopped the car and the motorcade stopped with him.

Zee and his family attended the parade every year. When he heard me yelling his name, he looked my way and leaned his narrow body back, singing, "Ayyy!" Becoming the beat that the mas bands played, he smoothly danced his way through the crowd as only a man from the islands could. I ran to him and we hugged. Just to clarify things, I don't usually run, but I was happy that day. Things were finally looking up for us, that, and Jeri and I had a little puff-and-pass thing going on in the car.

66

"Yuh here?" Zee yelled, grabbing my waist and whining up on me. It was like their holiday—National Caribbean Act-A-Fool on the Parkway Day. "Wine ya wais, wine ya wais…," he gleefully sang.

I stood on my toes and yelled into his ear, anxious to introduce Jeri and point him out. Jeri held up a finger and nodded toward us. Zee seemed confused but returned a head nod anyway. Maybe he recognized his competition? He looked back at me and gave me one of his boyish smiles, even Jeri couldn't ruin his holiday. It was the last day of our summer vacation. Zee swiftly turned me about, grabbed my waist, nuzzled my neck, and danced with me like he wasn't holy. Taken by surprise, I laughed in a boisterous manner. That boy knew he had my whole heart, yet that morning, when Jeri walked through the door, I felt the universe shift. I looked over toward the Beemer. Jeri was getting out to dance again. No one was stopping his show either. So, I grabbed Zee's hands, placed them on my stomach, and became one with his rhythm. We danced in merriment. We danced in freedom. We danced in celebration of being young and Black. Jeri was FYNE! I found myself wanting to be with him more than anything else, but I scared myself with how much I loved Zee. I quickly turned to face him. A broad smile that connected his eyes and cheeks painted his face. *Is this just a dance?* We were best friends. My heart raced. My flushed cheeks burned as thoughts of friendship were replaced with the curiosity of becoming lovers. With Zee, it wasn't that simple. I would have to be committed to him, and I wasn't even committed to myself half the time. I took another peek at Jeri; I couldn't stop watching him. He was dancing with more women, and for some reason, to me, he felt easier to love. We were full of the same toxin. Zee scared me; I could love him forever. I gazed up at him, bewildered, he rested his forehead on top of mine, then closed his eyes and continued to dance with me, sharing souls.

"Come with me," I yelled, interrupting the intertwining of our spirits. The dance was about to make me cry.

"Okay." I took Zee's hand, and we ran over to where his parents were dancing. "Moomi, ah go wid Solo. Ah meet you back by Tanty Bev's house later." They nodded, Anna kissed his cheek and mine.

We got in Jeri's Beemer and ate, drank *Kolas*, and laughed. Whenever we wanted to, we got out and danced and danced and danced.

When the parade was finished, Rah slowly limped her way back toward us. The way she danced and interacted with the crowd, no one would have known that she was in pain. She was determined to prove to Jeri that she could do whatever he needed of her. I bet she didn't anticipate eight straight hours of high adrenaline dancing. Jeri proudly smiled when he spotted her through the crowd; people stopped her for pictures, and she still danced with them. Jeri got out of the car, and he and a few of his henchmen rescued her. He picked Rah up, carried her back, and then gently sat her on the hood of his car. She smiled broadly and wrapped her arms around my man's neck. He kissed her in a manner that made me pucker up as his crew oohed and ahhed, whistling and clapping and carrying on. I tried not to appear jealous in front of Zee. He was caught up in the merriment. Oddly enough, he and Jeri clicked instantly.

Jeri removed Rah's shoes. He rubbed her feet as she squinted and flinched in pain, so he kissed them. "Aww!" The crowd reacted. I couldn't help it; my mouth fell open. Yup, he's the one. I had to become a woman to please him. Not a shy girl, like Rah. She covered her face from feeling embarrassed and tried to pull back her foot. Jeri, a ham for attention himself, suggestively sucked her toes in front of everyone. *Jeez! It's not fair!*

"Geem di whole foot!" Somebody yelled. "Stick dem all inna yuh mout!

His crew went crazy, and Jeri laughed and hugged Rah's neck. She hid her face in his broad chest as he whispered something into her ear. Then, he motioned for everyone to quiet down. Blu, along with two other guys dressed in white, reiterated his request by whistling loudly.

"Forreal tho! Mi just want fi tank, Miss Voodoo Doll fah representin' mi mother and Island Bwoy Promotions. Big up! Yuh represented hard, baby. Yuh set a standard fa everybody out here!" He pounded his hands, emphasizing how serious he was. "I appreciate you, and I look forward to doing business with you…mmm, mongst ah few oddah tings. Mek sure yuh wear dat later…lawd-a-massi!" Everyone but me laughed. The thought of her working my man out like she worked those feathers earlier enraged me. I folded my arms and pouted with a few other women in the crowd.

As for Poo, she was sold—hook, line, and sinker. She laughed and clapped like it was income tax season. She was high as a kite, but she should have known that when the good times end, that's when people show you who they really are.

This Virgin is in My Way

I'm forward. I'm stubborn too. I want what I want when I want it and no leftovers. After meeting Jeri, I was on some next level ish. I no longer wanted to aimlessly sit around the house, feeling sorry for myself, missing Senior, and missing who I was when he was around. Jeri gave me a taste of what life could be like with him. He ignited a fire within all of us. Sy, Le-Le, and Baby Girl moved into one of Jeri's apartment buildings in Brooklyn. Le-Le made all the Video Vixens costumes, and Sy worked as a bouncer. Poo, who stayed wasted most days, and as mean as hell the others, took pride in fixing up our new home. Mr. Jenkins worked hard in our new building, and when he wasn't doing that, he sold fitted caps in Harlem. Rah ignited a fire in me as well. The kind that needs extinguishing. I hated her even more than before.

Voodoo Doll became everything that Rah used to brag about becoming—and more. She had my man. Jeri got her featured in popular hip-hop and rap videos. She choreographed dance performances and graced the pages of culture magazines. Voodoo Doll hung on the arms of handsome celebrities. Paparazzi followed her, taking pictures, and claiming she dated this one and that one. They made her into the trollop that she already was in my eyes, but it made Jeri, who played under the radar when it came to the media, grow angry with jealousy. I guess we both were. Jealous.

When I met Jeri, I was a freshman in high school, and I was still a virgin. I used to be the most forward and fastest kid you would ever want to meet, but after Daddy died, my interest died too. Zee was safe with me, but I could tell that he had a growing interest. We hung together most Saturday nights into Sunday. We went to the movies and had many memorable nights skating at *Empire* in Crown Heights and *Skate Key* in Mott Haven. I also got Zee to do something that he usually wouldn't, which was hanging out on the avenue near Charlotte Street. He knew why I wanted to be there, and it infuriated him, but he did it for me.

I was dead set on getting with José Rivera. I wanted to have sex. I needed the experience and Zee wasn't trying to play along. That's okay, though, he wasn't the type you experimented with. I needed the experience for him too. I wanted to give him my best. You see, I was doing this for us. José was a two-cent hustler, a wannabe. He sold dime bags and did petty robberies but wore the latest gear and wasn't that fat, dirty-faced kid anymore. We both matured nicely. By the end of 1988, I had lost weight, and Poo finally let me get one of them *Hawaiian Silky* perms that all the girls wore. My hair hung midway down my back, but my sides were shaved down close because some jealous girls at school jumped me and slapped *Nair* across my head. Now that I was flyy, their wack boyfriends wanted me. I didn't want any of them, though. Before Jeri, I was the cute fat girl who stayed to herself and kept her nose in books. I was feelin' poetry. Nobody bothered me. After Jeri, I blossomed and became about *that life*. Yeah, I would have worried about my man too.

When the family found out about me getting jumped, Rah and Le-Le showed up at the school the next day in a souped-up 1988 royal blue *Jetta* with *Louisville Sluggers* in hand.

"Who out here is messin' with my little sister?" Rah yelled, profiling hard in front of her new whip. It was three o'clock, and them busted behind chicks were planning on jumping me again.

I amped up the situation getting in a few faces. "Yeah! Now whatcha gonna do?"

Before it got too hectic, Jeri and Blu stepped out of the car with guns visibly showing, tucked into their pants, and all my enemies parted. After that day, I gained a clique of girls that followed me around. Okay, Rah is alright sometimes.

Zee went to *Bronx School of Science*, one of them nerdy magnet specialized New York City schools. He was a senior there. When Zee graduated, his family planned to send him off to Northern Caribbean University for seminary. He wasn't thrilled about it, but he let Anna run his life like the good little geek he was. I hated the idea of losing Zee to Jamaica for four or more years. We both knew his parents didn't have the money to bring him home to visit often. He did receive tons of scholarships so, his tuition wasn't the problem. The problem was me. I was in love with Zee and Zee loved me too; although we played like we didn't, Anna knew. When my fire for Zee started to flame again, she did everything in her will to break us apart. On the weekends, Anna had him speaking and teaching in Seventh-day churches all over the NYC metropolitan area to break up our weekend dates. She said it was for the extra money, but we both knew the truth. Zee was torn between his mother and me. He knew that I liked Jeri and didn't want me to do anything stupid like sleep with José for the experience. Zee was there for me, though, as much as he was allowed. He stuck by my side through the extreme dieting and the dramatic changes in my appearance. He knew I was serious.

"Solo, meh like meh women thick, yuh know. Weh meh boomsie," he joked, but he jogged with me and made sure I wasn't starving myself.

When Anna took Zee away, I moved in hard on José. I hung around his building, reading books on the park bench until he came down. That sad negro didn't have the sense that God gave him. He always sold drugs in the park, and I knew it was a matter of time before he got busted. That day, I had on my flyest outfit, it was spring of 1989, and I was slim and cute in pastels with matching Reeboks, *54.11's* if you will. I was pretending to read *"Beloved" by Toni Morrison* again when José came over. He had just made a sale.

"Yooo! Is dat you, fatty boom-boom?"

I hate him. "Excuse you?" I looked over my book, giving him much of an attitude.

"Nah, what I mean is—you look different. Mad flyy." He sat on the arm of the park bench with his feet on the seat, biting his lip and whatnot. I gave him a screwface once over then put down the book.

"And you are?" José stared at my parted lips; I knew they were popping. Fuchsia does something for my complexion. My *Luster's Pink* shining black hair was pulled back into a tight ponytail with a blunt bang hanging over my chinky looking eyes.

He nervously laughed. He must have remembered those whippings I gave him. "It's me, José! José Rivera from PS61."

I acted clueless at first and then shocked. "Wait, the chubby José that used to talk mad junk and got his butt handed to him on the regular...or tall José?"

"Okay, okay. You got jokes." He nodded with his head held down, chuckling. "What you up to, ma? I see life treatin' you real good." He played with my hair, and I swatted his hand away. "You wanna go get something to eat. Let me treat you to lunch?"

"You got a car?" I rolled my neck. I knew he didn't.

He looked simple for a moment. "I can get one." That excited me.

I was getting ready to live on the edge. All I had to do was groom that sucker and motivate him to step up his game.

José stole a car. A black *Honda Accord*. We drove to 72nd Street on the Upper Eastside and abandoned it along a side street. José got lucky and found a one-hundred-dollar bill in the glove compartment. We went to *BBQs* and I made him spend every single stolen dime on me. We went to a movie and had popcorn then ice cream afterward. *Watch your diet*, I kept telling myself. We walked and talked until I felt better about being a glutton. Before we knew it, it was way past dark. José wasn't all that bad. If anything, he was funny, and I'm a sucker for a sense of humor. We took a cab to some random building near my block and then ran out on the bill. We laughed and ran all the way to my building. I brought José home because I wanted the family to see that I could get a man who was cute and had loot too. I brought him into the apartment, but no one was up. It was almost midnight. José was impressed by our neatly kept building with its shiny marble lobby floors. It didn't smell like urine and it always had working elevators. Our basement apartment had windows, and the furniture was new and modern.

"Yo, y'all hit the *Lottery* or something?" If I didn't know better, I'd swear that punk was sizing up the place for a robbery. I handed him some cherry *Kool-Aid* to rebuild his strength after all of that running we did.

"My sister's boyfriend owns the building, you might know him. Jeremy Cole. He owns the—"

"Yeah, yeah. I know Cole. He ain't here, is he?" He looked uneasy. Maybe he wasn't going to rob the place after all.

"Nah, my moms and stepdad are in the back, though," I warned, taking his empty glass, just in case he wanted to act stupid. I led him to my boudoir and turned on *Friday Night Videos.*

He sat on my bed.

"This is nice, who sleeps there?" I had another twin bed in the room.

"My niece, when she comes to visit, which is all the time." I walked over to him, standing in between his legs. I removed his navy-blue *Ralph Lauren* cap and fluffed his thick, curly, untamed fade. He had hair like Sy. He leaned back on my bed, rubbed his goatee, and smirked feeling he was going to get lucky.

Should I do it, or make him wait? But dang, how long? I mean, I've been waiting.

I sat on his lap and leaned on his chest, playing with the buttons on his shirt. "So...you think that cabbie is still looking for us? It's late." I gave a hint for him to leave.

José grabbed my face and kissed me, pushing me back on the bed. My first French kiss. I aced it. He hovered over me, rubbing me up. I let him get to first and second base before I stopped him.

"What kinda girl do you think I am?" I turned my face. He lifted my blouse. I got nervous and tautly pulled it down. Maybe I wasn't ready for anyone to see my tetas yet. "I don't fool around with petty thieves...I wanna playa." I sat up.

"Pfft! I ain't no petty thief!" I could hear the Puerto Rican accent coming out. "Yo, bee, look at me!" He was referring to the hard situation in his pants.

"Hmm," I got up and handed him his hat. "I want the finer things in life." I turned around, whining my behind up in his face. He latched on. "What do you have to offer me? I don't want no little boy fooling around with me on a twin bed in my mom's apartment. I want a king-size bed at the *Marriott* on Broadway. I think I'm worth it." I played with his manhood and his ego fell for it.

He stood up.

"What's your number?" he asked, looking for some paper.

"You know where to find me when you ready. I want to be wined and dined like Jeri does."

"Like Jeri does?" He sucked his teeth and turned for the door.

Too much? Those were big shoes.

He found a pencil and wrote his pager number on my wall. "Page me in a few days...607. I'll be ready then." He grabbed me and kissed me again. My heart raced.

"We'll see." I played like I wasn't fazed by him.

I gave José two weeks and beeped him 607 (I miss you). He showed up a few hours later polished and dressed in dope gear with car keys in hand. An older *Lexus* that he said belonged to him. I introduced him to Poo and Mr. Jenkins, Rah and Jeri were there too. Jeri wasn't impressed. José and I went to dinner on City Island, and I ordered the most expensive thing on the menu. Jeri told me to do that before we left. He also slipped me some money to get home just in case. Afterward, we drove into the city and checked into the *Marriott Marquis* on Broadway. That was that. I wasn't a virgin anymore. I probably wasn't the best José ever had, but I was the only one who ever challenged him to be more. That, and he was excited about being my first. After that, we challenged each other to do more and be more. He taught me some tricks, and I kept him curious enough to keep coming back. That is until he got picked up for selling drugs at the park. But now I was ready for Jeri.

PART 4: 1990

Dear Diary, *December 10, 1991*

How did I get here? I don't know. Who knew that so much could change in a year? I don't even recognize this life that I'm living in. It can't be mine. I feel like I'm being digested inside of the beast that swallowed me. I'm being broken down by bile acids and about to be passed as a stool. The beast doesn't even want me anymore.

Is there a friend? I have one. A he/she friend, and he means more to me than these pointless bodies posing around as human beings. God gave me one. A lifeline. Timothy.

I'm Lost

Kotex, Please

The year 1990 was a capital B. She came in on her menstrual cycle, and that sister didn't stop bleeding for that entire year. On the other hand, 1989 was the best year ever! I was trim. I had flawless amber-brown skin, and I was young, sexy, and in love. It was an exciting time to be alive without a care in the world. That *Regina Belle* jam, *"Baby, Come To Me,"* was my love song to Jeri. He had it goin' on, and something was telling me that a fire was going right up his spine for me too. In 1989, we spent a lot of time together. When I wanted to see him, all I had to do was go uptown to his club or ring the bell to his penthouse apartment. "Whassup, Go?" he always asked. I loved it when he called me that. "Nufn much, whassup with you?" I answered, and he put his strong arm around my neck and drew me in. I made sure to wrap my arms around his waist and quickly inhale his amazing scent. I mean other guys wear *CK One*, but Jeri...his body chemistry owned it! I was just the right height to fit under the nook of his arm. Not like Rah who wore heels to get up there. Jeri knew that I wanted to be around him. He entertained my crush. We mostly chilled. He taught me how to drive. He taught me how to shop for unique clothes, not the stuff that everyone else wears. We practically lived in *Dapper Dan's* of Harlem. We ate in fancy restaurants. Yes, I was the infamous third wheel. Jeri invited me to a few industry parties. I met celebrities and probably could have dated a few, but Rah stayed on me like a mother hen. She guarded my reputation because she couldn't have hers. She's Voodoo Doll to the public. That title came with a lot of shame, so she never gives out her real name. It's all she has, but not me. Tarnish me, baby! I wanted to drink *Cristal*, smoke blunts, and ride in fancy whips with hoodlums that meant me no good.

I almost died when I met a certain famous rapper and he acted like he wanted my number. Oh, my goodness, was he fine! I played it cool. Rah and Jeri cold blocked me. I knew Jeri was jealous. I was becoming a woman before his eyes. I would soon be ready to pluck. He claimed he didn't want me messing with his clients for his business' sake. "You too young. You mad trouble. Nothing but jailbait," he said. But I noticed him looking. Those cute outfits that his pockets were funding were paying off. Guys were all over me. Rah and Jeri kept me laced in dope gear. But by the fall of 1989, they weren't coming home as much anymore.

The more Rah was gone, the more I realized I wanted her life. She didn't have to deal with suffering. When I saw her on television, or in a magazine, I didn't even recognize her. She was oozing with seduction. Her popularity was at its peak, and she and Jeri were living in the limelight. He wasn't the drug dealer I assumed him to be; he was an entrepreneur. Jeri owned several apartment buildings throughout the city, so he and Rah weren't always home in the Bronx. Which meant my gear wasn't always where I needed it to be. Mr. Jenkins worked in our building for Jeri, and in return, we lived rent-free. He still collected his Veteran's benefits, Social Security, and hustled in Harlem selling hats, but that wasn't enough to maintain my newly acquired lifestyle. He had Poo, and eventually, Baby Girl to take care of.

Sy moved to Brooklyn and started acting a fool selling and using drugs. By 1990, my handsome brother was a full-blown crackhead. Le-Le was out there too, she worked for Jeri. She got into all the parties and drank and blew lines like everybody else, but by early 1990, she called the house looking for Rah. The next thing we knew, Baby Girl was living with us. Rah said Sy was in over his head. He lost his job. He lost their apartment. Le-Le and Baby Girl were living in a shelter, and she didn't know where Sy was. Eventually, he called the house looking for money, and Poo and Rah found a way to wire him some. Every time was the last time. I felt sorry for Baby Girl. We were the same. Fatherless.

Zee went to college in Jamaica. I didn't think it would affect me as much as it did. I was out of control. Not to blame him for my misconduct, but had he been there, maybe I would have acted somewhat sane. We both knew when he left that our relationship would be on pause. In retrospect, I guess we needed the space to find ourselves. Zee left in August of 1989, and he didn't return until the summer of '90. By then, I wasn't around.

I wasn't with dumb José either. He was in jail more than out. When he was gone, I acted a fool stealing guys from girls, and I really couldn't care less about them. I had to keep up my appearance, I needed resources. I wasn't sleeping with them. I didn't have to. They got to tell their lies, and I got what I wanted from them, money. The year 1990 was dark. I was trying to keep up my clout. The kids in school envied me and lived vicariously through me.

I did stupid things out of desperation. I didn't see that life was already going well for me until one day when all the *Pradas* hit the fan. Rah and Jeri were back home. I went upstairs to their apartment to get some things and I saw money just lying there. It was a nice thick wad of cash. I told myself, *who knows when the superstars are going to be back home again? Jeri won't miss it.* So, I skimmed off the top. Okay, maybe more than the top. I ravaged that stack! I mean, I went in.

Rah stayed that night with us. She wanted to spend some time with Baby Girl and give Poo and Mr. Jenkins a break. They took the opportunity and went out for a movie and dinner. I was reading a book, and Rah and Baby Girl were watching cartoons and coloring when Jeri came storming into the apartment. Rah stood up, ready to greet him. He didn't say a word. He walked over and pimp smacked the living daylights out of her. She flew off her feet, and I think she blacked out. Baby Girl screamed and I froze. My instinct would usually say, *fight*, but this time it stated, *you better sit down.* Jeri yanked Rah by the collar of her shirt.

"Where the hell is my money?"

I swallowed hard.

"What money?" Rah yelled, and Jeri pulled out a gun.

Oh, shoot! I almost peed myself, but instead, I involuntarily confessed. "I have it! Don't kill her."

Before I could blink, Jeri was in my face. Baby Girl was screaming, one of those piercing high-pitched screams that little girls do. Jeri looked down at her with anger in his eyes and with that gun in his hand. I emptied my pockets; Baby Girl couldn't help it. She froze like that.

"Please, Jeri. I'm sorry."

"I give you...whatever you want. Dis is how yuh do me?" He stared at me with an intensity that shook my bones. He put the gun back into his pants and marched over to Rah, yanking her off the floor. Her lip was busted. Jeri pulled her out of the apartment; he didn't even take the money.

Later, I tried to give it back, but he threw it in my face and stopped speaking to me.

"Okay, be like that!" I bought some things, but nothing worth his absence.

That was the first time I saw Jeri hit Rah. I don't know if it was her first time, but she stayed with him, and I still loved him. We women can get out of hand sometimes.

Tam

José got out of juvie in January of 1990. I told you that year came in on its period. Of course, we got back together, and he jumped right back into the game. This time, he was a little more aggressive than before. I found that attractive. He stopped selling his merchandise in the park, and I thought that we could make it work this time. We could become a power couple, hotter than Jeri and Rah. But José smoked too many *Phillies* blunts and drank too much. He stayed high. The corner on the block was more attractive than Park Avenue. I was about to set my goals higher when we found out that I was pregnant. We were at our spot downtown. We had a free night because the city was snowed in from a blizzard. José was watching porn and getting high. We usually watched together, that's how I learned all my tricks, but I hadn't seen my period and was getting a little concerned. I stole an *e.p.t.* from the pharmacy the day before. My intentions were to take it at home, but since we were stuck at the hotel, I decided to use it. And that sucker came out bright pink. Pink means you're pregnant.

"Yo, ma, come on...we miss you," José sang from the king-sized bed. I was pissed like he planned to ruin my life.

"You should have never got with him again," I told myself in the mirror.

The beast looked back at me and said, *"You're gonna get fat."*

"Oh, hell, no!" I stormed to the bed and dropped the test on José's chest.

He was naked and ready for a good time, and just like that, I lost interest in him. It was a long hard night. Literally. He begged and promised that everything was going to be alright.

"Das me, babeee! I take care of mines!" He rambled on in a Bronx Spanglish accent, getting upset. "I'm no títere de la calle! I'm a man." He even told me that he loved me. I wasn't trying to hear it. He got me pregnant. How was I supposed to be the diva I wanted to be, pregnant?

"No, you don't understand! I'm not FEELING maternity wear."

I got José to promise to take me to the abortion clinic. There was nothing inside of me that wanted to keep his baby. There were no feelings of attachment at all. He already had two kids, by two different girls, in the same project building. There was no way I was letting Jeri find out. I was already skating on thin ice with him. He didn't like José. He said he was a bum.

I didn't cry. I didn't flinch on the table. I didn't even want José there. I just needed him for the ride home. The only babies that would ever pass through my canal were Zee's, and I knew that even then. José and I stopped speaking, and a month later, he was arrested again.

The whole pregnancy thing kinda scared me. I got on the pill, but I really wasn't trying to be with anyone. The only problem with that was I needed my gear. I started traveling uptown on Friday and Saturday nights to Club Vixens, hoping to bump into Jeri and Rah. I visited a few times before they showed up, looking fine and smelling rich. Security was all around them, but Blu let me through. I had the notion that I could become a stripper. I could give guys all the feelings without going through with actual sex with them.

"No!" I should have known that Rah would say that.

"You too young. You mad trouble. You jailbait." I heard that before, but at least he was speaking to me. Jeri gave me money and told me to get out before he got shut down for entertaining minors.

I sucked my teeth and picked my pride up off the floor. *That's okay.*

The next day I went to this spot on Fordham Road that sold intimate apparel. I picked up a few pieces then went to the sleaziest hole I could find downtown. I needed someone who didn't care.

It was Saturday night, March 24, 1990. That's when I stepped into hell. The devil met me at the front door and put me on a pole. I was nervous at first. I stood there, trembling and clinging to it, wearing a black negligee with the butt area cut out. I can laugh at myself now. I was so naive. All I could think about was the *dollar dollar bills*. I...loved...money. Period. I did it all for the Benjamins. José's porn tapes came to mind. I looked at that pole like I looked at him and blocked out the heckling men. *C' mere, lover boy.* I acted out the scenes. My mind turned off the wack music that the club was playing, and I encouraged myself thinking, *Louis...Prada...MCM* bags...get dat *Fendi*, shake your booty for a *Gucci*. I wore that pole out. I could hear lust shouting, begging for more, then, dollars multiplied in my hands, guaranteeing I would give them what they wanted.

Afterward, the devil asked me, "Do you wanna make more money?"

"Hell, yeah! I'm not here to make ice cream."

He led me to the back of the club and up some stairs, I could see men in line paying to get up there. *The boom-boom rooms.* I exhaled deeply.

"No touching, right?" I turned to ask the devil.

He took the cigar out of his grimy mouth. "I get the admittance fee; you get what you make inside."

"But what if I don't make anything?"

He laughed. "That's up to you. How far are you willing to go?" He opened the door to the pit, and I could feel the heat. It felt like an inferno.

Darkness flew off the walls like bats in flight. They filled the room. I started to walk out, but the devil closed the door and locked me in. I could hear wailing, young girls crying over the thump of music coming from downstairs. I walked to a corner and stood there like I was on punishment, trying to cover myself. The doorknob was turning. Suddenly, the dollars collected in my garter belt meant nothing. It was semi-dark in the red-lit room with filthy mirrors hanging all around me. A tall, slender young black man entered. He was nicely dressed and immaculately groomed. He sat on the bench and crossed his legs, sitting straight and tall. He stared at me for a minute. What was I supposed to do? *How did Rah do this?*

"Well come on now, chop-chop!" he snapped in a high-pitched tone clicking his fingers.

I edged from the corner. Something was different about him. His polished shoes swayed back and forth, and his hands rested upon his knee. Suddenly, lousy music blared from an overhead speaker, and we both jumped. I awkwardly attempted to whine to the detestable non-beat...it was like porn music or something. The man shook his head and lowered it.

"No... please stop." He extended his long arm and fanned his hand out toward me. "You are doing yourself a disservice."

I inhaled deeply and exhaled. "Okay...let me...let me try this again." I rolled my shoulders. I knew I could do it; my nerves were getting the best of me. I tried to catch the beat and rolled my butt to the rhythm. If anything, my butt was big—it demanded attention. The man held his head back and covered his mouth in shock.

"What are you doing out here, chile? Please...stop while you're ahead." He heartedly laughed.

Okay, I see what's going on here. I turned around, figuring no real man would deny a big butt. I stopped dancing and slowly paced in front of him with my mouth twisted in a manner that stated, *I'm on to you.* "The better question is...what are YOU doing here?"

"Baby girl, DO...NOT flatter yourself. Big doesn't always mean better...okaaay!" He uncrossed his legs and flamboyantly stood. "I'm here doing you a favor." He sashayed to the door showing his true colors.

"My sister...Voodoo Doll, she started out on the pole, and now she's rich and famous," I yelled before he left. "I just figured...that maybe I can get discovered too." I held my head high. *It could happen to me.* He looked like he was someone important...not only there for a cheap thrill.

"You need talent to get discovered, sweetheart." He laughed. "Voodoo Doll...now that's talent. You impressed me with that one." He pointed at me and quickly took it back, saying, "You're not a good student, are you?"

"I got talent!" I was offended and ready to smack the smirk off his face.

"Anyone can grope on a pole. It takes TALENT to make it disappear and become an extension of your body." It was the way that he said it that irked me. "Chile, you just can't come up in here thinking..." He shook his head. "You just ain't ready. Now somebody needed to tell you that today."

I sucked my teeth. "I can learn."

"You in trouble or something?" He gawked down at my stomach. I was eating a lot since the abortion. Nerves, I guess. "Why you need this so bad?" He tilted his body to the side and rested a hand on his hip.

"I don't NEED this." I held my stomach in. "I WANT... the lifestyle."

He thought about that for a moment, rocking his head from side to side. "Now that I can understand. Let's get the heck out of here. I got just what you want."

The devil tried to lure me back, but my new friend and I, we both *sashayed* and *shantayed* out of there. And two Black people caught a cab in 3.5 seconds downtown Manhattan at night because my butt was all the way out. I left my clothes, sneakers, and coat in that rat trap. My friend promised me better things.

He cleared his throat and, in a deep harmonious masculine voice, said, "I'm Timothy A. Moore, from Lystra Projects in Red Hook...but out here..." His pitch rose with the theatrical movement of his arms, wrist, and hands. "I'm Tam!"

The cab driver stared through his rearview mirror.

"You a drag queen?" I asked.

"Please, chile. Don't insult me!" He clenched his chest. "And you, little miss are...?"

"I'm Gomer." I extended my hand to him. "They call me Go-Go."

He stared momentarily then squealed, "I love it! Tally-HO, Go-Go! Purr-fect." He cracked himself up.

"Whatever!" I laughed. "You never told me why you were at the club. You on the down-low? You bi?"

"Oh, pfft!" He fanned me off. "I love the theatrics. I usually go to finer places, like that spot uptown your sister works at."

"Runs." I corrected him.

"Whatever. The costumes are to...die...for, but they haven't been up to qual lately..."

"Hmmm," I mumbled. Le-Le wasn't there anymore. After the shelter, she took a job at a local fast-food restaurant and went back to school for her degree in fashion.

"I don't know why I was in that sleaze bucket tonight...I guess God led me there to save ya sorry tail." He rolled his neck and blankly gazed out of the cab window, stoned faced like he was sorry for turning his back on someone.

He's a believer. I could tell.

Still gazing off, he continued, "You looked so young and new, and those wolves looked hungry. I outbid a fart as old as dirt just to get in with you." He turned to say. "You owe me, chile. I didn't want you to have to go through that. You know what happens to young girls out here?" He took my hand. "There wasn't going to be any money in it for you...only sorrow. But I got you, boo!" He smiled, winked, and fluttered his eyebrows.

Tam went on to tell me about his business. His boyfriend...well he said friend, but I knew what that meant, ran an escort service. Tam found potential escorts in strip clubs and such then introduced them. Together they dolled the girls up—refined them, and then turned them out on commission. The same thing Jeri did with his Video Vixens.

"So, you a gay pimp?"

"Chile, please! I create opportunities. What ho you know gets to live like a millionaire every day and doesn't have to feel dirty about it? You don't have to lie, cheat, or steal to feel fabulous. Chile, I do it myself. We get male clients who want to spend an evening with sexual chocolate like me." He laughed; he didn't take himself seriously, but I was all in.

We went to Tam's studio apartment in Greenwich Village. It was spotless, modern, and sleek. He said the rent was sky high there. We had mimosas and Chinese takeout. He taught me how to use chopsticks, how to sit without slouching, how not to act my age, and fake an orgasm. We talked until I fell asleep in his arms. I liked Tam a lot. He was real and he spoke my language. Money. Everything else can walk. We instantly became fond friends.

What the? My eyes popped open. "Do I feel what I think I feel?"

"I said I'm gay, not dead! Now turn that big thang the other way before I slip up tonight."

"Mmhmm, so, BIG is better?" We laughed.

The Streets - One

I started working for Rowe Escort Services in the spring of 1990. I was a little intimidated at first, but Tam was right. For a moment, every day, I got to vicariously live someone else's life. The best part was the money. I received a percentage of the booking fee plus whatever bonuses the clients paid out...clothes, shoes, purses, jewelry, and of course mo' money, mo' money, mo' money! I was living out that ridiculous movie *Pretty Woman*, and secretly hoping for a similar happily ever after with Jeri.

I moved away from home. I wanted Jeri to be my hero like *Richard Gere*, but at the same time, I didn't want anyone to know what I was doing. I woke up and went to school one morning and didn't go back home. I called Poo that night. She sucked her teeth and said, "Whatever problems you got, go right along with you. Ain't nobody gonna treat you like your family."

"That's what I'm betting on...cause y'all ain't worth a dime." We ended our conversation on the wrong note as usual.

I moved in with Tam, and we shared the bills, rent, and his bed. Tam was gentle and kind. He was also a nudist and encouraged me to be one as well. We harmlessly flirted with each other, shared secrets, and acted like kids who were left *'Home Alone'* on a regular basis. Everything seemed perfect, but there were three problems. One, after a while, I felt like smut—dirty. Two, Tam showed me how to not feel smutty. He had a drug problem that soon turned into my problem. Three, let's not talk about three yet.

I started out with a few clients. They were three unique guys who encouraged me to continue going to school. I could have dropped out, but I wanted my diploma. I wanted that diva life and divas aren't dropouts. It was hard, but I pressed through. I went to school during the day dressed in the freshest gear that you'd ever wanna see a teenager in high school dressed in. Even the teachers were sweating me. I did my work and passed my grades, so no faults could be found in my academic performance. But the evenings were a different story. You know how doing wrong always starts off as feeling right? You get caught up in the make-believe. Like my three clients. They were a smokescreen.

Dan the Man

Dan had a food-fetish. Yeah, you read right. Food was his thing. It kept him calling on escort services to hide his dirty secret. He was a ridiculously cute Caucasian guy with tanned skin and deep dimples. An Italian Stallion. My first white guy. He had more money than he knew what to do with. My job, at the time, was to help Dan enjoy spending it. Every Tuesday evening, we met at a different hotel. Dan sent a limo for me after school. He always left notes that made me smile and accompanied them with detailed grocery lists that made me blush. Dan was a freak, but so was I. I bought all the items that the average person would foolishly consider as just food. I did too, before Dan.

For Dan, food was an aphrodisiac. It highlighted the sensual senses. The fruit had to be a certain ripeness for a smooth consistency. Certain sauces and dark chocolate tasted better on sweaty skin. He knew it all. He was a famous chef; Tuesdays were his slow days. He spent his mornings off with his fiancé and his evenings off with me. I went shopping after school for the necessary supplies. I always made an extra bag of groceries for Tam and I. Dan could have had a different girl every Tuesday if he wanted, he said that he used to before me, but it was always awkward for him to introduce his habit even though he paid for the services. Dan was kind and sensitive to the feelings of others. I knew what he wanted from his profile and treated him like it was a regular thing. I made it fun, and he felt free to explore with me. When he did something that I didn't like, I smacked the taste out of his mouth, then laughed, and we did something else. I liked Dan. We talked a lot about our dreams and people in general. He loved his fiancé but was afraid to tell *Miss American Pie* about his fetish. "She's timid," he said. I told him, "You'll be surprised by how freaky quiet girls are. My sister is quiet. You should give it a go." He always declined. He enjoyed the secret that we shared, the rendezvous, and the expensive food fights. We left a massive mess in every hotel room, but Dan always left an even greater tip.

Tam and I lived on shrimp and steaks for dinner while Dan was around. Tam was an excellent cook; although, he wouldn't have been allowed to cook in anyone else's kitchen but his own. He cooked in the buff and was obsessed over his body. He hung full-length mirrors all around the apartment just to observe himself at different angles. Tam was tall and lean, not overly muscular but just right. His skin was soft and flawless. His butt was round and tight. If he weren't gay, we would have been lovers. He was caring and a good friend. On the nights that I made it home to our apartment, he made sure to cook me dinner. "How do you like your steak?" he always asked, knowing I would say, "Without pube hairs, thank you." We laughed, and I puffed on the weed that he kept nearby. We ate, smoked more blunts, watched *Arsenio*, and talked about life and love.

Richie Rich

Dr. Richard Foster was elderly. He was a retired cosmetic surgeon and philanthropist. My first old white guy. He called on me every Monday, Wednesday, and Thursday night like clockwork. He had an enormous appetite. I was his night nurse. I showed up at his apartment on Madison Avenue in full costume, ready to give him his medicine. All Richie wanted was a little company. His wife died two years prior to meeting me. The other escorts made him feel like an old man. I made him feel like a dirty old man, and he liked that. We talked about how he *used to be*, and the things that he *used to do*, then reenacted his love life. I made living fun for him. Richie was impotent, so he had a pump implanted. That made him feel like a man. His kids would have died if they knew what he was doing.

Hey, the way I figured it: we're all misfits. We're all in search of something more. Richie never made me feel dirty or less of a person. When he did, I smacked the wrinkles off his face, and he apologized. I laughed and we did something else. I liked Richie Rich. We slept in each other's arms every Monday, Wednesday, and Thursday night. He reminded me of Paw-Paw. He pulled magic quarters from behind my ears and gave me extra money to buy clothes and candy.

Tam had an expensive candy habit, which is why he could only afford a studio apartment. He supposedly made good money with his "business partner," who only came over on the nights that I worked. I smelled his cheap cologne lingering on our bedsheets and saw the sadness in Tam's eyes when he left. Tam's "friend" didn't have the nerve to claim him as his lover.

"I ain't trying to fly on one wing, Go-Go," Tam used to tell me in his dramatic rendition of *Sister*, from *Sparkle*, while blowing lines of coke as we laid naked in bed.

After a while, Tam's friend stopped coming over all together. He sent Tam out on more and more escort jobs with closet men instead of rendezvous with him. Tam felt dirty and betrayed. Nose candy was his freedom, a way out. I liked what I did. It didn't make me feel dirty, I laughed it all off and enjoyed life. Cocaine wasn't my thing. I got a high off life.

Leo the Lion

Leonard was a squealer—a 'say my name' type of brother. My first African American guy. He was short and comical looking—not only in the face. Let's just say that his height wasn't his only complex, he had a lot to make up for. Leo was a very married politician and father. We met in random secret places and had mission impossible type sex—in the limo on his way home, in parking garages after meetings, in his office, in bathroom stalls at restaurants during his dinner dates. Whenever Leo called, I was there. He sent a limo to pick me up and whisked me off to some remote location for five minutes of high adrenaline, macho, Napoleon complex sex. This made him feel like a big man. I gave him what he wanted. I had fun with Leo. I played along like there was nothing wrong with him. When he got too freaky, even for me, I smacked that egotistical smile right off his face—he liked that also. We laughed and did something else. I enjoyed it all. Until things changed.

Rowe Escort Services was all about politics. If the clients were happy and spending lots of money, you got to stay. Tam's nose candy got in his way. His clients were complaining about his conduct, and his "friend" released him of his contract. It was September 1991. I was in my senior year of high school when Tam convinced me that he could start his own business. We would bring over my clients and pick up girls with existing clients and pay them more of a percentage than they were getting elsewhere. It sounded good. Dan the Man and Richie Rich felt their services were limited enough to make the transfer. Leo the Lion had too much on the line to make noticeable changes. He stayed with Rowe Escort Services. Tam decided to expand my clientele. He felt I was experienced enough to send out on bigger jobs like dates, travel, and fabulousness. So, in November 1991, I went on my first public date as an escort. He was a tall, light-skinned brother. He was suited and polished for a night of drinking and dancing at his job's annual fundraiser. I acted my age and not my shoe size, as Tam taught me. Dressed in an elegant black sequined gown, I mesmerized Mr. Polished Shoes. He was pleased and came on to me all night long. We slow danced, and he asked, "Do you want to get away from this noisy crowd?" I loved the atmosphere and was having fun amongst adults, but I knew that I was working. I politely nodded, and he hailed us a cab. On the ride to his house, we pretended to be old lovers—nibbling ears, patting legs, and holding hands. He held doors for me and made me feel like I was on a real date. I took him for a Dan the Man or a Richie Rich, I let my guard down. He took me to his brownstone in Brooklyn where he fed me grapes and champagne. But when he closed his bedroom door, he changed. His face was that of a man ready to take his stress and anger out on me. Someone had to pay. I guess he felt it was me.

"Look at you..." He whipped his belt off and laughed. "...pretending to be a lady. Someone you're obviously not." He pushed me down on his bed. I couldn't figure out his game.

His profile read: *Young and ambitious male, seeking fun companionship for social events. Enjoys young, aspiring Black women able to communicate with others of similar goals. Classy and fun. Safe sex.*

You never know what you're really gonna get. Tam was inexperienced in client profiling. He was also desperate and hungry. He didn't do any background checks; he just took the money.

"Take that dress off and hang it back in my closet!" He ordered me as he undressed.

Have you ever felt fear? You can feel it in the air when it's coming. It feels like the devil's boom-boom room—hot and heavy.

I removed the dress as seductively as I could, thinking maybe he enjoys things a little rough. *Let me just roll with this.*

I was wrong. Mr. Polished Shoes was nasty. As I hung his dress back in the closet, he called me every degrading name he could come up with. I stood there in my black lace *Vickie's Secret* ensemble feeling small and hot as hell. I was boiling over. When I couldn't take it any longer, I turned around and smacked the mess out of him. He slapped me back. Then, he proceeded to push me to the floor. I fought and it was as if he expected it. *That* was his thing. He beat the crap out of me, smugly reminding me of how he paid for my service, then he raped me. He didn't even look at me. He drooled on my back and stained my ensemble removing his condom. He kicked me down then told me to go home. He said I wasn't worth the sweat. I let my guard down thinking that I was on a real date. I allowed my emotions to get in the way of work and got my feelings hurt. I cried when I shouldn't have, but he kicked me out of his house into the rain. All I had was my purse and a shawl in Brooklyn. I didn't know anything about that borough except that they have wonderful parades on Labor Day. Somehow, I made it home.

You would think that I would turn around and run home, be done with that life. Instead, after a few hot showers, I tried a taste of nose candy with Tam. It made me feel good. But feeling good is a lie. We laid in bed naked, airing out as Tam called it, and we floated above the world. Tam was sorry. He held me in his arms, kissed my scratches and bruises, and told me his story. He cried while I slept because he knew that I still felt dirty and ashamed.

The Streets - Two

Tam was born Timothy Anthony Moore from Lystra Projects in Brooklyn. He was a child prodigy like Zee. His voice was, and still is, that of angels. He was raised by women in the church, where he sang and played the organ from the age of four. His grandmother, Mother Lois, partly founded The Peoples' Baptist Church in Flatbush. His mother, Eunice, is a prophetess. She got pregnant with Tam during her time in the streets. Like his mother, Tam had been acquainted with the scriptures since childhood. He became an actual believer when he witnessed a crippled boy be healed by a guest speaker named Pastor Paul at his church.

"Can't nobody tell me there ain't no God," Tam often expressed with tears in his eyes, feeling like he disappointed his maker.

Tam, a particularly handsome brother, said there was a time when he boldly professed the name of the Lord through sermons of song, but his light was dimmed early on by a deacon and his uncle who thought him particularly handsome as well. He became timid and reserved to the point where he felt suffocated. Tam met a man while in high school who helped him breathe again. He ran away from his family to avoid the embarrassment of being gay but became his own embarrassment when the man pimped him on the streets of Times Square. I stuck with Tam because he was the real deal. He didn't try to sugarcoat life...except when he used drugs. Then, he avoided it altogether. Which brings me to problem number three.

Mr. Polished Shoes was crossed out from our client list, although he did me a favor. I was living in a fantasy world, smiling and enjoying life like I was really a part of it. What I did was lose layers of toughened skin. Mr. Polished Shoes made me remember that you must have your own back in this world. After him, things got worse for Tam and me, but because of him, I was prepared. Dan the Man married his girl and grew a conscience. Tuesday nights were lonely, and Tam and I missed our surf and turf dinners. One Wednesday night, Richie Rich and I were pretending to be on his yacht in the South of France when his daughter burst into his room and caught us with our anchors down. She almost called the cops on me, claiming something about elder abuse, but Richie Rich swore he'd never see me again and allowed his granddaughter the rights over his personal care. After that, Tam lost his business and our apartment. We rented sleazy rooms, and I went back to dancing on poles while Tam supposedly looked for clients, but he was mostly looking for a high.

Pole life became easy. Stocked well with condoms, Listerine, and plastic wrap, the boom-boom rooms were my place of expertise. The bats that once flew off the walls, making the room thick with darkness, parted when I entered. The cries of young girls became moans of pleasure and every man that I entertained was a soul trapped in darkness, with me as its keeper. This is the life that I get high on! I don't give them my joy; I give them my pain. I give them the poison that runs through my veins.

I met Nick the night that Tam left me. It was Christmas 1991. The year was on its way out and left me with its spawn. Nick. He was one of the regulars at the strip club, but he never visited my lair. Nick was dirty. He frequented clubs to get his jollies off like everyone else, but he also came to release his anger on helpless women. When Nick found a girl that he liked, he took her home to become his sex slave, and after a few weeks or months when he was done with her, no one ever saw her again. Nick came into my room looking for a new mate, and we left together because he fed me his poison instead of taking my pain. He blew lines of coke and laid out a stack of hundred-dollar bills. I followed him like a sheep to its slaughter.

That night, I was permitted to leave his house full of contraptions and devices, with a purse full of money. His plan was to feel me out a few times. I had no idea I would be moving in. I took a cab home to Tam, thinking he and I would be moving out from the sleazy motel room and back into the village where we both belonged. When I got there, Tam was already packing, and I hadn't even spoken to him.

"What happened?" I thought maybe we were being put out.

"Hey, Go, girl. We gotta talk," Tam said, busying around the room. I took a seat on the edge of the bed where his suitcase laid, then thumbed through it checking to see if anything belonged to me. He snickered and shook his head. "Listen, I gotta get out of here." He laid more clothes on top of my wandering hands, then paused and said, "Now you're welcome to come with me...but I just can't do this...not anymore."

"What you talkin' bout?" My harsh tone sounded like my mother's. "Go where? What happened?" Maybe someone hurt him? Tam zipped his suitcase and slid it over to sit by me. He lightly patted my thigh then looked directly into my eyes.

"Chile, my wings are gone." He was referencing *Sparkle* again. "I can't make it out here without a crutch...and I'm not *'feeling'*..." He emphasized the word, giving it life with hand and arm gestures. "This anymore. I'm moving back to Brooklyn... I'm going home."

I stared at him like he had two heads. We were a team. "What? Pfft! You letting your conscience beat you, that's all." Tam often spoke about the church and his grandmother. I got up, took my coat off, and opened my purse. "Here you go. Are you feeling this?" I dumped the money into his lap. He was fully dressed. Tam was never dressed at home. I looked at him for real this time. "Merry Christmas," I said halfheartedly. Tam collected the money, shaking his head as though convincing himself not to fall for the okey-doke.

"I'm done, Go-Go...and I want you to be done too," he whispered, placing the money down and taking my hands. "Listen, sugah, the love of money causes all kinds of trouble. Some people...and by some, I'm referring to you and me, want money so much that they have given up their faith and caused themselves a lot of pain. Go, this life is death. It's killing whatever is left of us. Nothing makes me feel good anymore, and watching you throw your life away hurts me even more. You're so young.

"I tried to pull my hands away from him, but he grasped them harder and stood up, towering over me. "I love you, girl...and I know that a beautiful person is hiding somewhere beneath all this anger." His voice was deeper and more natural.

The beast that swallowed me uncomfortably shifted. I yanked my hands away, stood up, and instinctively started to undress. *One of us has to be naked.* We had our best conversations in the nude. Tam stared at me in confusion. *He's really trying to leave me.*

"Gomer, I'm serious." He grabbed my busy hands. I quickly tugged them back, grabbed his face, and did something that I hadn't done with anyone in a while. I kissed him, hard—then softer. I kissed him with the hurt I felt, with my pain, and with all my desire to keep him. Tam opened his mouth and kissed me back.

We did it. We did it to feel something other than miserable. We did it to end questions and desires. Me, searching to see if I could change him. Him, searching to see if he could change. To see if his body was telling him something his mind hadn't yet grasped. It felt awkward. Suddenly, I was embarrassed by the same body that Tam had seen a million times before. He was gentle with me. Tender. Giving me what he never received. But for me, it was of no use. I couldn't tell where he began, and Nick ended. I wanted it rough. Tam was leaving me. I needed to feel pain. Instead, he held me and treated me like a new toy. The next morning, I woke up to an empty bed and a note.

I guess I still have some soul searching to do. Listen, do us both a favor and go home where you're safe. I can't be worried about you. I took two hundred dollars. Don't wanna go back empty-handed. Merry Christmas, and Tally-ho, Go-Go, you're a wonder.

Love you forever, Tim

I cried like a baby. *I hate Christmas.*

I moved in with Nick after the holidays then went back to school without the flare that I previously possessed. Nick didn't give me any more money, but I didn't need any. My aspirations had changed. By that time, all I wanted was my diploma. Nick drove me to school and picked me up every day in one of those cop cars—a black *Crown Vicky*. My classmates didn't know what the heck was going on. But I didn't care. There were only a few months left before graduation. All I needed was shelter and time to figure out my next step. I wasn't going back home. Anything was better than proving Poo right. I figured all I needed was me, and a boo thang to get by. So, I hid behind books during the day, and at night, I hid behind garter belts, whips, and chains. I laid up eating fast food and getting fat. Nick liked me well enough. He liked the idea of a schoolgirl. He came home drunk most nights and fed me his fist the others. But I stayed. I needed the pain like he needed a punching bag. Nick did drugs and tried to force me to use too, but I always told him the truth.

"I wanna feel the pain, I don't wanna mask it." That turned him on. We fought a lot.

One day while driving in the Bronx, a cream-colored *Lexus RX* cut Nick off and blocked him in the middle of the street. The driver's car door quickly popped open. *Super Cat & Heavy D's "Dem No Worry We"* blasted from the speakers as a man rushed to get out. Nick reached for his gun in the glove compartment. When I saw who the man was, I slammed Nick's hand in the door. Before he could scream, Jeri punched him in the face with brass knuckles through the open window knocking him out.

"Get out!" he ordered me. I quickly obeyed, allowing Nick's head to fall into my seat. He moaned as I popped the trunk to get my bag.

Jeri swaggered back to his car, kinda looking around but not really worried about anything. He had stopped traffic, and angry motorists were blowing their horns at him. Nothing phased Jeri. He rolled his shoulders and adjusted his customized fitted *Yankees* cap. The man was fine, dressed in baby blue and denim, with matching *Air Jordans*.

It was the summer of '92, and I had just graduated. Nick was getting antsy with me. I wasn't a schoolgirl anymore. I think the road trip was goodbye. Maybe he intended to sell me off to someone else like he did the other girls. He told me to pack all my things. He said we were going on a trip, but he forgot to bring his luggage.

"Get in!" Jeri demanded, shutting his door and lowering the music. "Hurry up!" I ran to him and we sped off. "What the hell? You trickin'?"

He asked with a disgusted expression on his face, briefly looking me over.

"NO!" I straightened myself. I looked cute. My designer gear was from last year, but Jeri hadn't seen it. The white denim skirt that I wore was short and tight, maybe a little too short and tight. I wanted to pull it down, but I didn't want him to notice my hands. Tam sold all my rings and bracelets for drugs, and I was in dire need of a new set of acrylics. I was confident, however, of my *Cross Colours* shirt, matching *Nike Air Trainer SC* kicks and cute crossbody *MCM* bag. My perm was growing out. Nick didn't understand the need for a black girl to visit the beauty salon every four to six weeks. So, I wore two long and thick cornrows with my baby hair slicked down on my forehead with *Dippity-doo*. I thought I looked Indian, but apparently, Jeri thought differently. He was pissed.

"This is what the hell you doing? Got ya moms and Rah worried about you and you out here trickin' for pennies, like a two-dollar stank. Pfft!" He sucked his teeth. I sucked mine too because I couldn't care less about what they thought, especially Rah. Jeri got mad and abruptly pulled over. "Listen, I don't have the time to be out here, babysitting...fix ya face before I smack the black off it!"

I fixed my face. But I was pissed too.

"Ain't nobody told you to do all this! I'm grown." I rolled my neck and head, gesturing with my hands.

"Pfft!" He rubbed his goatee and slid back into his seat with one hand on the wheel. "Fix this...NOW." His tone was calm, but I could tell by his temples racing that he was mad.

"Jeri, I'm aiight. I graduated high school last week and—"

"Yeah, I know, ya sister was there."

"What?"

"Fah sum reason shi care bout ya ungrateful rass. She been calling the school keeping tabs on you—"

"Did Poo go?" He shook his head. I don't know why I asked. "Well, if Rah was keeping tabs on me, they should know that I'm aiight. I went to school every day...I can have my own life."

Jeri shook his head and bit his lip, staring off at nothing and everything like gangstas do.

"Yuh right bout dat." He started the car. "But yuh can show some respeck. Your choices suck!" He pulled off into traffic.

"Whatever." I smiled and sat back, feeling good to be right about something.

"So, if you ain't trickin' what you doing? You look healthy, clean..." He took his eyes off the road to swiftly examine me. I melted in his boyish smile.

"What you think I been doing? I been workin', dawg! I had me a little friend. We were livin' at this spot in the village."

"Hmm? Village rent is expensive. So, ya boo sellin'?"

He had mad questions about everything.

"I said, I *had* a friend..." *Let's make that clear.* "...and maybe he was."

Jeri shook his head again. He understood the game.

"Ya lil' boyfriend is back," he said, taking his eyes off the road again to see my expression. I wanted to straddle him. "He's been looking for you."

"Who? José...please!" I fanned him off.

"Nah, my boy. Preacher mon." Jeri likes Zee. Who doesn't? Some time ago, Jeri and Rah were in Brooklyn checking in on a business. Zee and his family were in front of a church nearby. Zee had a crowd drawn around him. He was preaching and teaching to passersby. Rah told me later that Jeri stood there for an hour hanging on Zee's every word. Zee has a way of bringing the Word to life, although his messages are full of doom. Jeri gave a large donation that day, and they swapped numbers. "If you were smart, you'd get with him."

If you were smart, you'd get with me. I crossed my legs; my thighs were thick and tight. Jeri looked down at them.

"What's that bruise?"

I quickly unfolded them and fidgeted with the length of my skirt.

"Who was that dude anyway?" He roughly moved my hands aside and lifted the skirt.

I sucked my teeth. "Stop! Don't worry about that ol' head." I shoved his hand away.

"Let me see!" He wanted to see much more, and I wanted to show him.

"Stop it...I got in a fight. You know I'm always fighting." I laughed it off.

"Well, fix that too!" He stopped playing and refocused on his driving. He was making an illegal turn. "You gonna go see Zee tomorrow."

"What?"

He stopped in front of the train station on Fordham Road.

"I'ma call Blu and let him know that you staying with him tonight...since you carrying luggage and all," he said like he wasn't entirely sure. I could have been transporting guns for all he knew. Jeri leaned back in his seat and pulled a clip full of money out of his pocket. Nothing but hundreds. "Guh fix up yourself. Get ya hair and nails done. And tek dem WACK played out sneakers OFF! Mi neva teach you better dan dat?" I smiled wide like a kid in a candy store, then squealed and leaped over to hug him. He laughed, slipping his arms around my waist. There was an awkward moment of silence as I breathed up toward his ear and him down on my neck. "Get out of here." he softly said. "I don't got time to be babysitting."

I sat up and grabbed my Louis duffle bag. I cleared my throat. "Thanks, Jeri." He gave me an upward nod sitting in a gangsta lean. *I bet I'm not too young anymore.*

PART 5: 1992

Dear Diary,   June 15, 1992

    I don't say this often, but I miss my family. I don't know why. They're probably not missing me. They all have their little cliques, and they exclude me from everything. Poo is always in the bottle and Mr. Jenkins is in there too trying to get her out. Sy and Le-Le are like Run DMC, they're tougher than leather. Rah and Jeri are never home, and Baby Girl is a baby. Everyone loves her. I don't fit in. Maybe it's my imagination. Perhaps it's because I was the baby of the family, or maybe it's because Senior loved me the most. I don't know, but I do know that I miss them. It gets lonely out here. Maybe it's time for a visit.

Diva Status on Hold

My Diva Status

Blu let me use his car to go see Zee. I parked on Charlotte Street across from the Felix home with the tinted windows rolled up. Zee and his dad were in the yard doing some landscaping. Zee was taller and more robust than I remembered. *Where is my lanky childhood friend?* This man had facial hair, contacts instead of glasses, and muscles. I smiled, watching him in a wife-beater working and getting along with his father. Then, I got sad thinking about the time that escaped us. I felt stumped for words. *What do I say? Do I just walk over and say hi, what's up?* I hadn't seen him in almost three years. Things had changed, I wasn't the innocent girl he remembered. We abandoned our friendship. *Well, he left me first!* I thought about all the men I had been with. I started to doubt my choice of wardrobe. *Maybe this is a little too much for Zee. He's simple.*

"Freak it!" I took a deep breath and got out.

Zee noticed me instantly. Who wouldn't? I wore tight, faded denim shorts with a backless crop top, *Air Jordans,* and a blue-printed *Gucci* bag. *Yasss! I'm a big fan of myself.* To finish the look, I was rocking Blu's thick herringbone chain along with his royal blue Beemer. Somebody was going to notice me that day.

"Aye, Solo!" Zee yelled, cheesing and waving from his yard. He wasn't ashamed to express his excitement. We met in the middle of the street and he picked me up and spun me around.

Whoa there! I didn't know he could do that. Especially with the little weight that I gained at Nick's.

"Wow! Yuh like an angel to meh eyes."

I wouldn't have said all of that, but my *Janet Jackson, 'Pleasure Principle'* cut and perm was impressive. I smiled and fanned my hair from my face like a white girl. Zee was mesmerized, and I was at a loss for words. I felt like a harlot sinner entertaining a priest.

"Come nah, let's go see the fam." He took my hand.

Zee's parents were happy to see me, although Anna stared like she knew my secrets. And, after a while, I relaxed and enjoyed them and the trip down memory lane. Zee was still a comedian; his laughter was contagious. He was going back to school in August to complete his final year. His parents bragged like he was the President of the United States. As they should, Zee was exceptional.

"Gyul, wha yuh been up to? Wha yuh do fuh ya' self?" Anna had to ask. The room fell silent as all eyes fell on me. They were probably wondering about the royal blue Beemer parked out front.

Making them wait, I guzzled down the end of the peanut punch that Zee made special for me. It was extra sweet and extra peanut buttery like I liked it. He knew how to spoil me.

"Well..." I wiped the milkstache away with the back of my hand. "I just finished high school a few weeks ago—" Before I could continue, Zee and his dad, Barry, cheered me on. Zee gave me a sideways hug. I guess it was an achievement. When I put my mind to something, I usually do it. Unfortunately, my mind gravitates towards the wrong things.

"Whas next?" Anna went on, searching for my faults. I twisted my face and leaned back in my seat with my thick legs crossed at her kitchen table.

Two can play this game. I took Zee's hand into mine and our fingers interlocked.

"I've been thinking about cosmetology school...for hair mostly, but if Zee keeps getting this fine, I just may sneak off with him." I bit my glossed lip and winked my eye at Zee. He smiled like it wasn't a bad idea. The hair thing was true, though. The more I thought about the future, owning my own salon made sense. I'm good at doing hair. At that time, I didn't know if I had the patience for school again. I preferred driving around town in sweet looking cars like Blu's and Jeri's, looking beautiful and causing havoc.

"Eh-heh, cosmetology, dats a fine idea. You good wit dat," Barry said, breaking the awkwardness. His wife was turning all shades of red.

"Thanks." I nodded, then coyly smiled toward Anna. Our mother and daughter relationship was being severed. "Let's get outta here, Zee." I directed my attention toward him. "We have a lot of catching up to do." I swung his arm and smiled. I knew my dimples were popping.

Zee and I were together every day after that. He convinced me to sign up for *Wilfred Beauty Academy* on Fordham Road and paid for the tuition and supplies. I went to school during the day while he interned with a large telecommunication company downtown. We hung out after hours, it was a great time to be young in the city. It felt like we never left each other. We held hands, ate dirty water dogs in the park, and continued our scary movie date nights. Most importantly, we laughed. I don't remember ever laughing so much. We talked a lot too. Healing our relationship.

Zee had a lot of questions, and I did a lot of lying. I told him that I got with José and we lived in the village for a while, but we broke up. I was stupid. My lies weren't even consistent. When you lie as much as I do eventually, you don't even care. When you get busted, you just make up another one. I could tell it broke Zee's heart, learning that I was with someone else. I wasn't a virgin anymore, but he was. He said he dated a girl at school, and it had gotten serious.

They were taking a break over the summer to see how far they wanted to go into the relationship. The girl was talking about marriage. That green-eyed monster crept up on me real fast. Although I desired Jeri, the fact remained that Zee was mine. I never considered him in someone else's arms. That thing hit me like a ton of bricks. Someone else kissing my man, laughing at his jokes, and holding his hands. *Hell no!* I missed and loved Zee. I didn't realize it until that moment, but I still did.

The beauty school wasn't the only thing that Zee convinced me of that summer. He persuaded me to visit my family. Poo hugged and cried over me like I was a dead relative who came back to life. She was still drinking, even heavier than before. Whenever Zee and I came over, she was already drunk no matter how early or late it was. She looked good, though. Her skin was flawless, and she even put on some weight. It was good to see her. I guess I missed them all. Sy, Le-Le, and Baby Girl had come back home to live with the family. Sy got off the drugs, and he and Le-Le got saved, sanctified, and full of the Holy Ghost power. They finally became husband and wife. My brother co-leads a street ministry in Brooklyn on the weekends, and Le-Le makes costumes for Jeri's dancers, but now she also comforts and prays over them in passing. They moved back to the Bronx because Sy caught wind that Jeri was possibly beating on Rah. But I already knew that. A man like Jeri demands respect and uses force to get his way. It's part of the game. Rah had to learn to play or sit the hell down.

She and Jeri moved back to the penthouse apartment in the Bronx permanently. Jeri ended her lucrative career in showbiz and put her in charge of the girls at his clubs instead. Rah trained them and choreographed their routines. Her celebrity status drew people to Vixens from far and near. Her and Jeri's efforts played off. Instead of one person causing all the fanfare, all the Video Vixens had celebrity status and bad contracts with Island Boy Promotions. Jeri was rolling in the dough, and although Rah was the real star behind the dynasty, she had to ask for money and his permission to do anything. I told y'all from the beginning that Jeri was from hell. You either love that type of man and roll with him or clear away.

Poo begged me to stay with the family, but I wasn't ready. She must have forgotten how we fought. I stayed with Blu a little longer than I should have. He hated it, but he didn't have any choice. He did whatever Jeri asked of him to do. I made sure to flaunt around him in skimpy clothing, torturing him and his dates. I had to make sure that I still had it. Blu was stern and loyal, though, he never budged, and I never gave up seducing him either.

Days before Zee had to return to school, out of nowhere, he asked me to marry him. I know...it shocked me too.

"Solo, marry me." He was on his knee and holding out a ring that looked like it cost a pretty penny. I hoped not his school money. Zee was still doing preaching engagements all over the city to earn extra cash. I went with him sometimes. His words were like fire purifying silver, you could see yourself in them. For me, it wasn't pretty.

"What are you doing?" I responded to his proposal, totally blown away. I did not see that one coming.

We were in his backyard—the pretend *Millennium Falcon,* sipping on iced sorrel punch, and trying to stay cool. It was the hottest day of the summer. Zee looked serious, but there was also another look that concerned me.

"You heard me right. Marry me, Elizabeth Gomer Williams." I gagged at hearing that name out loud, then laughed. "Ah get my love off on yuh, yuh know?"

Not taking Zee seriously, I got down on my knees with him and took his hands eyeing the ring before closing the black velvet box.

"What's going on, huh?" Zee held his head down like he feared what he was doing. Like it was a mission he was on, and it required strength and obedience. I could read him. I lifted his chin, and his eyes were wet. "You don't wanna go back to school, do you?" I assumed. We were having a great summer. I didn't want him to go either.

"Go-Go, I love you. I love you so much it hurts..." His voice cracked. "I'm always thinking of you...and when I think of you... I'm thanking God because I'm truly grateful. No matter what happens, it's Him who put us together. I've always known that you are my wife...and *a man who finds a wife finds a good thing."* I was blushing. My heart was on fire. Yes, we both knew it. Zee stood up and brought me up with him. "Now is the time. God told me so. If I save the world and lose you, I've gained nothing. And nothing else matters to me right now but you. Nothing!"

Well Damn. What do you say to that? "Are you sure it's me that He said to marry?" I wanted Zee to be correct, but maybe God meant for him to marry the girl that he was taking the summer break away from.

Zee said something, but I couldn't hear him. I looked away briefly, thinking about my diva status. *How can Zee afford me?* I mean, I knew that he was destined for greatness but not my type of fame. I know that sounds shallow; nevertheless, those were my thoughts. I must have been frowning because Zee lifted my chin, searched my eyes, and kissed me as I've never been kissed before. The earth moved beneath us. The world spun around us. I wrapped my arms around his neck, and he held me firm and tight. So, tight that the beast that swallowed me couldn't run away.

When I fell limp in his arms, he repeated. "Solo, marry me.

You...are...the...only girl for me—fuh troot. Yuh meh chookaloonks." He smiled and the universe twinkled in his hazel eyes.

Have I mentioned that I've always loved Zee?

"Yes...okay. I will," I heard myself saying in an out-of-body experience, but it felt right in my heart. Zee slipped the ring on my finger. I loved him; Lord knows I did. *But what about Jeri?*

Anna nearly died when we told her. She carried on about Zee's education and his career. She even cried. But Zee was stern and adamant. I never saw him act that way toward his mother. God had to tell him to marry me. He said that he wasn't returning to Jamaica. His calling wasn't there.

"It's here with Solo."

Anna contested wholeheartedly. She shook her head the entire time Zee was speaking. After listening to his son, Barry stepped in. "We cyah fight against God."

I wanted them to at least try. I wanted to see a good ol' fashion family fight, but the Felix household always disappointed me in that area. Anna sucked her teeth and ran out of the room, crying. *Wait until she hears the part about me moving into Zee's bedroom.*

The thought of romancing her darling boy under her roof made me giddy. Zee took a permanent management position with his job. He said he only needed a few months to move us out on our own. That part thrilled me too. A place of my own. Somewhere where I could be the queen bee and make all the decisions, a home for me.

Unlike Anna, my family was ecstatic. Jeri stood off at first but smiled like he was proud of his little brother. I knew that his feelings were torn between Zee and me; I was feeling it too. But I'll do anything for Zee, he's my heart. I can't explain it. I'm in love with two men.

Jeri offered to pay for the entire wedding, and Zee declined; he said it wasn't necessary. Jeri didn't argue; he knew what Zee was saying, but I was planning on some *Dominique Deveraux* type event, he should have said yes.

"Well, we're giving you a flyy-azz honeymoon then... and I insist." Rah hung onto Jeri's arm, her eyes looked glazed over, her smile plastic. Still, she nodded in agreement in her fancy designer wear. Jeri liked *Versace*. She looked like a canary in that yellow silk shirt with the big bow tied up under her neck. "And don't worry," Jeri added. "I'll use the clean money to buy it."

He and Zee laughed; apparently, they spoke before about dirty and clean businesses. Zee disagreed with Jeri promoting and selling sex through his various businesses. Jeri is who he is, dirty. But Zee saw more in him, and they counseled each other in friendship.

"Dred, the clean money we take!"

Zee and I married a month later at his family's home church in Brooklyn. As I walked down the aisle all dressed in white, I just knew that lightning was going to strike me down, but we had to give Anna a proper wedding. Sy gave me away. Mr. Jenkins' feelings were hurt, but I couldn't help it. There was something in me that wouldn't allow me to grow close to him. Rah and Le-Le were my bridesmaids, being that I had no friends. Zee's cousin Sheldon and Jeri stood for him. They looked so handsome standing at the altar in their black tuxedos with royal blue trimmings waiting for me. Jeri nervously held his head down. I was staring at him a bit too much.

Nevertheless, Zee stood tall and proud. He knew about my teenage crush on Jeri, but he remained confident. He boldly and loudly professed, "I do!" and the entire church laughed. I said I do too in a beautiful *Vera Wang* dress and a *Swarovski* crystal-encrusted crown with a veil. Princess Go-Go was in full effect. I used some more of Jeri's clean money because I wanted what I wanted. The wedding was beautiful, Barry and Anna had saved a pretty penny for their only child's big day. They went all out Trini style. The reception was held at the *Grand Prospect Hall*. The music was loud, the drinks were plentiful, and the whining was nonstop. Poo got wasted and Sy carried her out, as usual. Jeri may have been tipsy himself because he treated Rah tenderly, dancing closely with her, whispering in her ear, and kissing her neck. I tried not to look and prayed that he wouldn't do anything stupid, like ask her to marry him. It was my day, and Zee was so happy. Everything was perfect. He held me like he finally had permission to show the world that he loved me, including Anna. She and I bumped heads the entire time, but the wedding turned out perfect. It was a beautiful combination of African American and Trini traditions like the electric slide meets calypso. I couldn't have asked for a better day.

117

We honeymooned in St. Lucia at one of those *Sandals* resorts from television. It was my first time out of the United States. Hell, it was my first time out of New York City. Zee and I left right after the reception and were jet-lagged and hungover when we reached our destination. That first day was a bust. I don't even remember if we held each other. But that night, I woke up as Mrs. Hosea Felix.

Zee laid closely behind me, lightly brushing my arm. I opened my eyes. The room was lit with candles, and our dinner was on the table. Yes, my man knows the way to my heart. Feed her! I was starving. I hadn't had anything since the reception.

"Good morning, sleepyhead," Zee whispered, although it was clearly nighttime. I felt safe with him and I slept the day away. I rolled over on my back and smiled, even though my head was pounding. Zee handed me two *Tylenol* and a glass of water.

"Oh, ho ho, you are a *Jedi Knight*." We laughed.

"Yeah, well, you should have seen me this morning." Zee isn't a drinker; he does know how to celebrate, though. I took the medication and sat up. I was still in the sundress that I boarded the plane in. Zee looked showered fresh in cargo shorts and an opened plaid short-sleeved shirt. He looked fine in his Caribbean tan and married glow.

"I'm sorry. How long did I sleep?"

"It's ten o'clock."

"Holy crap! Why did you let me sleep so long?" We had arrived at six o'clock that morning.

"I didn't want to wake you; you were sleeping so peacefully...minus all the snoring." We laughed. No doubt, I was snoring.

I tried to run my fingers through my hair, but they got caught in my bun. I rubbed my eyes. I knew I looked like a hot mess. "Let me get up and take a shower." I pulled the sheets back.

"I ran you a bath." Zee held his hand out toward the hot tub that was in the room. I saw rose petals, bubbles, and champagne glasses through the flickering lights.

"Wow, nice." I smiled, throwing my legs to the floor. Then it dawned on me that we weren't just sleeping over anymore. I perked up. *I finally get to whip it on Zee.* That put a bounce in my step, and I headed for the bathroom to potty and shower. I didn't want any funk in my romantic bubble bath. "Keep that water hot, I'll be right out," I said, removing my dress before entering the bathroom so that Zee could see what he had to work with. He jumped from the bed and started to strip.

"I'm coming!"

"Hold up, partna! I gotta piss!" I held out an arm to stop him. I knew he wasn't ready for that type of freaky party, but the look Zee wore said "I don't care what you say I'm coming in."

"Meh been waiting!" He pushed and held open the bathroom door. I went through and sat on the toilet. Zee dropped his pants then underwear.

"Wow, you mean, I finally get to see yours?" He smiled and did a little dance. He wasn't bashful at all, he was confident. He wasn't a boy anymore; he was a man. Zee ran the shower and we got in.

The water was nice and hot. I put my head under the showerhead to rinse out the gel from my up-doo. Zee watched for a while, then reached out and traced my arms and face with his fingertips, drawing a straight line to my heart. Every hair on my body rose. I closed my eyes, and we kissed. I don't know where Zee learned to kiss like that, but it was the type of kiss that's electric, transformative, and enchanting all at the same time. It's the type of kiss that you want to experience again and again. No drug can simulate that kind of high. Zee turned me around and began pulling the hairpins from my hair. My body was his for discovering, and instead, he washed my hair. His strong hands massaged my head, and I was weak, moaning even. I thought about what measure I was going to take with him—*easy does it or work him out?* He kissed my neck. *Work him out! He's young he can take it,* I thought as he soaped and bathed my body. He was playing with me. We rinsed. He shut off the water and reached for a robe to dress me in. *Are you serious?* I stepped out with him. Zee took my hand and led me out of the foggy bathroom.

He started to head for the dinner table but changed his mind, then to the tub, but changed his mind again. I could hear his inner thoughts saying, *bunk that! It's time to get it on!* He led me to the bed. I sat down and opened the robe. Zee laid me back and kissed every inch of my body. I thought I'd give him some help just in case he didn't know where to begin, but he stopped me and continued to take his time.

"I wanna know my wife," he whispered. "I wanna know every inch of you." I smiled, kinda seductive, and sorta nervous. He didn't look like the Zee I knew. He looked like a man who intended to take good care of me.

Zee left no parts undiscovered from the soles of my feet to the crown of my head, he knew me. He stopped and noticed every scratch and keloid on my body. I have a few. Rubbing them with his fingers, Zee likely wondered about my past and what I did in the streets, but he kissed them anyway and perhaps said a prayer. Zee made love to me. I'd never made love before. He thought about me. He took mental notes of the sounds I made when he touched me in certain places. He wanted to be an excellent lover to me, and only me. I thought that I would show him a thing or two and, instead, he showed me how to be generous. That night, I felt no need for pain for the first time, and I didn't miss it, although I thought I deserved it. All those years of loving Hosea, so much so, that I wanted to cry because I couldn't have him. I finally did. I cried in ecstasy and loved him even more.

We arrived back in the states with *the dough* in the oven. Against Anna's cautiousness of me, she treated me kindly and spoiled the woman carrying her first grandchild. Six months later, I prematurely gave birth to Jezreel Hassan Felix, and I was scared out of my mind. He was so tiny. Every day I wanted to run—not from him, but away from what him and his father meant to me. I loved them and my love is toxic.

Diddly-Squat

May 25, 1993, I got a call from Poo at seven o'clock in the morning telling me to come over right away.

"It's an emergency!" she yelled, but she wouldn't say what. "Bring Zee and the baby too."

I sucked my teeth. "Are you drunk? It's Tuesday morning! Zee's getting ready for work," I rudely reminded her, secretly dreading my first real day home alone with Jez. We had just moved into our own apartment the day before.

"No, I ain't drunk! Let me talk to Zee."

"Are you serious?"

"Elizabeth...Gomer, I'm serious as funk right now."

After speaking with Poo, Zee took another day off. He wouldn't tell me the reason. All he said was, "Yuh must be there, it's imperative...and I wanna support you."

I started to act difficult. I didn't care diddly-squat about what was going on. If no one was dead or dying I didn't see the need to rush over so early in the morning. *I swear, Poo better be sick or something!* You know how difficult it is to travel with a baby in New York City without a car? But there was something about how Zee looked that wasn't there earlier. We caught a cab to Pelham Bay.

My heart instantly stopped when I walked into the living room of the basement apartment. I swear it stopped for five whole minutes because I died and came back to life. Senior was sitting on the sofa with his thin legs crossed around each other and his arm stretched out across the back. His bright smile reached his eyes. He was missing teeth, but it didn't matter. He was alive! The heavens opened and shined above his head in an angelic glow. My world actually stopped for five whole minutes. I climbed out of the beast that swallowed me and ran to hug my daddy. He didn't stand to greet me, he couldn't. My eyes filled with tears. Without any reservations, I fell into his lap like I was ten years old again and not carrying all the extra weight.

"Princess. My little girl, Go-Go", he cried, squeezing me weakly. I held him tight enough for the both of us.

I couldn't hear anything but our voices. I hadn't cried out loud in a long time; and it was a good hard cry, loud and ugly. Daddy held me as he rocked and moaned in my ear. I didn't care who was looking. I don't even remember who was there. It was only Senior and me. I looked at him. Maybe I was dreaming. He didn't look like himself, but I knew he was mine. My daddy. His hair was patchy and graying. His skin darker, hard, and drawn. His body was thin and narrow, but he smelled like *Old Spice* and *Irish Spring* soap. I inhaled a lifetime of missing him. If I could bottle that scent for all girls missing their daddies, I would.

"My, baby girl," he kept repeating. I looked over at Zee and his eyes were moist. If anyone knew my pain, it was him.

I was trying to be a good Seventh-day wife. Zee preached that *people without understanding will come to ruin*. I was trying to understand. I went to church in Brooklyn, on Saturdays, mind you; with my husband, who was a preacher, and I wore full-length dresses to appease him. Zee tried his best to make me happy. I wanted the marriage to work for him because he gave up so much for me. But each day I grew hungrier and hungrier for the streets. Hungry for the glitter, the chaos, and corruption. Marriage wasn't my thing. Zee could see the time bomb ticking in me.

"What can I do with you, Solo?" he often asked, trying to figure out if there was anything he overlooked. "*Your love is like the morning mist. I want to appreciate you while I can,*" he said as though he knew a secret, and it hurt him. He held me tightly at night and every chance he got, he told me and showed me that he loved me. He made love to me like I was precious. It made me sick to my stomach.

When we still lived on Charlotte Street with Zee's parents, I got just what I wanted. I was out walking the baby in his carriage when José rolled up on us in a black *Infiniti Q45*. A 1993 edition.

"Ayo, whassup, ma?" The words rolled off his tongue like honey. The diamond stud in his ear glistened and the gold Rolex on his wrist told my time.

I made a *damn he's fine* face. Then, I attempted to fix myself. I was rocking mad baby weight and trying to walk some of it off. Let's not get things twisted. I was still as cute as ever. My curves were in the right places and Zee had me feeling real sexy about myself. He loved the weight.

"Where you going with that baby?" José stopped the car. "I know you ain't giving my nani away." I smiled and was instantly smitten.

Jez was about two months old. We got in José's car and rode off with him downtown. He took us to *BBQs*, and I laughed at all of his tasteless jokes and talked filthy trash myself because I hadn't done it in so long. José had been out of jail for a year and he was trying to build an empire for himself. His mentality had finally changed. He stayed away from the block and moved to Co-Op City. We only bumped into each other because he was coming from his abuelita's home-going service. He told me that he was looking for me when he first got out. He said that I was MIA on the streets. I revealed to him that I was married.

"My condolences for ya loss," he joked, mimicking what he heard earlier that day. "Whatever I can do to ease ya pain, let me know."

The conversation turned hot and heavy. We drove to a local telly. I put Jez to sleep then gave his milk away. José and I were wild and reckless as Jez slept comfortably in the $200 carriage that his Auntie Le-Le and Uncle Sy bought for him.

After that day, I gave my baby's milk away every Wednesday and Thursday afternoon. I took the bus to avoid nosey neighbors getting into my business. I did it for Zee. If I hadn't, I was going to lose my mind. The affair spiced up our marriage. I was able to smile throughout church services, thinking about the dirty things that José and I did. During sex, I moaned like I used to, putting a different face on my man's body, and taking over in the bedroom. I didn't want to be loved. I wasn't lovable. At least that's what I thought before Senior showed up.

When I finally let Daddy loose, he explained to me why he left the family. He felt he was no good for us. He confessed about his drug use, the women, and his street life. The rest of the family heard the story the night before, so he spoke directly to me, feeling he owed me an apology. I totally related. Then, he told me that he was dying. He contracted AIDS from a woman that he used to prostitute for drugs. They had a baby together, a girl. When he said that, I voluntarily crawled back into the beast, and, for the duration of Senior's life, I loved him from my safe place.

Charlotte "Cookie" Williams was eight-years-old. If I didn't know myself, I'd swear she was me. We shared the same color skin, the same long black cottony hair, the same dimples, and chestnut-shaped brown eyes. I was pissed. She's a sweet girl, everyone gets along with her. She has Down syndrome and can't help herself. Senior came home to die and leave her on us.

Poo stopped drinking as soon as Daddy returned. In him, she saw her future. She loved him. I could tell by the meticulous way that she fussed over him. She instantly took to Cookie, treating her like she was the link that held her and Senior together. Before Daddy died, Poo and Mr. Jenkins put in paperwork to adopt Cookie. That took a load off Senior's chest. Cookie's mother preceded him in death, and her family disowned her a long time ago, so Cookie had nowhere to go.

As Senior's condition worsened, he required hospice care. So, the family agreed to take on caring for him from home. I used the opportunity to move back in and gain some baby-free time with José. I left Jez with Poo or Rah when he wasn't with his dad or grandparents. The situation was perfect for an affair. Everyone was pitching in to help me. I blocked out what was happening with Daddy, dressed up in the fancy clothes that José bought, and went on secret rendezvous with him. Every now and then, I returned home to remind my husband how good I felt. I lied to Zee and everyone else while shacking up with another man, sniffing coke, and getting high. I couldn't even breastfeed my baby anymore, and I didn't even love José like that. I loved his lifestyle. I sniffed coke to forget about my love for Zee and Jez. Coke helped me to be that perfect Seventh-day Adventist wife. Eventually, none of it helped, my dresses got shorter and tighter, and soon I stopped going to church

124

altogether. Zee knew something was wrong. I was turning back into the Gomer who left him for the streets - *the early dew that disappears*. The more he loved me, the more I ran.

Free Minutes After Nine

One night, I was taking care of Daddy and talking dirty with José on my cell. Remember those "free after nine" conversations?

"What you wearing?" he asked me.

"A tee. What you wearing?" I laughed, reclined on the other twin bed in my old bedroom. I had the television softly playing and was eating a popcorn, pretzels, and ridged potato chips mix from a bowl.

"Take it off...and do that thing."

I sucked my teeth. "Boy, I told you I'm here with my daddy. I ain't doing that. You do it." He was silent for a moment then I heard moaning. I turned the television up a little and peeked over at Senior. He cleared his throat like he could hear José too. He was loud. "Hold on, babe." I walked over. "Daddy, you okay?"

"Every closed eye ain't sleep...I mostly be thinking," he mumbled.

"Babe, I gotta go. I know. I'll see you tomorrow. Keep that going for me, aiight," I laughed. José had said something dirty. "Bye, boy, you crazy." I ended the call because he wasn't about to stop talking. "Daddy, can I get you something?" I fluffed his pillows.

"What you up to, Princess?" he asked without opening his eyes. "That's a fine young man you got at home. What you doing messing it up with some punk?

I wondered how much of my conversation he heard. "Senior, what you talking about?" I laughed uneasily.

"I know what you doing." He rolled over on his back and opened his eyes looking at me through a television lit room. I felt ashamed. "I guess that's my fault too. You got too much of me and ya mama roaring inside of you." He took my hand. "I wish you would learn from our mistakes. Take another direction in life." He yawned and closed his eyes again. "I love ya, Go-Go...something awful. Lord knows I do."

I choked up. "I love you too, Daddy. I'm okay. I promise. Zee and I are fine."

"Go, you lyin' through your teeth. That conversation didn't sound fine to me. Stop hating yourself, baby girl, and give life a chance. When you start loving yourself...I promise you...love won't feel so much like a stranger when it comes around."

"Daddy...you don't understand." I wanted to tell him of my many sins. I wanted to tell someone about all the changes I was going through, but I couldn't because of the knot lodged in my throat.

"Don't miss out on love...like I did...you smart... you'll figure it out…" he said before dozing off again. I sat on the edge of the bed near him and wept like a baby.

Then, I called Zee.

"Aye, hun!" Zee answered cheerfully. But I could tell that he was half asleep. "Whappen? Everything good?"

"Yeah, yeah! I just wanted to hear your voice." It was true. I was losing my grip on reality and needed a solid reminder.

"Wha-happenin' dey? You need me to come over?"

"That would be nice. But, nah, I'm okay. It's late."

"I'm comin' jus-now." I could hear him struggling to get out of bed. Zee and Sy are the hardest working men I know. They both work long, crazy hours, and then turn around and do their ministries. Helping people.

"No, Zee. That's okay. I'll see you tomorrow."

"Tomorrow may never come. I'll be there in thirty. Pull out the sofa for me."

I smirked. "Okay."

"Love you, Chookaloonks."

"Me too."

I spent that night lying in my husband's arms. No sex, just company.

127

He held me and played with my hair. It reminded me of Tam holding me at night, scratching my scalp, and humming old hymn-book songs that were stuck in his head.

Naked, come to Thee for dress;
Helpless, look to Thee for grace;
Foul, I to the fountain fly;
Wash me, Savior, or I die…
Rock of Ages, cleft for me,
Let me hide myself in Thee.

I could hear Tam's angelic voice singing and it haunted me like the creaking sounds of an old house. I closed my eyes and said a prayer for him. I was sorry about everything. I'm a sorry ass person.

Senior died the next day. A month after he had returned. The house was busy that morning. Rah relieved me from my night duty and was up early with him. She came to grips with whatever past she and Daddy shared and helped us care for him like he was her father too. I must say, I respected her for that because I remember how Senior used to beat the crap out of her. She wiped the drool from his chin, held his hands, and spoke into his eyes. They whispered and cried a lot when they were together, and I know it must have been full of apologies. Senior had changed. He was full of that Holy Ghost power that had Le-Le and Sy on fire.

Senior requested that Rah make a big breakfast for the family like she used to. Rah was up early, fulfilling his request. He also wanted a big dinner and had a menu in mind. So, I stayed home from José's house that day and went grocery shopping instead. I watched Rah, Le-Le, and Poo cook for Daddy. I played with Jez, Baby Girl, and even got to know Cookie a little better. She sang and danced to *Michael Jackson* a lot. That was her way of communicating, and I totally got it. Sometimes creating your own world to live in is more comfortable than accepting the one you're actually in.

I also got the pleasure of watching Mr. Jenkins befriend and care for my father. He lifted Senior into his lap and carried him from one place to the other when Sy wasn't around. It was Mr. Jenkins who brought Daddy home to us. Just like that, I loved him. I probably always did. I guess I needed Senior's permission to finally start calling Mr. Jenkins "Pops."

These were the things that were going on every day in the basement apartment. I just tuned them out. We are a loving family. We have problems like everybody else, but at the end of the day, we have each other's backs. I'm the black sheep. I make life difficult for myself.

That night when the guys returned from work, we put on music and danced, laughed, ate, and enjoyed each other. Daddy sat reclined at the kitchen table, wrapped in two blankets. He was always cold. He couldn't eat anything, but he enjoyed watching us. He smiled, nodded, and dozed off into eternity.

One month later, I discovered I was pregnant again.

José or Zee

Not too long after burying Daddy, I found out that I was pregnant. This time I didn't know who the father was. José or Zee? My mind told me to abort it to avoid the hassle, but my spirit wouldn't let me. So, I told myself that it was Zee's baby. The last time I was pregnant with José's, I didn't feel anything but hate. This time around, I was at peace. Besides, I didn't want to take any chances on killing none of Zee's babies. God would surely strike me down. Once again, I stopped the drugs and José, and like clockwork, José went into hiding. His cousin reached out to me, speaking of a drug deal that went wrong. José was in over his head doing shady business with a big-time drug lord in Brooklyn, and they wanted his head on a block. For his safety, José had to lay low for a while. His cousin said that he wanted me to join him. I believe he was somewhere down south. Any other time I would have jumped at the opportunity to run, but this time, I stayed...and it was the longest and hardest nine months of my life. I knew I was having a girl because she didn't give me any breaks. She spread my nose, gave me heartburn, split my ends, and took my looks. At six months, I was put on bed rest or I risked losing her. Sitting still for three months was the hardest thing I ever had to do. No coke, no cheeba, no nookie, no moving around too much. No nothing. It was like trapping a lion in a small cage. I wanted out.

Zee's cousin, Jemimah, came to stay with us. She was in the states on a green card and was looking for work. Zee hired her to care for Jez and me while he worked. I was miserable and fat and had to deal with Jem chattering all day long. She could gossip up a storm, and I hardly understood her talking about *the ting and ting* all the time. Jem's accent was thick, but she was on point. She cleaned and cooked for us, and I was grateful, but after a while, I couldn't take the smell of her seasonings anymore; they made me sick. I wanted American food. I wanted to smell the aroma of bacon frying. I mean, I liked Jem well enough, I'm just not the one for no females. Poo could relate; we're more like each other than ourselves. She, Rah, and Le-Le took turns coming over to keep me company, bringing good old *yang-kee* food with them. Sometimes a girl just wants some fried chicken, collard greens, and baked mac and cheese, not callaloo and macaroni pie.

In February 1994, I gave birth to a beautiful, healthy baby girl, but I'm afraid she's not mine and Zees. She doesn't have a dark golden honey complexion or dusty brown hair with sparkling hazel eyes like her father and brother. She isn't an alluring amber color like me either. She's marshmallow white with pink heart-shaped lips and curly jet-black hair like José, but even José has more melanin than her.

My heart sank when I saw my baby girl for the first time. *What the...? What have I done?* It didn't even phase Zee. He acted, clueless. He cried as he did when Jez was born, then handed out pink bubblegum cigars to all the men in the maternity-ward. But I saw all the cut eyes and heard all the whispering coming from our visitors. Poo had my back, even though I fed her lies about my trysts with José.

"Aww," she mouthed, googling over the baby. "She looks just like Rah as a baby. I wish we still had those pictures of her that mama sent Tante Mags." Poo's eyes were wet, remembering the baby she abandoned. "You know my father, Richard? He was mulatto...and his mother too." She explained to Anna and Barry, who were there. Anna didn't bite her tongue.

"Ah cyah say des child my son's."

"Well, you better get over that. We Creole!" Poo informed. "No telling what type of babies y'all gonna get. Look at my kids! Just pray that they don't inherit our temper." She smiled again at the baby she held in her arms. "She's perfect...yes, she is." Poo was in love, and she had my back.

None of it mattered because Zee was utterly in love with her as well. I named her Lorah Tam Felix, after Timothy A. Moore and *Laura Ingalls* (without the white girl spelling) because I wanted her to be a different kind of woman than me. I wanted her to be kind, smart, and close to God like Laura and Tam. Zee said it was a perfect name. He noted that Lorah/Laura means "Victorious in Spirit." Yes, that's what I was going for. I never wanted her to feel like she has to hide. I want her spirit to be free.

PART 6: 1994

Hey you!   *September 5, 1994*

I lost my diary out here in these filthy streets. My whole life was in that book. If I weren't so angry, I would cry. Now I'm writing on pieces of a brown paper bag.

Brown paper bag letters
Words written for no one to see
Brown paper bag type situation
The trash in the street
Brown paper bag livin'
There go my dreams
I'm just hoping these brown paper bags don't stifle me.

Man, I'm mad! I hope no one is reading my secrets. May the lids of their eyes burn off, and their souls go straight to hell if they read my stuff. Amen.

Lost in the City

Cuchifritos on A Spring Breeze

Zee and I had our first real adult argument six weeks after Lorah was born. I was all healed up from the delivery, and I wanted to be intimate with my husband. We hadn't been together in quite some time. It was a rough pregnancy and an even harder delivery. Jez just popped out, but that little girl tried to do me in for real. All I could think about was what Poo used to tell me, "That's okay, sistah friend! One of these days, you're gonna have a little girl, and you're gonna get back all the hell you've given to me." This kid wasn't even crawling yet and I was paying for my past. In her first month, she had jaundice, cradle cap, she was colicky, and didn't sleep. Thank God for Jem. She stayed with us for a little while longer.

This is where the argument came in. On top of being frustrated with trying to be a good mother, I was craving marijuana. I know it's stupid, but I wanted a blunt so bad that I could smell it. But I couldn't smoke because I was breastfeeding. When the baby had her one-month appointment, I spoke with her doctor about switching her over to formula. I also made an appointment to see a GYN for birth control pills. My stitches were out, and I wanted to test and see if the kat was still good, but I did not want to get pregnant anymore. Zee was the problem. He didn't believe in using contraceptives, and he firmly believes in breastfeeding. His mother's thoughts and opinions, no doubt. When Jez was an infant, I lied and told Zee that I wasn't lactating because of all the stress over Senior. The truth was, I was sniffing coke, expressing my milk because the engorgement pain was ridiculous, then pouring it out.

One night, after one of our scary movie date nights, Zee and I were both ready for some lovin'. He was revved up on ginseng root drinks and the babies were with their grandparents. I hadn't seen a GYN doctor yet, so I didn't have any pills. Per Poo's advice, I was planning on keeping the birth control thing a secret.

"Can't we just use condoms for a while," I asked, interrupting the flow of our intimacy. "I really don't wanna get pregnant right now, Zee, for real, nah mean." The thought of another baby was killing my mood.

"Ahh, come nah. Don't do dis," Zee begged. His body was ready. "I'll pull out. Promise," he protested, continuing to kiss and caress me. I didn't trust that pulling out business...and isn't that a form of birth control? See these are the conversations you should have before marriage, but I couldn't say that. I knew that Zee wanted a large family. He's an only child.

"Okay…" I responded, as caught up in the moment as he was, "…but I'm getting on the pill after this."

Why did I say that? Zee instantly stopped foreplay. I forgot about how passionate he was over his beliefs.

"Yuh wah?"

We had a full-blown argument about our rights, my body, and his beliefs. Zee was working hard on purchasing us a home. Whatever God gave us is what he was willing to accept. We were young, vital, and fertile. I wasn't ready to put my body through all that. I used the argument as an excuse to leave the house before Zee apologized. It was all too much for me, anyway. I was fresh off a three-month lockdown from my pregnancy, and at the time, I was adjusting to caring for two babies, and one was trying her best to rip my nipples off. I grabbed my jacket and purse and left.

"Go-Go, way yuh go?" Zee yelled behind me, opening the front door.

"I need air!" I yelled back, intending on getting a lot of it.

I marched out of the building mad. An evening breeze with the scent from a Cuchifrito riding on it hit me in the face, and it smelled and felt good. I inhaled, smiling, and shaking my head. I knew I was about to get in some trouble. The streets of Harlem were noisy with the anticipation of summer. As I crossed the road, I looked up at our building and saw Zee staring at me from the front window. No doubt he was questioning why he ever got married. I didn't know why, but I wished we never had. It was ruining our love for each other. It was ruining our fun. It was turning us into adults and giving us responsibilities too high for my capabilities. I loved Zee, and the kids, but it was all too much. I jumped in a cab and headed uptown to see José's cousin for some weed and ended up staying the night with him and his family.

José called that night. I told him about what was going on with me, but I never mentioned Lorah. I didn't want him to get any ideas. He said that he was sorry for leaving me and had a plan on how he could get back sooner. He needed my help. Then, he told me something that blew my mind. He said that Jeri was behind the situation that he was running from. He said that Jeri was with the Jewish Mafia and ran the most extensive drug ring in Brooklyn.

"What! Please, you buggin'," I laughed; meanwhile, we all wondered about it. Jeri had successful businesses; he was an entrepreneur. "Jeri does not sell drugs, José. He doesn't have to." I defended my man. There was nothing wrong with the game, but Jeri was more than a typical hustler.

"I didn't say he was ya average street pharmacist. I said he's with the Jewish Mafia. There's a difference, shortie. He's like the whole damn pharmaceutical!"

Mafioso

José went on to tell me about a man he met in jail. This man grew up with Jeri. From José's description, I thought I remembered him from the West Indian American Day parades, but I wasn't sure. This man and Jeri, along with two others, were called the *Four Amigos*. Rodger Willis, Rowan Strong, Dexter 'Blu' Ivey, and Jeremy Cole were doing intricate drug deals on the streets of Brooklyn at the age of thirteen that most grown men could never accomplish. Jeri was their leader. He studied the streets and had heroes like *Frank Lucas* and *Frank "Black Caesar" Matthews*. He was well educated in his craft. Jeri's mother, Yvonne Cole, an immigrant from Jamaica, stayed on top of his education. She worked hard and sent Jeri and his sister, who was intellectually challenged, to the best schools. Yvonne was the lover and maid of a rich Jewish man in Manhattan, named Mark Canaan. Canaan helped to get Jeri out of juvie a few times. He also helped Yvonne pay for her daughter's funeral arrangements when she suddenly died of pneumonia. Yvonne shared everything with Canaan. She trusted his wisdom and advice.

Canaan found Jeri and his dealings on the streets to be impressive and reminiscent of himself as a youngster. Jeri wasn't the average hoodlum. He became Canaan's special project. When Jeri was fifteen his mother was tragically killed in a hit and run car accident. Canaan took the orphan under his wing. Jeri continued his top-notch education, graduating at the top of his class. He also resumed his street hustle with a little more wisdom under his belt and became Brooklyn's youngest drug lord. Jeri kept his mouth closed about his fatherly figure in Canaan. His boys were the only ones who knew him and even they were limited to information. All they needed to know was that they were making more money than they'd ever seen in their lives.

Eventually, the Four Amigos took their business off the streets and became entrepreneurs. They bought-out barber shops, restaurants, bars, and corner stores then leased them out for more than they were worth. Canaan sent Jeri to college to continue his education and keep his hands clean. The Four Amigos were happy with their lives. Jeri secretly handled all the drug dealings with the mafia and his boys watched his back making sure no harm came his way. In return, Jeri kept everyone's hands clean too. He bought businesses in their names, took care of their families, and treated them like brothers. All were happy, except for one. Rodger felt slighted. He felt that Jeri made all the money—he did. He was the one with the secret mob connections and preferred that everyone in his circle be businessmen with no drugs or criminal links.

To build his own empire, Rodger went behind Jeri's back and got involved with some up-and-coming suppliers named Solomon 'Solo' Webster and Kyle 'Ky' Banneker. He stepped on Jeri's toes then lied about it. Rodger was sloppy. He had started using drugs and forgot his business ethics. Later, he got arrested in a massive drug bust. Rodger met José in jail. Enraged with jealousy and fearing that his life was in jeopardy, he told José everything. He felt that José was the perfect person to bring down an empire. To bring the *Three Amigos* to their knees. He was right. José *WAS* the ideal person to bring an empire down. His own.

José was a hustler, and a hustler only knows how to hustle. Unlike Jeri, who values smart work over hard work, José wears prison stripes like trees bare branches. Every breath he breathes is already imprisoned. I'm not one to talk, but José doesn't think things through. If he knew how much I loved Jeri, he wouldn't have told me everything that he did. I wasn't about to let anyone ruin my man's life, especially with my family living up under his roof. José promised to take care of us, but he was buggin'; however, I was still interested in learning more.

Rodger asked José to meet him somewhere on the field the next day. He said that there were too many eyes watching them. He was going to give José the names of a few new contacts that would help build his empire and crush Jeri's. Rodger was found hanging in his cell the next day. The only connections that José could remember were Solo and Ky. He linked up with them upon his release. They were all doing well together, and money was coming fast, but José slipped up. He wouldn't say how, but I felt it had something to do with Jeri. He said his partners, Solo and Ky, started acting funny. There was a drug bust that José accidentally caught wind of before it occurred and was able to escape down south. He had a feeling that his ex-partners were working for Jeri. José wanted me to get close to Jeri and find out. He also mentioned a rumor that a few upper suppliers were pooling together to purchase sizable quantities of pure cocaine directly from the cartel. The profits from the stepped-on drugs would earn the lords and other business investors a seat in a huge casino deal. José felt that Jeri was behind it, and he wanted a piece of the action. He needed dirt on Jeri to pry his way in. It sounded like suicide to me.

"Ain't no strippers affording you enough money to build a casino! Think about it, Go-Go. Keep your ears to the ground and call me when you find something...be on the lookout for those two dudes, Solo and Ky."

I was intrigued and impressed with Jeri even more than before. If the story was true, I had to have him. I would leave everything and everyone behind for the lifestyle that I really wanted. I loved Zee, but I wished that I never started a family with him. I didn't want to be a boring housewife, budgeting money, pushing out babies, wearing off brands, and pretending to be happy. I'm all about the streets. I don't know why they call me, but they do, and I can deny myself of nothing that my eyes desire. My eyes wanted Jeri. Maybe something's wrong with my head. *I want to do what is right,* God knows I do, *but I don't do it. Instead, I do what I hate.* It's like I'm not the one doing wrong at all; it's this sin beast that I'm in. That night my mind said, *"Steal Jeri from Rah. No more Ms. Nice Guy, It's on."* José and I hung up. I smoked my blunt and took the conversation in.

The Streets - Three

Considering everything that José revealed, the only way I could fathom getting closer to Jeri was through Rah or Blu. I abandoned Zee and the kids and Jeri would definitely be upset when he learned of it. Without remorse, I would be catapulted into bad guy status. I had to come up with a plan to utilize everyone's vulnerabilities and get them to see things my way. Jeri had an inflated sense of self; despite everything, he would accept me if he felt that I needed him. He had to feel like he was doing me a favor, saving my life, and keeping an eye on me for his buddy. What I needed was to become a Vixen. I would be around him all the time, and he would finally acquire the opportunity to see me in a different light. I was not a little girl anymore, and he needed to know that. So, I decided to go back to the sleazy strip club downtown to brush up on my dancing.

The game had changed. Drugs were heavy on the scene, and there was more competition than before. The sleazy hole in the wall upgraded its services and the raggedy looking white girls that formally danced there turned into blonde bombshells and beautiful curvy women of color. I wasn't a dime in a dozen anymore. I was more like a drop-in-the-bucket. I had to step up my game to remain justifiable. I did things that I usually wouldn't...I told myself it was to obtain my diva status, but if truth be told, I got emotional and sloppy and started second-guessing myself. Regardless of the extending pit in the hollow of my stomach alerting me to run and go back home, I digressed. I missed Zee and the kids, but until I felt the warmth of a sable coat, the brief shivers from diamonds being placed around my neck, and Jeri's strong arms wrapped around me naked in bed, I wouldn't know if I belonged with him or with them.

It was all easier said than done, I experienced spurts of guilt and worried about my family. Jez was one-year-old. I missed his smile and sparkling eyes. My baby girl needed my milk, and I abandoned her. *Like Poo did Rah*, I told myself. *Rah turned out alright*, I rationalized. Using coke again was supposed to help me to forget everything, but it didn't help. It highlighted my situation, so I used more. I used so much that I forgot my diva status mission altogether and got washed up.

I was sleeping on a cold wooden bench in Penn Station when I was awakened by a man and his wife. They stood over me, calling my name. It was Dan the Man.

"Are you sure this is her?" the woman asked, looking nervous as she scoped out the area. It was after eight in the evening, and they had just departed from the Ronkonkoma train.

I ended up in that odd predicament, retracing my steps. My diary was misplaced, and I couldn't remember where I had been. I recalled a man from the strip club that I was with. He paid extra to take me on a little trip to Long Island with him. He must have slipped me a mickey because that's all that I remembered. I still had my pocketbook with all its contents, except my diary. Trying to figure things out and feeling woozy, I nodded off, laying across the train station bench.

"Honey, it's her. I'll never forget her face." Dan insisted, looking embarrassed after he said it. I saw him, but I couldn't speak. I, too, was embarrassed and stunned. Dan must have confessed about his past life, and his girl chose to stay with him. I wondered if she enjoyed his food fetish, or if he was a new man because of her. "Go-Go!" he repeated. "Honey, go hail a cab. I know what to do with her." His wife obeyed and nervously ran off. Dan waited until she was out of sight and pulled out some change for the payphone. He walked over to the side of me and spoke in a low voice.

"No, she's alive. Yeah, no one is with her...that I know of. Yeah. No. I guess so. Are you okay with that? I know. I'll have to tell her. Okay, we'll be there in about forty minutes...depending on traffic. Okay. See ya then."

Dan deeply exhaled, called my name again, then picked me up using a fireman's hold and carried me out of Penn Station into an awaiting cab. I blacked out.

When I woke up, I was laying in the bed of a strange room. It wasn't the nasty motel room that I stayed in downtown.

"Where's my purse!" I yelled into the air. I needed cocaine. "Where the hell am I?" I threw back the sheets. Thank God I was still dressed.

"Didn't I tell you to go home," Tam answered, walking over with a cup of coffee in his hand, black.

"Tam?"

He looked different. Masculine. He was in a yellow graphic tee and gray sweatpants. Home for the night.

"Didn't I tell you to go back home?" he repeated, smiling and showing his perfect white teeth. He was still handsome. I started to cry but couldn't. *Where is my purse?* He sat on the edge of the bed and offered me coffee. I shook my head.

"I just want my purse, Tam, please."

Hesitant, he got up and retrieved it for me. "I can tell you now—nothing in here is gonna solve any of your problems." He shoved me the bag, and I poured the contents onto the bed. I picked up a folded dollar bill.

"You want some?" I offered, unfolding the bill. Tam rolled his eyes. He wasn't that masculine. He sat on the edge of the bed, holding the coffee with two hands in a way to keep it warm. Using my pinky nail, I scooped up some coke, then sniffed it and rubbed the white powder across my teeth, numbing my gums. I refolded the bill and laid back, exhaling.

Tam handed me the coffee. He knew the fix was the only way to relax me.

"Can we talk now?" He looked disappointed. I laughed and sipped the hot coffee.

"How did I get here? Where's Dan?"

"Dan is home with his wife by now. A place where you should be—home." Tam climbed into the twin bed with me. My eyes widened. He wasn't a stranger, but he felt like one. "Tally Ho, I'm disappointed. I thought I knew you better." He rested his arm around my shoulders and pulled me close. I stiffened because I didn't know us anymore. We felt distant. I sat the coffee cup on his nightstand and eyed my dollar bill. I needed more.

"I did go home." I picked up the folded money.

"Nuh-uh!" Tam snatched the bill from me, crumpled it up and tossed it across the floor. "It's not gonna be that type of party."

I sat straight, looking perplexingly into his face. He wasn't a stranger, his eyes showed concern.

"Tam, I went home—"

"I'm Tim," he interrupted.

"Whatever! I went home. I got married..." I looked down at my ringless finger. I sold my wedding ring for drugs and a room. Tim drew me nearer; he knew how the story of drug addiction goes. I shook my head and started crying. "I have babies...beautiful babies. I named one after you."

"Aww, you did?" He hugged me tighter, kissing my forehead.

"I have a husband...and I..." I cried hard. Nothing seemed real. I rested my head on Tim's chest.

"You have a family, Go-Go?" His voice cracked. "Girl, that's great...what you doing here?" I shook my head again, I couldn't answer. "It's okay, Go. I'll help you get back."

Tim rocked me in his arms and prayed over me until the feeling of running away and jumping off a roof passed by. I wasn't usually suicidal. Well, not in that manner. My lifestyle was most definitely reckless. Every now and then, it got overwhelming, and I felt like everyone would be better off without me.

Tim sat with me for thirty minutes in silence. He most likely thought about his life, and what would have become of him had he stuck with a loser like me. I looked around the room. It looked like we were in a little boy's room.

"Where are we?" I finally asked, convinced that Tim had lost it.

He proudly smiled. "This is my grandmother's house. We're in my old bedroom."

"Ooh, okay. Phew." I sighed, looking differently at my surroundings. The beige walls were covered in old pictures of celebrities from vintage *Ebony Magazines*. Physically there wasn't much furniture, a toy chest, and a desk. I didn't see any mirrors, which was odd for Tim. What stood out most was a shelf full of Tim's trophies from singing competitions, and a beautiful framed 8x10 picture of little Timothy A. Moore with his mother and grandmother smiling in front of a Christmas tree. The room was neat and clean and had a homey feeling, just like our apartment in the village. But it was still a kid's room.

"Are you happy here?" I turned to Tim to see his face. He couldn't be.

"I'm very happy. Every day is a battle, but God is with me...helping me to fight all these demons off my back." He looked around the room, proud of his trophies and poster collection. "When I first got back here, Go, I was a mess. That money I took from you...I bought drugs. Unfortunately, I came back home high, emotional, and as confused as ever. But my family welcomed me anyway. I knew they would. I was honest with them and told them about the drugs, my lifestyle...you." I stiffened in Tim's arms. Telling the truth hurts. It's something that I never practiced. Not even to myself. Tim continued in telling me his truths. "I stood up in front of the entire church and confronted those deacons who molested me. I figured, why should I feel uncomfortable with everyone's eyes always on me like I did something wrong. Those men who rape children should feel the piercing looks. I don't know if the congregation believed me or not, but I do know one thing—there will always be doubt and questions in their minds. Folks will watch their children and start talking to them about these things. Those deacons, with their old asses, should be in jail. My uncle is. He finally got caught."

"Wow," was all I could say. I was impressed. I knew what happened to Tim haunted his spirit and he wore it like old bandaging that needed changing. *No wonder why there's no mirrors in here, he didn't love himself as a child.*

"I'm happy here now with my grandmother and moms. I know that soon I'll have to move on, or at least redecorate." He laughed. "But until then... I'm remodeling myself. I'm trying to figure out who I am...and I'm getting a lot of support... You wanna properly meet my family?" He asked suddenly. I must have met them coming in.

"No, I'm not ready." I was embarrassed. His mother was like a prophetess or something. "So, what do you do here...besides church?"

"It's all about the church. I'm singing again! I'm part of a music ministry. That's how Dan and I met in person. His uncle pastors a large church in Brooklyn. Pastor Paul. You remember I told you about him. He's the pastor who healed that crippled boy?" I nodded, thinking how small the world was. Then, I remembered that Sy co-leads a street ministry in Brooklyn with a Pastor named Paul. I wondered if they were one and the same, but I didn't want to dig into it. There were already too many signs leading toward God trying to tell me something, and I wasn't in the mood to hear it. "I attend Pastor Paul's church now..." Tim continued. "...because although I've faced my demons, I can't sit up in the same church with them every Sunday and carry on like nothing happened. I can't."

"True dat. So, you all saved now, huh," I said sarcastically, thinking of Dan, Daddy, Sy, and Le-Le. Tim laughed.

"Chile, I've always been saved. I told ya, can't nobody tell me there ain't no God! That still stands. I just wanna walk closer with him because even when *we are faithless, he remains faithful.*"

"So, you not gay anymore?" I blurted, looking in the direction of my tossed dollar bill. Tim was silent, so I turned my direction back toward him. He was looking off at the many smiling faces taped on his walls, eventually he exhaled and smiled.

"I learned something that night when...we were...together."

I was wondering when that would come up.

"What? That you're *not* gay?" It was possible. He held me in his arms that night like a man holds his woman. I turned my body toward him, cuddling up under his arm. I playfully put my hand up his shirt to feel his hard chest. I'm brazen and can't help it. Tim bashfully smiled and removed my hand, giving me a *you ain't no good look*. I laughed.

"No, I didn't learn that I'm not gay. I learned that I have a habit of becoming whatever, or whoever, people place on me...from my grandmother and moms to the deacons at church...my uncle and YOU! I wanna love Timothy Anthony Moore again. I think he deserves to be loved." He looked down at me. I looked back up at him and quickly turned away. I could feel the presence of a third party in the room, and it felt like a stranger watching. I felt uneasy but I wanted to feel unafraid and valid like Tim. He continued to speak. "Right now, I'm learning to be me again, and I'm neither gay nor straight. I'm a man with a wounded boy on the inside."

Sounds like a beast swallowed him too.

"I love the Lord, Go-Go. I feel free. I love to sing...and bring people to Christ. It's my calling *to fan into flame this gift of God*. I can't be timid anymore. *For God has not given us a spirit of fear, but of power and of love and of a sound mind*. I have to set an example *in life, in love, in faith, and in purity*. I'm learning to put the kingdom of God first and lean not on my own understanding. And because of this, my territory is expanding. I'm meeting new people and even learning how to sing in other languages. I want my ministry to be heard around the world. I sing...because I'm happy..." he sang in a beautifully carried riff, smiling with perfect white teeth. "Yo canto porque soy libreee! Su ojos está en el gorrión… and I know...he watches...me. I know that you don't understand, but I pray that you one day will. *Christ Jesus came into the world to save sinners*—and, Go, sometimes I feel like I'm the worst of them all. He's working on me. And I'll tell you what—I'm okay with just chilling right now. I know that great is my reward, so when, or if, love comes my way...chile, I'll be ready, and I'm gonna love them because I want to." He emphasized, pointing at himself.

I stayed with Tim that night and we talked until daybreak. He was a new person but still the same kind and gentle spirit. I listened as he spoke. He made a lot of sense but wasted it all on me. Tante Maw-Maw used to say, "never throw your pearls to pigs; they'll trample all over them." Tim's pearls of wisdom were useless on me. I respected him enough not to trample on them, but I don't know if anything sunk in. When Tim fell asleep, I retrieved my dollar bill off the floor, kissed his forehead, and quietly exited the house. Young Timothy A. Moore most likely was a timid young man, but he learned to love himself again through Tam.

Later, I woke up, and I was in my sleazy motel room again, and I couldn't remember if seeing Tim or Dan was real or not. But just like that, I weaned myself off coke. I saw something in the vision that was attractive. It reminded me of what I was doing. I think I know who I am? They call me Gomer, but who is she?

151

Exit, Stage Left

In the midst of confusion, there is truth and understanding. I was just too blind to see it. Street life was all I wanted or all I felt that I desired. I went back to the strip club, back to the pole, and back to the dirty money. Nothing changed. I was as vile as the things that I loved most. I thought I had a plan, it just needed execution. That's when Zee showed up.

The devil was acting strange; for no reason whatsoever, he fired me. I didn't even know you could get fired from a strip club. He was sweating profusely and acting nervous. He told me to gather my things and leave. I tried to be rational with him. I had a big-money client coming in that night, but he insisted that I go. He said, "Leave immediately," in a stern tone like there was a price on his head if I didn't. I later found out that there was. I changed clothes and exited the club yelling and screaming obscenities into the street. Every time I thought of something new to say, I went back in to cuss the devil out. He was messing with my money, and I needed new gear for my comeback. Up until then, I was sniffing my money up my nose and hadn't saved a dime.

I made it halfway up the block before I heard someone yelling my name. I turned around, thinking, *maybe the devil changed his mind.* The voice got louder like it was running towards me. Then through the crowded New York City streets, I saw Zee approaching. I felt like running from him. I was ashamed.

What is he doing in Times Square?

"Aye, Solo!" he gleefully greeted me and without any hesitation, grabbed me into an unexpected strong embrace. He looked great. I awkwardly hugged him back, worried that he noticed me leaving the strip club.

Attempting a smile, I stuttered, "What...what are you doing down here?" I fidgeted with the *smedium* sized jacket I was carrying. It was a cool late summer night. Zee stood back, quickly observing me with a distressed look on his face. My outfit was too revealing. I was wearing poom-poom shorts, four-inch heels that strapped up and around my calves, and a low-neck backless halter. You would think that I would have lost weight with all the dancing and drugs that I was doing but it was just the opposite. I was at a nice thick size, and it wasn't baby fat either. It was 1988 Go-Go size, only curvier and more confident. If Zee weren't taken aback, he probably would have enjoyed the view.

"I'm heading to...umm, our movie theater on 42nd to see that new thriller...uh...*Wolf*, you know the one with *Jack Nicholson*?" he explained, sort of nervous, or maybe just uncomfortable being around me. I was giving off bad vibes.

"Oh, yeah," I lied, but I hadn't been keeping up with the movies.

"You...you wanna come to see it with me?" He cleared his throat and scratched his head, even he couldn't believe what he was asking. His wife abandoned him and their children to roam 42nd Street like a woman of the night and here he was asking her on a date.

I tried to let him off the hook easily. I figured maybe he was trying to be nice. He was obviously out attempting to steal some alone time away from the kids. I hoped not with someone else.

"You don't have to invite me, Zee. I know my company isn't wanted. You go ahead. Enjoy your movie."

"Yuh makin' joke!" he responded, sucking his teeth and extending his arms, gesturing for me to come into them. "This is my happiest day in a long time. I found you. Yuh here. I miss you, Solo." I walked into his waiting arms. This time, I hugged him back and inhaled his magic. He smelled good. He smelled like home.

What I didn't know then was that a young woman found my diary on the Long Island Railroad. She was visiting a friend in Harlem. She saw the flyer for Vixens that I taped to the inside of the front cover. I circled

Rah's picture in a permanent marker and wrote under it: *My sister. I wanna be just like her.* The young lady was a fan of Voodoo Doll's. She decided to take a chance and went to Vixens to meet Rah about the book. As fate would have it, Rah was there that afternoon running dance numbers with the girls. Rah was thrilled. She took pictures with the young lady, gave her an autographed photo, and invited her back to a show. Once Rah retrieved the book, in her words, she thumbed through it. I believed her because she was still speaking to me. Taped to the back cover of the diary, Rah found a flyer of me in my skinnier days at the strip club where I danced. I circled my picture too and wrote underneath: *I'm on my way.* Rah shared the information with Zee. She told him that finding me there was a long shot because the picture was old, but Zee said that he would take his chances. It had been nearly six months since they heard from or saw me.

That night, Zee confronted the devil toe to toe. He asked to see me, and the devil alerted him that there were two other men ahead of him. Zee paid $500 to take their places in line and purchase his wife. After waiting a while in the scum hole and uncomfortably taking in all its splendor, Zee confronted the devil again. He changed his mind and wanted his wife out of the establishment right away. He explained to the devil who he was and why he wanted me. But the devil could care less. Zee then asked him if he knew of club Vixens. He did. So, Zee informed him that Voodoo Doll and I were sisters and that Jeremy Cole was family. He showed the devil the wedding pictures that he kept in his wallet of us all together. The devil started to speak another language. That often happened when mentioning Jeri Cole. Zee threatened to have Jeri come down and handle the matter personally. The devil quickly changed his mind.

"Don't tell her that I was here...just get rid of her. I'll be waiting outside," Zee said before leaving.

That night, Zee and I watched a corny two hour and fifteen-minute long movie, from the back of the auditorium of a partly crowded Times Square theater, just to be with one another. We shared popcorn, drank sodas, and before the movie ended, I was wrapped in his arms, wearing his jacket, and making out with him like a teenager. We went home together, and I showered in my own bathroom and laid in my bed with my husband. We weren't intimate because I felt dirty, no matter how hot the shower was. I lied, telling Zee that I was on my menstruation. Instead, we talked, and I lied some more. Before long, that little girl who wouldn't sleep as a newborn started crying. Zee got up and went for her before Jem could and brought her back into the room.

My heart melted and tore at the same time. Lorah was almost seven months old and sitting erect in Zee's arms. I couldn't help but cry. She was a beautiful, chubby, high-yellow baby. Her hair stood high on top of her head in mounds of jet-black curls. She smiled with my same dimples, one deeper than the other, and didn't act afraid of me. I don't know if I could have handled it if she did. I held her and inhaled her sweet-smelling baby scent while nuzzling my nose under her neck. She admired me, patting my face and pulling my ears and nose. Then, she laid her head on my bosom, just like her father, and she sucked her thumb and they both fell asleep. Silently crying, I held my beloveds, feeling sorry about the things that I had no control over. Mostly lost time. I didn't know what I was doing or why I was doing it anymore. I didn't know how to stop it either. I belonged to the streets, but my heart was caught somewhere between the moon and New York City. Before daybreak, I gently kissed Zee and Lorah's cheeks, and I quietly attempted to leave the apartment.

"I'm not exciting enough for you anymore?" Zee asked before I could escape the room. I exhaled. I couldn't turn around to face him. He was everything to me, and I hated myself for mistreating him.

"I'll be back...soon," I answered, choosing not to lie entirely. I wanted to see my family again.

"Aiight...go then...but memba dis, when you *sow the wind, you reap the whirlwind*...I don't know how many chances I got left in me..." I wanted to turn around, I wanted to see his face but couldn't. The guilt ate at me. "Blessings to you always...Gomer."

What could I say? Look at all that I did. Have you ever felt like dirt? I imagine it's what a pig feels like. All I desired was to waddle in the mud, and it didn't even make me feel good anymore. It's where I belonged. I stopped my tears from falling and walked out of the apartment. I went back downtown to my sleazy motel room, gathered my belongings, and checked out. I didn't know where I was going to live or what I was doing, but I found myself in front of Club Vixens around noon with luggage in hand. Luckily, Rah was there with the girls. When she saw me, she screamed then hugged me, crying. Being stubborn, I couldn't make myself hug her back.

"I have something for you," she hurried off excitedly and brought me back my diary.

This time I screamed, "Where did you find this!" I quickly hugged her then wondered if she read it. Ashamed of myself, I retreated from our hug. *All that stuff I wrote about Jeri!* "Yo, Rah...that stuff I said. Pfft! I don't even feel the same way anymore." I don't know if I was defending my thoughts or trying to make her feel better about how many times I said I hated her and loved Jeri in the book.

"Listen, Go, I swear to you, I didn't read it. I only flipped through to verify that it belonged to you. I promise."

"It's cool," I lied, acting like I didn't care. Rah still had her eyelids, so I assumed she was telling the truth. She smiled, gazing at me like a proud mother, then exhaled and hugged me again, still crying.

"I believe you, Rah. It's good...I'm good!"

"No...It's not that." Rah gestured for me to take a seat then crouched down in front of me. She took a deep breath, wiped away her tears, and clasped her hands together, possibly considering her approach in speaking with me. It can be difficult. "Go, I don't know what you're doing or where you've been...but I do know that we miss you, and we worry when you're gone. It's a bad feeling, not knowing where someone is." She was trying to contain the puddle of tears in her eyes from falling. *Rah is such a sap.* "You don't know if you should call the cops or just leave it alone—"

"Pfft, Rah..."

"No, let me finish...before you run off again." We sort of snickered, but it was possible. I definitely wasn't there to be lectured. "I know that in the past, I rejected you when you asked to dance here, but I'm thinking...how would you feel...about maybe dancing here now?" She said it as if she wasn't sure herself and was playing around with the idea.

"Word?" I blurted. I didn't even have to scheme, the opportunity just jumped into my lap.

"Well, of course, I'll have to run it past Jeri first, but I think that I can convince him." Rah looked apprehensive, but I felt confident that I was going to be a Video Vixen, or at least a dancer at the clubs. Instantly I got my spirit back.

Drop It Like It's Hot

Vixens 2.0 has a different type of vibe. First off, it's located in the heart of Brooklyn, and, secondly, most of the dancers are thick and curvy like me. The charming yet conspicuous club catered to its location. Instead of an elegant uptown smooth players-club feel, like Vixens in Harlem, Vixens 2.0 has Caribbean flair. Most West Indian men are known to love them some big gals, and I gave them all the feelings under one wrapper. Looks, I got 'em. Body, supreme. Personality, this is how I really win them over. Most people don't know this, but exotic dancing is sixty percent hustle, forty percent looks. All the beauty in the world with a dry behind sense of humor only gets you attention, but when there's a crowd drawn around a big behind beauty, like me, talking mad junk, gassing folks up, making sure everyone gets a piece of the action, you don't have a chance. One thing I know for sure is that people are always going to be curious. I can't dance as well as Rah, that's her gimmick. I got mine.

What can I say, I quickly grew in popularity, and I didn't do it for money, per se, I did it for Jeri. I desperately wanted to be with him. It was all that I could think of, and it wasn't even a matter of love anymore; it was about status. In my mind, Jeri's lifestyle could solve all my problems. His money, power, and fame could erase my feelings for Zee and the kids. They didn't need me messing up their lives. Jeri went out on a limb and hired me even though we barely spoke, and I knew he assumed that he could watch over me, but he must have cared too. As I figured before, he was mad as hell. He didn't give me any pocket change or half-smiles as he used to do. He only nodded toward me in crossing. He didn't even make sure that a sister had a place to stay. Rah tried to convince me to go home or stay with the family, but I declined. I was on a mission to steal her man. My home was his crib.

My first day at work was a rehearsal day and the first person I saw was Blu. It was as if all the planets were aligning just for me. The first opportunity I got, I backed him into a wall and pretended to be nervous about dancing at the club. I lied and told him that I would feel better if he was there for encouragement. He agreed, and that night I worked Blu over. I wasn't nervous. I was born for this. I drew him in with my eyes and hypnotized him with my hips. I danced solely for him, like he was the only person in the room. If I was giving a lap-dance, I seductively stared at Blu the entire time. I dropped it like it was hot, and I knew the game was over when he finally smiled. Blu is a straight-up roughneck. They call him Blu because that's what color he is. He's a scary looking brother who doesn't play around, but by the second night of seducing him, I moved into his apartment without Jeri's approval. We both agreed to keep it on the low. Blu owns a few apartment buildings in Brooklyn, but he lives in Harlem. He set me up in an apartment, but once we started sleeping together, we fluctuated between the boroughs.

Blu was a grimy lover. Every time with him felt like a night on the pole and always detailed lap-dances, alcohol, bad lighting, and cheap thrills. But no matter what, we practiced safe sex. Blu was adamant about that. For his own personal reasons, he didn't want any kids. It's a good thing too because I never got those pills from my GYN, but I did use a diaphragm from time to time. I enjoyed Blu, and since Rah and Jeri made sure that I didn't get any of the boom-boom room action, he was all that I had. I stroked his ego and made him feel larger than life. He was the man! I cooked for him when he wasn't cooking for me, and I didn't bother him with being exclusive like other chicks did.

Before I knew it, Blu was buying me things and taking me places. We quickly built a good rapport. He respectfully spoke of his family and fond childhood memories. Blu was born in Jamaica, unlike Jeri; he's a yardie tru and tru. He loves his women thick, his food hearty, and his life is mainly about family and his yaad-boys. He spoke of the dishonest things that he

159

and Jeri did growing up, but nothing like what José said, it was mostly mischievous kid stuff. Blu is most definitely a loyal friend. I could see why Jeri trusted him, but I couldn't understand why Blu trusted Jeri.

There's no doubt that Jeri is a smooth operator, but there's more to him than his looks and money. He's generous, kind, and trustworthy to those who find his favor, but even then, if you get out of line, there's no telling of what he'll do. Jeri's edgy, and that's what I found most attractive. However, in the little time that I was away, he took on a dark personality. Darker than usual. He was quiet and unapproachable, and most times, he seemed angry and didn't smile as much. I loved his smile. All he did was work. Maybe this was the side of him that I didn't know. The side that made all the money and built the empire. In all of his work, nothing seemed fishy. He put a lot of time and energy into the clubs and branding the Video Vixens as *Hugh* did with the *Playboy Bunnies*. Nothing that José said was panning out, except that Jeri and Blu were close like brothers.

What I did learn about Jeri was that he liked his women thick too, and he spent a lot of time in Brooklyn. He didn't mess with the strippers too much, but there were rumors. I also noticed that far too many times than few, my sister's body was covered in bruises. During rehearsals, when she danced, I saw them. The other girls did too. That first month, I got in a few fights defending Rah until everyone learned to hold their tongues around me. When I confronted Rah, she said things like, "I'm getting so clumsy nowadays!" I knew the truth. I lived that truth, but I must say it felt different witnessing her on the receiving end, especially because the main reason she was with Jeri was for the family's security. Rah's a different kind of person, not like me.

Jeri reprimanded me about the fights, but at least we were speaking.

"I can't have my girls walking around here all bruised up," he had the nerve to say, and the beast that swallowed me confronted him.

I sucked my teeth. "Nigga, please, get outta here wit all dat! I'll stop when you stop using my sister as a punching bag. I'm the one out here defending her name!" I clarified, rolling my neck and head like my mother.

Jeri tilted his head like he didn't hear me right. "Wah yuh seh," he asked sternly, holding a hand to his ear and removing the shades that he

160

was wearing like it helped to hear better. I noticed the fading shiner that he sported; Rah told me that he and Sy were fighting a few days before. Jeri was losing strippers left and right because of Le-Le. She held bible studies with them and prayed over them. Jeri confronted her about it, and she left crying.

"You heard me! Ya girls need to learn some respect. They not gonna be talkin' 'bout my family in front of me. Nah, it ain't going down like that." I twisted my lips and crossed my arms. Jeri doubled over in laughter like he was crazy or something, but I can play crazy too.

"What's gotten into the Williams siblings?" he asked, wiping away tears from laughter. "Whatever it is...dat crap need to end, NOW!" He said more sternly, getting up from behind the desk and walking around toward me. I showed no fear. You can't show weakness, they'll beat you senseless. "Mi look like joke to yuh? Nuh romp wid mi." He got in my face close enough to kiss. I could feel the hot air coming from his flared nostrils against my cheeks.

"Rah is kind...she ain't like you and me. You need to check ya' self!"

"Put clothes pon yuh argument." He tightly grabbed my face. That was his way of telling me to watch what I was saying.

"I go blow for blow." I boldly mumbled through squished lips. My squinted eyes attested to the statement.

What Jeri did next rocked my world. He kissed me on the lips, sloppy, wet, and long, and my composure fell completely apart in the beauty of destruction. I went limp in my seat. I didn't even see him walk back behind his desk.

"Now get yuh blow fa blow rass outta yah, mon," he laughed.

He wants me. Rah who?

Who's Ya Daddy?

I was told to go to Vixens in Harlem for an appointment with Le-Le. My popularity was growing. So, I was finally worthy of a Purple Palace creation. That's the name of Le-Le's boutique. What that meant is I was on my way to becoming a Video Vixen and having Jeri brand me under Island Boy Promotions. My big butt and I were already on publicity fliers circulating Brooklyn. I was proud of that, but I was also acutely aware that for me to become an official Video Vixen, Jeri would have to put his relationship with Zee on pause. That meant thinking more about the money than their friendship.

As I said before, Jeri's Video Vixens are like *Playboy Bunnies* or *Chippendale's* dancers; they're a commodity. The Vixens showcase in movies, magazines, and music videos. They're escorts, pin-ups, and porn stars. For the right price, you can have a dream come true with the girl of your choice. People come from all over to see them along with Voodoo Doll, the original Video Vixen. Rah choreographs elaborate shows featuring the girls twice a week, and they are geared toward everyone's likings, both men and women. The other strippers and I work the floor poles, cages, and boom-boom rooms. If I transitioned into a Video Vixen, there was no hiding that from Zee. He would find out, but I was prepared to take those chances. For the right amount of money, I knew that Jeri could put his feelings aside as well. The problem was Rah. There was no way she was letting me do any of that.

I was waiting for Le-Le in her office when an older Caucasian man entered without knocking.

"Oh, I'm sorry, doll face. Is Lydia here?" he asked, looking around the mound of hanging costumes in the room.

"Nah, I'm waiting for her. *WE* have an appointment," I clarified, letting him know that I was first.

"Okay, sweetheart. You tell her that I'll be back."

I half-smiled, and he left the room as quickly as he entered.

Le-Le ran thirty minutes late.

"Yo, what the? Hello?" I yelled, pointing at skin time as she entered, hauling a ton of things as usual.

"I'm sorry...I had to pick up Baby Girl at school, she's not feeling well." She threw the stuff on top of her already crowded desk. I don't know how she keeps everything in order. "And your brother's home today...so I had to take care of him too." She shook her head and quickly hugged and kissed me before heading back to the cluttered desk. I knew that Sy must have looked a mess if Jeri had a busted face.

"Remove your clothes and hop up on the stool, please, mama," Le-Le requested, looking for a pen and paper to write down my measurements.

"How is she?" I asked, following her orders.

"Who?"

"Baby Girl."

"Oh, oh, she's okay. I'm sorry, mama. I'm a mess today." She found her notepad and pen.

"Some old white dude came by to see you," I got up on the stool. I was attempting to get the fitting over with as quickly as possible. I had to take the long train ride back to Brooklyn. I was working that night. Blu usually drove me, but he and Jeri were keeping busy.

"Pfft, oh, that's Canaan!"

My ears perked. *Mark Canaan?* That was the first sign of José's story being true. "Who's he?"

Le-Le wrapped a measuring tape around my waist as I overlooked her work. My measurements had to be precise. I had a flat-ish stomach and a small waist for a big girl, and I liked my stuff tight.

"Don't tell your brother, but I think he has a crush on me." I lifted an eyebrow. "He stops by to flirt and gives me compliments every now and then. He's a fresh little thing too." She laughed it off.

"Well, who is he? What is he doing here?" I couldn't care less about the crush.

"Oh, you don't know? He's like Jeri's fatha or godfatha or something like dat," she said in a thick Bronx Latina accent.

My heart dropped. I don't know why. I started sweating like I was having a heat flash.

The Jewish Mafia. Oh, snap!

"Jeri's father, how's that?' I laughed it off.

"Beats me, girl." Le-Le wrote some measurements down then exhaled before moving the measuring tape onto my hips. "I've been running all day. I don't know if I'm coming or going." She stopped long enough to look me directly in my eyes. "How are you, mama? How is this all going for you?" She wrote more numbers down and then ushered me to step down off the stool; she's short and needed to take my upper measurements.

"I'm aiight." I didn't want to get into a conversation about Zee and the kids. I knew that I was an absentee parent. I didn't want to talk about it every time someone saw me. I went home a few times to be with the kids. Lorah loved me, Zee was praying for me, and Jez was afraid of me. He was Jem's son. She had him eating Trini food, like porridge and crap. *Who eats that but the Three Bears?* He even picked up her accent. I couldn't understand a word my child was saying.

"That's good." Le-Le stepped up on the stool and tilted my head back and forth examining my face under the light. "Dang, bee, your skin is flawless! You got the good genes!"

I smiled and did the crazy *Bill Cosby* eyes and voice, "I knooow...what can I say?"

We laughed.

"How do you feel about the color, fuchsia?"

"Oh, that's my shiznit!" Le-Le was on point with hers.

"Good, that color will definitely pop against your complexion. You're so pretty, Go. I can't stand you." She smiled, writing something on her notepad.

I had to figure out how to get more information on Canaan without seeming like I was snooping. Before I could, Le-Le started

164

doing what she does.

"Such a beautiful creation. Look at what you've done, Father!" she shouted, looking up at the ceiling, shaking her hands in the air with excitement. I looked up too, feeling a bit uneasy. "Go-Go, I would die for a shape like yours. Your brother wouldn't know what to do with me, bee!" We laughed.

Is she serious? I was getting suspicious, she was humming.

"You know, Go, life isn't perfect, but God is." She turned me around. "And you...my sistah are fearfully and wonderfully made. Don't ever forget that. I know that He will give you beauty for all of your ashes." Her hands felt warm against my skin. I don't know why, but whenever sincere people talk about *higher things*, I go numb. I feel small, and I don't know what to say or think. Le-Le could tell I was getting antsy. "I have a few more measurements and notes to take, and then I'll be done. Forgive me if I'm handsy," she said, measuring my breasts. I nodded, thinking of an excuse to leave. I really didn't wanna get saved. I hadn't been with Jeri yet. *"O child of God, wait patiently when dark thy path may be,"* Le-Le quietly sang, laying her hands on me. *"And let thy faith lean trustingly on Him who cares for Thee;"* She rubbed her warm hands up my arms and over my shoulders. *"And though the clouds hang drearily upon the brow of night, Yet in the morning joy will come, and fill thy soul with light. O child of God, He loveth thee, and thou art all His own; with gentle hand He leadeth thee, thou dost not walk alone..."*

Chills ran up my arms, I love poetry. I used to read and write all the time. I didn't know if Le-Le made up those lyrics, or it was a real song, but it felt like she reached into the mouth of the beast and laid hands on the girl cowering inside of me. It felt like a commission to come out and be set free. She looked up and smiled at me. I smiled back.

"I love ya, Go-Go—with a sisterly love that can never be broken...and I miss you." She kissed my cheek. I stiffened, rolled my shoulders, and exhaled. *Here we go.* "May the LORD bless you and protect you." She put her hand on my heart. "May the LORD smile on you and be gracious to you." She smiled again, staring directly into my eyes. "I'm done." She turned around and filed her notes in a folder and put it in a cabinet.

"Das it?"

"Das it."

I was nervous and ready to run off. If I had clothes on, I would have flown out of there. I felt light—like peace was hemmed into an invisible garment and sown onto my skin.

"Have a great day, sis." Le-Le hugged me like she wanted nothing but my happiness. "I'm praying for you," she whispered in my ear.

Join the club.

I didn't acknowledge the power that prayers possess.

I left out of Vixens that day feeling confused. Jeri had a daddy named Mark Canaan, which meant he also had a drug empire. That's all that should have concerned me, but I felt guilty. I wanted to rush to Brooklyn, find Jeri, and give him all the babies that Rah couldn't, and I felt horrible feeling that way. I sat on the train and pondered over the words Le-Le sang to me. *O child of God, He loveth thee, and thou art all His own; with gentle hand He leadeth thee, thou dost not walk alone.*

"I walk alone", I whispered to myself. *Step off! Just leave me alone, God.*

And just like that, I felt the anointing leave.

Fantasies Come True

That night, like clockwork, Strong was added into the equation. He and Blu came into Vixens 2.0 together. I remembered his face from the West Indian Day parades and had overheard his name. Rowan Strong. I made sure not to ask any questions, but I put my ear to the ground, as José suggested. Strong had a few drinks at the bar with Jeri and Blu. They appeared brotherly together, not stiff as Jeri was with other acquaintances. Strong didn't seem interested in any of the dancers, but Blu couldn't keep his eyes off me, and Jeri took notice. The men briefly spoke before Strong quickly left, leaving Jeri and Blu to wrap things up. Blu downed the rest of his drink, gave Jeri a pound, and headed straight to my station.

I worked Blu over more than I usually would. I knew that Jeri was watching. He often left after meetings and headed uptown to Vixens, but that night he lurked around checking me out. I worked Blu over so much that Jeri finally had to come over. When noticing him approaching, I ended the lap-dance and walked back up onto the podium and to my pole. Jeri stood with his back to me and whispered something in Blu's ear. Blu looked irritated. He rolled his tongue under his bottom lip and then followed directions, rushing off. Before Jeri could leave, I seized the opportunity to trap him. I threw my thigh over his shoulder and held him firmly with my calf. He started to toss my leg away, he was pissed. Instead, he slowly turned around as I freed him. The men enjoying my set were amping him on.

"That's you! That's you, bwoy!" they chanted, knowing Jeri was the owner.

He smiled, reached into his pocket, and pulled out a wad of money. He sat down, facing me with his legs ajar in a sprawling fashion as if to say—*okay, show me what you got, ma.* I stepped down off the platform, both elated and prepared to accept the challenge. I roused my fans talking dirty and getting them involved, while signaling toward the DJ to play *Mad Cobra's "Flex."* Like a rude gal, I teased and seduced the hungry men, waiting for the songs downbeat to drop to straddle Jeri. I wanted the message to be loud and clear. *Flex —(Time To Have Sex).* The guys nicknamed me "Hydro" because I could rev it up, drop it, and make it bounce on the drop of a dime like I was hitting hydraulic switches on a lowrider. Rah taught me that trick. I owned the group of gawking men by giving Jeri the lap-dance of his life, and he fittingly rose to the occasion. Before I dismounted, I slowly licked up the side of his face, marking my territory. He tasted like chocolate. We stood together.

"Walk with me," he ordered in a whispery voice into my ear. I had him in a bad way. I gestured for another girl to take my position and sashayed off with Jeri close behind. Blu was watching at the door, I nervously looked away. He put on his cap and left the club. "Wah mek yuh do dis to a bredda?" Jeri laughed, grabbing my shoulders from behind. He had lost his cool. I stopped walking, turned around, and placed my arms around his waist.

"Isn't it my job to make fantasies come true?" I purred as *"Flex"* turned into *"Batty Rider"* by *Buju Banton.*

"Tru dat." Jeri licked his lips. He saw something tasty. He held me around the arms and gazed into my eyes, possibly battling with his inner desires. It was apparent why Blu couldn't get enough of me. "Be at Vixens for rehearsals tomorrow." He kissed my cheek, catching the corner of my lips before he diddy bopped away. "You got it, girl!" he yelled back, before leaving the club like I had passed an audition.

That night when I walked through Blu's door, he knocked the wind out of me with a punch to my stomach that hauled me over. He commenced beating me for the first time, making sure not to touch the face. Afterward, we had make-up sex, and it was just as angry and grimy as the fight.

The next morning, I waited patiently for Blu to leave for work. I wanted to call José's cousin because I needed him to get me in touch with José. I was debating on whether to let him know about all that transpired before I left out for rehearsal. My inclination told me to wait and see what he said first. If it was something stupid, he wasn't getting any information from me. I stood at the window and watched Blu leave the building. Before getting into his car, he looked up at his second-floor window and blew me a kiss. I waved, then he got in and drove off. I waited at the window a few seconds more to make sure he wasn't coming back. A car that looked like Jeri's pulled out from a block behind and followed Blu. I stepped away from the window. I knew it was Jeri and I knew he saw me. I never mentioned it, but I didn't have to.

In typical José fashion, once again, he was in jail, and his cousin said it would be for quite a while. This time, I was grateful. If Jeri was executing a casino deal, he didn't need any of José's mishaps. I had to figure out a way to include myself into his dynasty, not pull it apart.

Steppin' On My Toes

On the train ride to Harlem, all I could think about was my lap-dance with Jeri. I had to hide my face from smiling so hard. We were in sync, and if that ride was any indication of the real deal, I was sold. There were sparks between us, even Blu saw them. I mean, in the past, I may have souped-up our attraction just a little. In reality, it was mostly on my part. At that moment, I knew for sure that Jeri wanted me as much as I wanted him, and not only physically. He knew my worth. I could replace my sister. Rah was getting older, and she was too soft for the game anyway. Jeri could do so much more with a real playa like me. I was giddy. My dreams were finally coming true. In my mind, I was days away from his bedroom even though he saw me at Blu's apartment. That was Blu's problem to sort out, not mine.

I reached Vixens early for rehearsal and was excited about finding out if I made the cut. Rah wasn't at the club yet, so I sat there waiting and noticed a few other girls from 2.0 coming in. *What the heck are they doing here?* I returned their fake smiles and bluntly rolled my eyes. Some other floor dancers from Vixens uptown showed up too, and my bewilderment grew. This was supposed to be a Video Vixen rehearsal. I realized that all the strippers there were the best floor dancers at both clubs. Maybe we all made it, but it seemed like a lot of dancers to me. Right on time, Rah walked in laughing and talking, with the Video Vixens following behind her. Before the doors closed, Jeri entered behind them.

He seemed lighter than usual. A smile brightened his face. I stood up to greet him, but Rah intercepted.

"Good afternoon, my sistah!" She squeezed me around the waist and rocked me back and forth. Jeri walked away in the other direction. Rah started to tell me something but then remembered that she needed to call the girls to order. "Oh, wait a minute, Go." She quickly retreated from our hug and turned to them. They were loudly laughing and talking amongst themselves. "Listen up!" She whistled by pinching her bottom lip together to draw their attention. "Listen up, ladies, before warm-ups Jeri has some exciting news to share...babe," she said, gesturing for Jeri to take the stage. "I have some exciting news for you too, Go! I'll be right back." She ran off, practically skipping like a kid in a candy store. I was confused but getting excited myself.

Jeri took the stage and waited for Rah to meet him. "Good afternoon, ladies." He smiled, looking down at us and melting hearts.

We swooned over him, saying, "Hi, Jeri!"

Rah joined him, taking his hand. My stomach turned. I couldn't stand my sister with her corny *New Edition* liking, *Prince* dancing, fake *Lisa-Lisa* body double wanna-be self.

"As you probably all noticed, we have de best of de best dancers here tideh." Everyone looked around nodding their heads. I took a seat in the back of the room closest to the door. My spirit is always ready to leave. "This is because I want the best...to help me celebrate." Jeri looked at Rah and kissed her hand. I leaned in on my seat and placed my elbows on my knees. *Hold up!* My heart raced. "One month from today, Vixens will be hosting a monumental celebration in anticipation of a large casino deal that's finally coming into fruition...for myself and my partners." His speech grew in excitement with each word. Everyone clapped and chattered amongst themselves, not fully understanding. Jeri ushered for silence. "For the celebration, you chosen ladies will be granted the opportunity to be a part of the greatest show this club has ever seen...along with the opportunity to advance alongside me...into bigger and better things. Mi chattin' bout large productions...STAR-DOM! Yuh hear mi, doah." He had my attention. "A lot of game-changers will be here that night, and I want nothing but the best for them. We have a sound and lighting crew coming in, an event planner and caterers. Le-Le is creating da bomb costumes, and my girl here...my bay-bee..." He seemed like he was gushing over Rah. Jeri didn't normally do that. "Voodoo Doll has agreed to take the stage in a show-stopping finale performance!" He announced with excitement, egging her on.

The Video Vixens went crazy. They knew that Rah was the magic behind every show. They ran up on stage to congratulate and hug her. But I was confused. I knew that my sister vowed never to strip again. Jeri was the one who took her off the pole, now he was putting her back on? Something was up. A loud whistle brought the excitement back down.

"Thanks for the well wishes, I'm gonna need 'em." Rah squeezed Jeri's hand and held it to her heart. She looked nervous but still excited. "Ladies, the fact is we have a lot of work to do and not a lot of time to do it. This show has to be perfect!" She released Jeri's hand and started talking with hers. He stood off nodding in agreement. Rah is a ride or die type chick. She had Jeri's back one hundred percent. I briefly thought about Zee and what he could be if I had his back, but that thought was useless. "On top of everything else," Rah, continued. "We have to keep up with our weekly shows and treat them with the same perfection." She briefly gazed across the eyes of everyone in the room. "Jeri and I feel like we've chosen the perfect people to execute this plan and make this celebration worth...all...the...hype!" The girls were amped. "We need those who will be committed... and like Jeri said there will be an opportunity to expand your personal brands as well as the Vixen brand. So! Do we have your cooperation?"

There was an explosion of "Yes!" They were glad for the opportunity. I was too, but I didn't like all that touchy-feely stuff that was going on.

"Okay, okay, so let's start warmups...and get to work!" Rah yelled over the clatter. I stood up and started to pull off my hoodie. Jeri noticed me still in the back of the room, and he and Rah walked over, well Rah ran over, taking my hand.

"So, what do you think?"

"It's something alright." She wasn't getting any jumping out of me. "I thought you vowed never to strip again?" I kinda whispered toward her as Jeri approached. Rah stiffened and cleared her throat before fake smiling. I knew something was up.

"Yo, Go!" Jeri yelled, pulling me into a half hug like I was one of his boys. "I know I been frontin' on you. I ain't really been feelin' you doing all of this...you know...because of my boy, but after last night..." He twisted his mouth and nodded his head upward like—*you know what I'm talking about.* "I know that you a star in ya own right, and ain't no stopping you," Jeri admitted, pounding his hands as he did when speaking seriously. Now that excited me.

"Right, right!" We dapped hands. "Give me my props, okaay!"

"But do you feel like you can handle it... I'm not gonna take it easy on you," Rah warned, crossing her arms. I knew she wasn't a fan, and if the event was as big as they hyped it to be, I knew the guests would be expecting more than lap-dances. But would she allow that?

"What? You sound stupid. I was born for this." Jeri and I dapped again, falling on each other and acting silly. Rah looked jealous.

"We have some more good news..." She twisted her lips, eyeing Jeri. He stopped joking around and cleared his throat but said nothing. Rah sucked her teeth and exclaimed, "We're getting married!" The lights went out in Gomerville. "Go-Go! Did you hear me?"

"Yeah," I said, quickly nodding. "Uh-huh."

"We're getting married as soon as this is all over...no wedding, just us. We ain't' trying to let everybody know either..." Rah wrapped her arms around Jeri's waist, and for the first time, he looked stupid to me. "We're finally doing it! Are you excited?"

I didn't even know what she said. I went deaf. I looked at Jeri. He couldn't face me. It was just the other night that I indecently grinded whatever dignity I had left away on his lap. I thought we had sparks.

"Excuse me...I have to pee!" I pushed past Rah and ran to the bathroom. *How could Jeri do this to me?*

The following weeks were different. I threw myself into repetitive work, figuring at least I had a chance at getting paid, lovely. I was confused. I didn't know if I wanted to pursue Jeri anymore—or the money and fame for that matter. That's how much of a jacked-up space he had my head in. I couldn't even hear the streets calling, but because *the very root of me is evil,* I wandered with no purpose anyway. My sin was like a spreading vine that only brought forth selfish fruit.

During the month of rehearsals, Jeri hardly came around. Neither did Blu. He came home late every night and collapsed on top of me.

I thought about Zee and the kids a lot, but I couldn't bring myself to go see them. Thanksgiving had passed, and I didn't even bother to call. Blu and I ate at his mom's house early and then at the club. Rah, Le-Le, and Jazmine, the top Video Vixen, prepared a big dinner there; even Poo, Pops, Sy, Cookie, and Baby Girl showed up. Rah was beside herself with happiness, and I couldn't stand it. That chick was straight-up living my life. She told the family about her and Jeri's engagement, but I didn't see any ring. All she could talk about was getting married and having babies, but she never answered my question. Why was she getting on the pole again? Then, I figured it out.

The casino deal meant everything to Jeri. I started seeing a lot of Mark Canaan and the Three Amigos hanging out together. They were all working hard and keeping long hours. José was trying to figure out if Jeri was a part of the merged investments, buying and selling cocaine straight from Mexico. He had to be. There was a lot of activity going on. It all looked like club and casino business, but the faces I saw lurking around were grimy. Rah kept preaching to us about how perfect everything had to be like the President of the United States was going to be there. I knew for sure that Jeri must have conned her into dancing by asking her for her hand in marriage. That's the only reason she would do it. To clear her name as Jeri's personal prostitute and instead secure the title as Mrs. Cole.

It was a sweet fairy tale, but as the month progressed, Rah realized that Jeri had no intention to marry her. For him, it was all about the casino deal. She cried on me and Le-Le's shoulders, saying, "He never registered for a marriage license. I don't think he ever plans on marrying me, and I'm tired of being used." After a while, Rah started looking depressed. The routines that she put together for us were the bomb, and her finale performance even better. But one week before the show everything changed. Rah walked into rehearsal late and angry and said that she was changing her act. She wanted all the dancers to take part in it. A surprise for Jeri, she slyly insisted. From the looks of the changes, it was going to be a surprise for her too. There was no way that Jeri would appreciate what she was going to do. That thrilled me. Maybe it wasn't too late to take Rah's place. All I had to do was figure out how to pick up the pieces and become her replacement.

Mickey D's

I was standing on Third Avenue in the Bronx, getting ready to fetch a cab. I had just come up from the train station. Having stayed the night with Blu in Harlem, I promised Baby Girl and Cookie that I would come to see them the next day before heading back to Brooklyn. It was noon and the streets were already busy with Christmas shopping. I was about to flag a cab when I noticed Jeri's midnight blue *Lexus GS* drive by on the opposite side of the street. He parked in front of *Mickey D's*, rolled down his window, and proceeded to rap to this chick crossing the street.

"Excuse me, miss...yeah, you with the braids...c'mere right quick, shortie."

She was a pretty young lady pushing one of those duo strollers. That's right, that means not one but two babies. Without shame, she rolled the *Cadillac* of strollers over to Jeri's opened window and stopped to speak to him. Even from across Third Avenue, I could see why he cat-called her. She had a banging figure and looked more like *Janet Jackson* than *Janet* looks like herself. Her *Poetic Justice* braids were freshly done and hanging loosely from a head wrap. I let the cab go by and stood behind a light pole to spy on them. Jeri was chewing on a licorice stick and giving her mad game. *Hold up! Is that?* I looked around the pole the other way. Rah was sitting in the passenger seat of the car. Her arms were folded, and she looked pissed. The girl smiled gloatingly; her dimples must have been playing games with Jeri's right mind. *How dare he?* But I smirked.

Why does Rah waste her time with him? She can't handle this.

The girl pushed her stroller to the sidewalk as Jeri rolled up his window. He and Rah must have been arguing because she exited the car angrily. But peep this. The girl took Rah's place in the car and left her kids with my sister. Even I got a little bothered. Jeri literally traded a seafood dinner for a *Happy Meal*. They drove off, leaving Rah standing in front of *McDonald's* with the fake Janet's kids. I laughed. *Ooh...snap!*

"Whassup?" I yelled like *Martin*, taking a seat at the booth with Rah and the kids in the mega stroller. A three-year-old and a sleeping infant. Rah quickly wiped away tears. I felt slightly empathetic for her, but no one told her to play this game.

"Hey, Go. What you doing here? What you up to?" She helped the toddler open his hamburger wrapper. I stole one of his fries.

"Same crap, different day. Better question, what are *you* doing here? You babysitting the stank's kids now? You the nanny?" Rah shifted in her seat and nervously looked around as she removed her coat. I was loud.

"No." She quietly answered, looking down and then over at me. "She's doing a quick interview." I raised an eyebrow. She didn't even look like she believed that story.

"Ketchup!" The kid insisted. Rah bit open a package and started to squirt it on his fries. I held her hand back.

"Excuse you," I told the kid, rolling my neck. "How do you ask?"

"Ketchup, please." He smiled. Little rascal knew what he was doing. Rah gave it to him.

"Now, what's that you say..." I reminded her, staring her dead in the face. "Jeri's giving her a quickie?" Rah reddened and sucked her teeth.

"You know that's not what I said." She tried to give me an attitude.

"Humph!" I stole a few more fries from the kid and he whined. "Boy, you bet not!" I threatened with clenched lips.

"Stop, Go." Rah kept looking at the door. I shook my head and stuffed the fries in my mouth.

"One of the prettiest girls in New York City used to have big dreams of dancing...and she had so much potential." Rah looked at me. I rinsed the fries down with the drink that she wasn't touching. "Now she's hiding behind fear. What's Jeri pushing into you besides his knuckles?" Her mouth fell open. "Tell me something, Rah." I crossed my legs and took

176

off my coat. This was going to be a long conversation. I sensed it was the reason why she couldn't move forward. If only I knew mine. "What happened with you and Paw-Paw?"

Unexpected tears instantly invaded Rah's eyes as she nervously fidgeted for a napkin.

"What? Paw-Paw? What brought that on?" She dabbed at her eyes.

"Brought it on? Hell, it never went away!" My eyes glassed over, but fortunately, no tears escaped. Rah searched my face then tucked her hair behind her ears clearing her throat. She knew she owed me something.

"Well...Paw-Paw came home by himself that night from the bar's Christmas party," she started to explain, losing herself, drawing imaginary doodles on the tabletop. "I guess somehow he slipped away from Tante Maw-Maw and was picked up by an old cabbie friend. He had had a glass of champagne... and you know he was on medication. Anyway, he confused me for P - someone else. He had that Alzheimer's. He got out of hand...then…" Rah swallowed like it was a hard pill going down, she then said what I knew she would say. "He raped me...but he was demented, Go!" She reached for my hand and I moved it. I didn't want her to touch me. Rah was always trying to make up for people. Always paying debts she didn't owe. She drew her hand back and continued her story. "Next thing I knew, Tante Maw-Maw was there with a gun drawn to his head." Rah looked at the door but her vision was past looking for Jeri. It was distant and scary. "Paw-Paw was begging her for mercy. He was confused. He didn't know who I was...but...but she said she couldn't forgive him anymore. She said, I was her blood...their blood. Then, somehow he...somehow he grabbed the gun from her and...he shot himself...in the head." Rah's voice cracked and her spirit outwardly moaned. Tears traced her face. A knot lodged in my throat. I wanted to speak but couldn't. Nothing good would come out anyway. Even the kid looked like he wanted to cry. "Sy heard the shot and ran into the room just in time. Tante Maw-Maw was going to kill herself. Sy wrestled her down and I threw the gun out the window. She went crazy, Go. She snarled and lunged out at us. Le-Le must have called the cops because the next thing I knew they were there, too...Tante Maw-Maw had to be put away—for good. The doctors said, her condition will never change...I'm sorry that no one told you, Go." She quickly looked up and into my blaming penetrating eyes then ran from them back to her doodling hiding place. "It was hard for all of us..." Rah explained. "...and the part that's worse than losing Paw-Paw like that...or getting raped and then being pregnant, having to have an abortion, it was the dreams..." *Dang!* I looked over at her differently. I never knew any of that, and instantly I felt ashamed for blaming her. Rah looked at me with nothing but love in her eyes and said, "Every night, I dreamt of Paw-Paw dancing me around that room, humming a jazz tune in my ear that I'll never forget...and I couldn't, I still can't, determine if it's a nightmare or the most beautiful dream I've ever had. I loved him, Go...so much." She cried into her hands knowing that I was incapable of giving her affection. I passed her some more napkins.

I loved him too. I deeply exhaled, satisfied with finally knowing the truth but my stomach hurt. I don't know if it was the story or those fries that tore me up. Paw-Paw and Tante Maw-Maw seemed so distant then. I held my belly thinking about my own rape and how disgusting it made me feel, but also the power it gave me to fight for what I wanted. Rah doesn't defend herself. She bears the weight of all her fears by covering them up—helping everyone else but herself. She wiped her eyes and looked up at the door again. We both noticed Jeri walking over with the girl hung on his arm like a cheap rabbit fur.

Lord, please don't let me bust this chick in her face.

"What's holding you back from leaving this sorry behind negro?" I whispered from the side of my mouth. I don't know if I said it for myself or for her.

"Why? So, you can have him?"

My mouth fell open. Maybe Rah did read my diary.

PART 7: End of an Era

Dear Diary,   *December 20, 1994*

Stained sheets
Broken hearts
Tears that shouldn't be
Misery replaced hope and left me dead in a beast.
Blood everywhere.
Lives gone.
I feel I'm all to blame.
Where is God?
Where am I?
A dark path I lead
In my soul, there is no light.
O child of God, does he loveth thee?
I don't know?
I walk alone...Gomer, who is she?

Elizabeth Gomer Williams-Felix

Darling Nikki

On the night of the grand celebration, I had an out-of-body experience. I was obviously there, and the event was just as dope as Jeri imagined. However, I felt like I was floating outside of my body, viewing everything as it happened from the perspective of my former self. I was outside of the beast, but the beast had full control. The house was full of ballers, glitz, and glamour that evening, and I was accumulating one hundred-dollar bills faster than I've ever done before, and I didn't even have to sleep with anyone to get them. Still, something was hanging over me. It felt like my spirit was trying to check me, but as usual, I wouldn't listen to wisdom.

You could see the humiliation spread across Jeri's face during Rah's pornographic performance. He loosened his tie and took a handkerchief to his sweaty forehead as she danced to an older *Prince* song that seemed fitting for her rash return. Inviting us strippers back on stage for the show-stopping performance, she became *Darling Nikki*. We were the backdrop to debauchery. Against purple projected strobe lighting and lightly scented fog, we performed lewd acts with one another. It was hot and naughty. Rah moved with sensual grace between each dancer taking part in each forbidden action. She danced and teased back and forth between the hungry men and us. For her finale, she lay arched over the stage, partially naked and flushed with adrenaline, reaching for the grabbing men as they filled her hands with money. We crawled in alongside her like lionesses coming in for supper, licking and clawing at her body as the lights dimmed to *Nikki's* cries.

When Rah rushed off the stage, crying, I floated toward Jeri. There was an apparent unrest in the *Galactic Empire*, and *the dark side of the force* was pulling me his way. I didn't fight against it. I wanted to see how things would turn out. Jeri was beyond mortified; he was enraged. His business partners were shamelessly howling for more Voodoo Doll, and everyone there knew that she was his girl. They showed no indignity in their reaction. Jeri's face was stern and tight. I could see the steam coming from his head. He downed three shots of Tequila before opening vindictive bidding to sleep with Rah—like in an auction. Canaan was the auctioneer. I stood over Jeri with my arm encased around his shoulders, encouraging him. He searched my scheming face, smirked, then wrapped his arm around my hips, pulling me closer as he clinched a cigar between his teeth and anxiously watched the bidding. He started to stand and intervene as it looked like the offerings were coming to an end, and a tall, heavyset white man was winning, but I held him firm and worked his shoulders. Blu was staring and I didn't care. I was on auto-pilot. Fifty thousand dollars! Rah sold for fifty thousand big ones. As Jeri ordered three more shots, the men cheered on the winner they called Doc. Then, Canaan, giddy with devilry, rushed over to give Jeri a pep talk.

"I'm gonna go talk to Rah now," he reported, sort of roughhousing Jeri around. Jeri was acting dazed and distorted. "J-boy! You did the right thing. Don't punk out—not now." Canaan dotted his beady eyes up at me, and I caught sight of the stronghold he held over Jeri blazing in his pupils. I turned away like I wasn't listening. "Everything we've ever worked for is tied up in this room." He continued. "Don't blow it romanticizing over a chick. I taught you better than this." Canaan held Jeri's face firmly. He was showing signs of drunkenness, or was it heartbreak? "If Rah accepts the money I'm gonna offer her for sleeping with the doc...she ain't worth the stress you're feeling right now...and she's out of here!" My heart raced. How could I stand by and watch? It was the out of body experience and I had no control over what the beast was doing. Jeri's feelings were wrapped up in Rah, and my feelings were acting like they were divided between both. "Look at all of these beautiful women here tonight..." Canaan resumed. "You can have any or all of

186

them! What da hell?" Jeri laughed, and in concern, I glanced at him from the corner of my eyes. He downed another shot. When I looked back up, Blu was standing in front of me. His white eyes were all that I could see of his face in the dimly lit room. He grabbed my arm.

"Blu!" Canaan yelled like he was glad to see him. "Show the good doctor up to the Throne Room, Miss Voodoo Doll will be there shortly." Canaan left the table with Jazmine by his side. She was his stripper of choice. Blu's thin lips pursed as he tossed my arm down and left, following orders. When I turned back, Jeri was gone.

That same cunning dark force told me to leave the club and go to Jeri's apartment. As I headed to the dressing room to collect my belongings, a weird sensation came over me. It felt like I was tripping off drugs. But I hadn't had any. I wanted to move quickly, but I couldn't. Everything around me appeared highlighted and defined. The cocky looking man they called Doc was following behind Blu in slow motion. My stomach turned. The techno lighting Jeri ordered lit the room in flashing colors. Everyone seemed to be enjoying themselves but moving at a snail's pace. Before I left the club, I noticed Jazmine, moving robotically as she spoke with one of Jeri's partners, the one he called the "Indian-looking mofo." It appeared she was going to trade Canaan in for someone much younger and finer. The room spun around me, but all I could think about was getting to Jeri before someone else thought to.

Pon De Replay

"What the—?" Jeri spontaneously yelped, reaching for the gun strapped under his jacket as he entered his penthouse apartment. It was early Sunday morning, around five.

He was startled, but I didn't move an inch. I continued to seductively pose. I stood in his hallway, buck naked and awaiting him with my stretch marks, baby fat, dimples, and battle wounds from this struggle-life glistening in Rah's oils. You would think that I would feel self-conscious or ashamed, but I felt no remorse.

"Why don't we stop playing games?" I coyly smiled and struck another sensuous position against the wall.

"How the heck did you get in here?" Jeri grilled me, regaining his cool and lustfully gawking like I was a steak dinner that he was about to indulge. He removed his mink-trimmed leather coat and tossed it to the floor. I inhaled deeply.

The smell of expensive stuff does something to me. A brisk chill ran over my spine. *This could all be mine.* I exhaled, trying to play it cool, but the excitement had already reached my breasts. I revealed the spare key that Rah made in case of emergencies, dangling from a rabbit-foot keyring hooked around my pointer finger. I bit down on my bottom lip. *Eeeooowww, it's about to be on.*

"Pfft! I should've known that key was a mistake," Jeri removed his pagers and loosened his tie. No doubt, he was referring to giving Rah the key to his world when he should have given it to me.

I boldly strutted down the hall, wearing only a pair of black patent leather stilettos and stopped mid-way for Jeri to absorb all my lushness. I tossed him the spare key. He caught it midair, with one hand, without taking his eyes off me. I swallowed hard. *Hmm, a multi-tasker. That's what I'm talkin' bout.*

"So, what you wanna do?" I popped my fingers and rolled my neck.

Jeri advanced toward me; I could feel the rhythm of Jamaica beating in sync with his diddy-bop. He licked his lips and moved in fast. *Oh, snap!* I braced myself. *This is really happening?* His favorite rap group was *Wu-Tang Clan*, and as he approached, I swore I could hear the chorus to "*Shimmy Shimmy Ya*," by *Ol' Dirty Bastard*, playing from the back of his mind. Raw isn't what I was expecting. Naively, I anticipated something smoother like *Denzel Washington's* character *Bleek Gilliam*, with his sexy self, playing the trumpet. Some rose petals and candles scattered about and Jeri lifting my big butt off the ground, but he didn't. He ripped off his shirt—the buttons and all. He was built like Adonis. I melted.

"Damn!" I said out loud, mentally scanning his god-like image for future reference.

Jeri's eagerness made me nervous. I led him into his bedroom. Hoping the change of atmosphere would conjure up a more romantic and gentle side of him. I wanted this dream to play out in high-definition slow motion, not fast forward to end. The bedroom setting only excited him more. He didn't give me a chance to become a part of the moment. Before I knew it, Jeri was kneading my body like dough, but no shivers ran up my spine. His strong clammy hands grabbed me but didn't hold me in an embrace. His juicy lips were sweet but not as sweet as I imagined. His mouth was cold, his kisses lacked the transformative ability to carry me away. I was still where I wasn't supposed to be. Instantly guilt and remorse set in, but it was too late for that. Jeri was grunting, humping, and speaking in tongues on top of me. I tried to psych myself into enjoying the moment that I dreamt of all these years, but I couldn't. *This negro is high, and he smells of too much tequila.* My eyes were on my chocolate dream, but he didn't return my gaze. *Yo, don't you realize that this is us...or maybe it was only my dream?* Jeri roared in prematurely released pleasure.

Damn, I should have had a V8...like really!

I was just about to cuss him out when Rah, hysterically yelled from the bedroom door.

"Go-Go! What are you doing?" Her eyes frantically dotted over the forbidden scene. From her expression, I could tell that she didn't fully register what she witnessed.

Jeri and I scrambled in shock. I shielded my naked body with my arms, while he instinctively jumped for his pistol on the nightstand.

"Damn," he mumbled under his breath, placing the pistol down and picking up a cigar instead. "Well, isn't this a blip," he teased with impish laughter, leaning back on the plush white pillows that Rah decorated the bed with. He lit his stogie, laughing harder. Payback was written all over his face, and that's why I thought I loved him.

"How could you? Why would you?" Rah asked, mainly toward me. The betrayal was tearing her delicate heart apart, and I was embarrassed, but gloating never-the-less in my achievement.

I leaned back into Jeri's outstretched arm. All those years, I waited for Rah to familiarize herself with the pain of defeat. *Yup, I'm taking this front-row seat.* An arrogant mien smeared across my brazen face, but at the same time, I couldn't help wondering, why I was doing what I was doing. My eyes locked with my sister's. Suddenly, I felt like I was that 8-year-old girl, again, meeting her for the first time. Rah's eyes were red, her lips pressed together. She exhaled and tugged at the red satin sheet she wore tied like a toga around her neck. *Why is she wearing that?* I pulled their pure white sheets up over my sullied body as Rah shifted her intensified gaze toward Jeri. His laughter stopped immediately in her silence. Flames of fire were in her eyes.

"Weh yuh friends?" he calmly asked, straight-faced like he knew a secret.

"You tell me since you know so much," she responded, mumbling under her breath, "I'm outta here."

Jeri jumped out of bed, grabbing his gun, and awkwardly hopping into his boxers. I didn't know what to do, but I knew he had a gun. I pulled one of the sheets off the bed and wrapped it around my body, then cautiously followed behind him as he cautiously followed behind her.

Hell hath no fury as a woman scorned. Jeri must have been thinking the same way.

The Real Fighter of the Family

A wise man once said, *"In love, one always starts by deceiving oneself...and ends by deceiving others. That is what the world calls a romance."* I brought on a tragic romance by loving two men. I desired one and needed the other and dragged my family through hell, pursuing them both. Then, there I was standing afraid in Jeri's apartment, like the third wheel I had become in his and Rah's relationship, watching as he tortured my sister. I said before that I wouldn't know if he and I truly belonged together until I felt his naked skin against mine in bed. Well...we didn't belong.

Rah stormed into the living room. Her eyes frantically searched the area before focusing on an oil painting by an urban artist with whom Jeri was acquainted. She strutted across the room and tossed the canvas picture on the floor, revealing a safe. Even I know that messing with Jeri's money was a no-no. He grabbed Rah by the arm and swiftly twisted her around from the safe.

"Yo, don't touch my money. I ain't even playing." He forcefully thrust her against the wall, wrapped his hand around her slender throat, and placed the gun he held to her temple.

I tiptoed into the living room. *Maybe this street life ain't for me anymore.* The sight of the gun held to Rah's head instantly divorced me from my past and I wanted nothing to do with the things that I previously wanted.

Jeri's temper was easily escalated. It could go from zero to one hundred in a matter of seconds. He curled his lips and aimed the pistol at

Rah's head like he dared her to say something. Her lips curled in anger as well, but she stood as still as a statue with her face turned away from him. Jeri carefully observed her body. He was probably wondering, as I was, why the heck she was wearing the linen from the Throne Room and thigh-high stiletto boots. He scowled in disgust, perhaps with the image of her raunchy performance still hung up in his head.

"Chaz said he monitored that Indian looking mofo and his boy, Ky, going into your room. What's that all about?" Using the gun, Jeri maneuvered Rah's head forward facing him.

I moved in closer to hear. Chaz oversaw security at Vixens. The Champagne Room and the Throne Room were the two most expensive rooms at the club. The floor that they were on was always monitored. Because I left early, I didn't know the outcome of Rah's fate. All I cared about was mine and Jeri's together.

"You tell me," Rah related sarcastically. Jeri must have tightened his grip on her throat because she yelped, and like an idiot, I slowly approached, afraid.

"Jeri…please don't kill her," I cowardly whispered, as if I had some sort of authority or say so in the matter.

"Shut di hell up! Wah yuh still doing here?" he barked, waving the gun. "Leave, mon," he ordered. I slipped out of his view, but I didn't leave. I couldn't. This was my fault. I wanted to live my sister's life, not take her life. "Where were you, and why did it take you so long to get back here?" Jeri continued interrogating Rah. "Weh yuh wid dem pretty boys, anh?" He tossed her to the floor, and she coughed, attempting to regain her breath.

"I wasn't with anyone."

"So where did they go? Better question, why were they there in the first place?"

"What do you mean, why were they there? You sent them! We didn't have a tea party," Rah got back up on her feet.

"Mi neva send no one but the doc, and that was a test of your loyalty, which you obviously have none. I told Canaan you would never take that money, and you made a fool of me!" He pushed her head as hard as he could, and she stumbled backward but regained her footing. I stood hiding around the corner, feeling like I was snooping in on their life, but

I couldn't believe Rah took the money either.

"I have no loyalty?" Rah repeated. "Your money, your drugs, and your women have always come before me! Don't try to play down what happened last night as my fault. We both know that you and Canaan want me out. You have bigger plans that don't include me, and that's aiight because Rahab will be okay. I do want my money out of this safe, though."

Jeri chuckled with a contemptuous undertone. He paced the room then noticed me standing nervously in the corner. Walking over, he licked his lips in remembering our escapade. It was only minutes ago that he had fed me his manhood. The essence was still running warmly down my thighs. He towered over me, I laid my shaking hands on his bare chest, in surrender, but he stepped back. His mouth twisted in repulsion like he wanted nothing more to do with me. He laughed, taking notice of my attire and Rah's similar one in red. He probably considered us one and the same, whores. Jeri took a seat nearest Rah.

"You want YOUR money?" he asked her sarcastically.

"Yeah! The money I worked for all these years. The money I earned training them superstar vixens," Rah yelled back, rolling her neck in grand Poo fashion.

Now isn't the time to grow a backbone, Rah, I thought—wishing we both could leave.

"You worked for? You did it all, huh?"

"That's right. Those clubs would be NOTHING without me, and you know it. Ya so-called Bonnie. Ya ride or die. Remember that, bruh?"

Jeri jumped up abruptly and forcefully grabbed and squeezed her face. He aimed the gun between her eyes and pushed her against the wall. I shrieked, coming out from the corner.

"Let me tell you something and don't you ever forget it. I'm the Head Negro in Charge. I run this show; everyone else is a pawn. Got that!" Rah grimaced and tightly shut her eyes.

I could see the strength crawling up in her like a sunrise. She pressed her lips firmly together. The tears running down her cheeks stopped. In her strength, I fell apart and wished I never left my life. I can take a beating. A beating is like an initiation, a rite of passage in the streets where only the strong survive. Jeri was seeking blood. This was about betrayal, a matter of loyalty and respect. The end of the road for a playa. I wasn't ready to die, and I knew that Rah didn't deserve it. I covered my mouth as she opened her eyes and stared Jeri down past the black steel pressed between her eyes. He squeezed her face a little harder in spitefulness and moved the gun under her chin.

"I'm…still…in…charge," the words rolled off his lips like poison.

"NOW you are…because I'm out." My heart stopped.

"If you don't shut ya lip, you'll find your way outta here quicker than you think. Yuh tink yuh run dem gals? I pimp you hoes." Jeri turned his head and looked at me, making sure I too felt the sting. "I'm the one turning y'all out!" As quickly as he looked at me, he turned back to Rah, and my feelings were crushed. I felt belittled and started to tear up as Jeri gloated on telling secrets that we all thought we knew but needed to hear out loud. I didn't care anymore about who he was or what he did. "This dope ring, that's me, Jeri Cole. I run the largest operation in Brooklyn. Don't think all I have is because of ya cheap two-step." He released Rah's face forcefully. "Dis deal going down tomorrow isn't because of you. Mi nuh tink suh. I got over twenty of my *boyz* waiting to *cut rocks* tomorrow. This whole building is gonna be crack central, and I'm getting rid of all you lazy mooching mofos." He stretched out his arms as if displaying the apartment. "You think *all this* is because of you? You're stupider than I give you credit for. I'ma push so much snow out of this building all five boroughs will be white by Wednesday. I'm the mickey-fickey man! Not dat wack Indian looking mofo, his tired bucket head partner, dat hillbilly doctor, or any of them other suckers you *bonin'*. They all wanna piece of what I got!" He quickly spun Rah around by the arm, slamming her down on the chaise lounge. She shrieked, and I ran over to help.

"Please, Jeri, don't hurt her." Jeri can't stand a weak woman. He commenced to back-slap me with the gun, but Rah rushed him from behind.

"Don't touch my sister!" She jumped on his back like a lioness and he fended her off beating her knuckles with his gun. "Get out of here, Go-Go. Now!" Rah demanded, ready to die for me. Just like that, I hated Jeri with the same intensity that I loved him.

I ran out of the apartment into the hallway and began pacing. Dragging my hands across my face, I screamed with anger, with hate, and with fear. I know I said that it's all a part of the game, but until then, ain't nobody ever held a gun on me before. I pressed the elevator button to leave then kicked the door. I thought about going to get Sy, but I was torn. *Either way, Jeri will kill one or all of us.* The elevator doors opened, and I let it close again. *I can't leave her! Get it together Go-Go!* I walked back to the apartment door. I crouched down on my knees and slowly cracked it open just as Jeri flipped Rah off his back against the wall nearest me. Rah quickly stood resisting defeat. I started to stick my arm through the door to retrieve her, but Jeri noticed and forcefully slammed it, nearly crushing my fingers. Breathing heavily, I put my ear to the door and tried to quiet myself. I heard a thump.

"It's too early in the got-damn morning for this crap!" Jeri yelled, seeming further away than Rah was.

"I'm okay, I got this," Rah announced, speaking into the door. She knew I was still there. She believed in me, although I didn't.

All I could hear was a roaring sound, like an animal charging and then another thump. I cracked the door slightly to listen better and possibly see.

"I don't owe you jackbone!" Jeri's fist was balled around a wad of money that he pushed into Rah's face. "But you gon' need me tho. Get outta here. You nothing but a trick." He opened the door and I fell through. He then attempted to push Rah out over my body. I had to scamper into the house to keep from being crushed. Rah fought, pleading, and acting distraught.

"Give me back my money, you son-of-a..." She gathered the satin sheet she wore in her hand and jumped for it like a dog for a bone. Tears built in her eyes. *What if this is all she has?* I thought of helping, but my legs felt like jelly. "Jeri, give it back to me. I worked for that," Rah insisted, and with that, Jeri smacked her, and she fell to the ground. "You're a beast," Rah patted blood from her lip as Jeri laughed in a sinister fashion, falling against the wall thumbing through the money in his hands.

"Don't sweat me. It's not becoming of you."

"Pfft. Sweat you? Please, your birth was a misfortune."

"Wow. That was raw for you. I'm a god out here...and when that delivery comes, I'll be living like the *Rockefellers*. I don't need this rasclot building, or ya burnt down borough. I'm from Brooklyn, baby." He bent down and rubbed the money in Rah's face. "But you, on the other hand, what you gonna do, huh? Go try-duh find you a little boyfriend and pimp him for money? Work the streets like ya floozy sistah?" He spat on me, and I whimpered. The flames from Rah's eyes rose and kissed his face. "You wanna act like a tramp?" He asked before forcefully kissing her and pushing his weight on top of her.

Rah scrambled beneath him then bit down on his lip. Jeri bellowed in agony. I looked for his gun; he didn't have it in his hand anymore. Rah clenched down on his lip harder, forcing him to stand with her. I stood too. Jeri dropped the money and grabbed Rah by the neck. Choked out, she released his lip so that he would allow her to breathe.

"I should kill you and spare you from poverty," he uttered, wiping blood from his mouth and loosening his grip on her throat. I stood flat against the wall, thinking of tiptoeing down the hall into the living room where the gun laid on the chaise lounge.

"You already have." Tears fled from Rah's cold eyes.

Pressing her against the wall, Jeri palmed her bosom. "I've given you everything, and this is how you treat me? Yuh want fi nothing." He started to pull up the scarlet sheet she wore. I closed my eyes and quickly prayed before taking my first step out toward the living room.

"Jeri, please. He raped me. Please, not again. Am I nothing?" I opened my eyes. *Raped?* Jeri released her, and Rah slid down the wall. He backed away, bumping into me.

"You think you know everything, well, you don't. I'ma tell you what really happened last night." Rah stared between the both of us. We both were guilty of mistreating her. Her eyes were dark, and her face was beginning to reveal her battle with Jeri. "What you did last night was introduce me to my biological father, so thank you." She nodded sarcastically. "And you know what he did? He raped me. Just like he raped Poo." *What is she talking about?* Both Jeri and I grimaced in confusion. "He didn't care how much I screamed. I'm nothing to him, just like I'm nothing to you. He raped me, he hurt me, he insulted me, and then, he invited your partners into the room to finish me off." Rah's cold tone broke in sadness.

In anxiousness, Jeri began to pace. He looked back at her, possibly to see the sincerity in her eyes. I looked for it too. *Was she talking about the heavyset white guy, the doc? Her father?*

"I was in so much pain and feeling so disgusted that all your partners could do was try to help. One of them said he was going for help, but when the lights suddenly went out, they were ghost—just like the rest of you money-hungry cowards."

Jeri stopped pacing. There was a perception in his eyes that read he somehow cared. "Are you telling me that that fat white bumbaclot is ya father? And he put his hands on you and raped you?" He pointed his finger in Rah's face while briefly noticing the multiple bruises on her arms. He wasn't the only one who roughhoused her.

"Did I stutter because who would make this up?" She pushed his finger away. "I'm tired of this...and I'm done. It doesn't matter how much you hit me or kick me or threaten me anymore because nothing hurts more than what you did last night. I've tried to love you, Jeri, and I've done all I know how to make you happy. But this is how you love me back?" I started to cry for her because no tears would come out of her eyes.

"I didn't have nothing to do with that," Jeri declared, visibly upset. He started to pace again. "How did you know he was your father...what's his name?" He stopped pacing and stood in front of Rah.

"Well, he was acting sort of nervous and having breathing issues, so we talked for a bit and had a brief introduction. I recognized his name and called him out. He grabbed me, thinking that it was a setup, but when he realized I didn't know anything, he switched gears. He got angry...and raped me," Jeri covered his face and rubbed his temples.

"What's his name?" he asked again, digging for reliable information.

"The Honorable Judge John Fontaine, Jr., JD," Rah calmly declared.

"Judge? He's a doctor." Rah shrugged her shoulders.

"According to him, he's a doctor of law."

Looking puzzled, Jeri stormed off in the direction of his office, then prematurely stopped and headed back towards us. "Get out!" He snatched the front door open. Rah and I quickly shuffled through, but he grabbed her back in by the hair. "I want you and your family to remain in this building until I verify this story, understood?"

"Yes."

"Yo. I didn't have anything to do with that," Jeri reiterated, solemnly staring into Rah's eyes. She nodded. "Get ya money off the floor and get out of here," he quickly added before storming off into his office.

I dived for it, piling each one-hundred-dollar bill into my hand like I won the lottery. I looked up at Rah, narrowly smiling. At least she got to keep her money. She stood depleted against the door crying. I gathered all the money, and we ran.

Truth Be Told

The elevator ride down to the basement apartment was mostly silent. The only sounds were our hearts pounding loudly through our chests. This wasn't the way I imagined the story to end. The dark chocolate addiction I craved since the age of fourteen gave me cavities. I thought I could win over his affection even though I knew he was gully through and through. I took his kindness to heart, and he gave me his butt to kiss. Like I did to Zee. People like Jeri and me do whatever you allow us to get away with. Rah had enough of Jeri. I hoped that Zee wasn't done with me yet.

I looked at the money in my hand. It felt like a good twenty stack, but it was useless. It couldn't buy back time nor heal strained relationships. Then I looked over at my sister, in her thigh-high stiletto boots and her body wrapped in red satin; she was tragically beautiful. But even on her worst days, her spirit stood higher than mine. She couldn't help it, that's how she was wired. I nudged her hand with the hand that I held the money in to give it back. She turned her head slightly toward me, then looked down at the cash and back up at me again. We both cried loudly, hugging each other. A unified agreement of apologies and forgiveness was established through tears. I had just lost the one I thought I loved all these years, and suddenly found myself in the arms of the one I called my enemy. I never knew they played opposite roles. Nothing in life made sense anymore, but being in Rah's arms at that moment felt real.

We held each other's hand as we rang the doorbell to the basement apartment at seven in the morning. We were both dressed in sheets, and neither of us had our key nor a pocket to place one. Poo answered, and seeing Rah's condition, she instantly fell apart.

"What happened to my baby?" she yelled, leading her into the house. She glanced at me with a logical facial expression that read—*this is your fault*. It was, I had guilt written all over my face.

Poo and Rah disappeared into the bathroom, leaving me alone as they usually did, in a quiet house with my thoughts and money. The old me would have run out of there, but I prayed a foxhole prayer that day, and Rah and I made it out safe. I was grateful. I promised God I would change my ways, but you know these things take time. After an hour with myself, I grew discontented and pounded on Sy and Le-Le's bedroom door. *They should be getting up for church anyway.* I couldn't let Jeri get away with what he did. He couldn't just beat the crap out of Rah and walk away like nothing happened—threatening us to be good little puppets and stay put until we heard from him. I wanted Sy to take that gun that he hid in his closet and march upstairs to kill Jeri.

"What is it?" Sy shouted, opening the door in his underwear. Le-Le sat up in shock. He rubbed his eyes then took a good look at me. "What the hell happened?" he questioned, already growing angry.

"Jeri beat Rah, and—" was all I had the chance to say.

Sy swore under his breath and turned around, picking his pants up off the floor. He swore again this time out loud, pulling them on.

"What happened?" Le-Le asked, concerned for her husband. She grabbed her robe from the foot of the bed.

"Jeri held Rah at gunpoint and—"

"Shut-up!" Sy issued. "Don't tell me no more," he said in a quieter tone, running a hand over his bountiful black curls. He was afraid of his own anger. He slipped a shirt over his head and went for the closet.

"No!" Le-Le cried. "Papí, let's tawk to Rah first," she begged.

I continued egging Sy on, but I think he tuned me out. He removed a safe box from the closet, and Le-Le ran off to wake up the house for help, yelling, "Sy is going to kill Jeri!"

Sy headed for the front door with the gun tucked in his jeans. I marched behind him, amping him up. Le-Le blocked the door, bearing her weight against it, the unmovable weight of a true mother and wife. Love was her strength, and it was strong.

"Move, Le," Sy gently requested, annoyed. He was trying to keep his cool and not break fool on everyone. He pulled the knob, and Le-Le shut the door with her backside standing in front of him. "Get out of the way!"

Le-Le cried, pushing Sy back from the door. Then Pops rolled over in his wheelchair and pulled Sy by the waist, and Poo held him by the arm. Sy grew angrier, pulling and banging on the door, attempting to leave the apartment.

"Let him out! That jerk needs his butt kicked." I instigated over the chaos, still wrapped in white linen. Waking the family and alerting them to what happened to Rah was more important than washing debauchery off my body.

"Papí, please, no!" Le-Le wailed. "You're not thinking clearly. Let's all sit and talk it over. Please."

"Get out of my way! This is my fight. I'm a man!"

"Over my dead body, Sy. Sit down!" Poo demanded.

"Come on, Sy; he's not worth it, son," Pops attempted to persuade him.

Unknowing of the unfolding drama, Rah exited the bathroom wearing Poo's robe.

"What's going on?"

My blameworthy face must have told it all, and if it didn't, I professed, "Don't worry, Rah. Sy is going to handle this. That negro needs to know he can't run us over."

Rah rolled her eyes at me and shook her head. "Sy," she gently called, taking hold of our brother's tense shoulders. He hesitated to face her.

"What kind of brother am I if I can't protect you?" Sy hung his head. "This has gotta stop." He turned to look at Rah. The state of her face sent him into a blind rage. He banged and pulled at the door harder. He almost made it through.

"Minton Silas Williams, Jr., God has a plan and a purpose," Rah loudly declared, silencing the room. Only Poo was aware of what was really going on. She smiled as Rah's face brightened when she spoke. *"All things are possible to him who believe.* Isn't that what you always say, Sy? Please listen. We can't interfere. This is our opportunity to get out of here forever. Allow me to explain the whole story." She looked at me, knowing I gave my hyped-up version, but she extended her hand to me anyway.

The more I wanna do right—I do wrong.

It was time for healing, doused in salvation, for a family firmly bound through turmoil. Poo cooked and served us a large Sunday's breakfast while we quietly listened to Rah's story. Although ashamed, she left nothing out from the previous evening. We knew the consequences of her lifestyle. Many times we turned a blind eye to the truth for comfort at Rah's expense. We were all sorry.

Rah admitted that she did the performance because Jeri said he would marry her. She knew all about his secret involvement with the underworld of drugs, crime, and sex. Not wanting anything to do with it, she allowed information to slip past her processing. All Rah wanted was what was best for us, and with Jeri as her husband, she figured the one-time-only performance was worth her embarrassment. Jeri turned on her. He and Canaan had other plans. They offered Rah twenty thousand to sleep with Doc and secure his sizable investment in the casino deal. Rah knew nothing about the auction, but she was smart; she knew it was a setup. It was Canaan and Jeri's way of saying goodbye—an exit payment. She took the money for the family so that we could start over. She had no way of knowing that the same crooked and despicable man who raped Poo as a young lady would come back and rape her too. They say that your past has a way of catching up with you—Lord knows, that's what I was afraid of. Trust and believe, Doc paid for that.

"I've never felt so belittled and disgusted in my life. I can't even begin to express how I felt. What happened with Paw-Paw shocked me. I was scared, hurt, and incredibly sad but this…this was different. It was more like an awakening. I remember thinking, why are you screaming? Aren't you Jeri's personal prostitute? Isn't this what you do?" Rah disclosed, looking at the hardly touched plates of food on the table that Poo kept nervously replenishing. No one had an appetite except the kids who were eating in the living room and watching cartoons. "Sorry, I know y'all are trying to eat." She apologized to empathic head shakes of excusal. She paused and gagged. Most likely, Poo's food, along with reliving the incident, was making her queasy. Tears lined her face as she tried to compose herself.

"Ay, dios mio," Le-Le whispered, cupping Rah's hand and crying herself.

"If it wasn't for the hate building up inside of me, I probably would've thrown up. The crazy thing is, my hate wasn't toward T-John." That's what Rah and Poo called Doc. "I hated God, and I was sure He hated me, too," Rah confessed, trying to fight back tears. Her words were my thoughts, and it hurt to hear them spoken out loud. "I prayed, Le-Le, I did. I asked Him to remove me from the situation. I bargained with Him for protection."

Unprompted, I interrupted in an overgrown outburst of unrestrained sobbing that gushed out from deep within the beast. It's no secret that I'm *the brash, rebellious type* who's *never content to stay at home.* But Rah's tragedy hit a raw nerve. Her situation wasn't uncommon to me; I fought many battles and privately bottled and shelved them inside myself. It was at that moment that I realized that the gist of my running was mostly from God. I was running from His eyes because they dissected and convicted me. They made me feel peeled apart and unworthy of Zee. It's not that I don't want a decent life. *While I desire to do good, evil is always present.* No amount of money, drugs, sex, or food can hide me from God. Hearing Rah's confession opened and burst my shelved bottles. Poo instantly stopped her nervous fussing around the kitchen and tightly held me, and I allowed her. The girl inside of the beast needed a hug. I was hyperventilating and couldn't breathe.

Sy got up and started to leave. The crying was too much for him.

"Wait, Sy." Rah quickly wiped her eyes and took his hands. "I THOUGHT God hated me, but He actually loves me more than I love myself," she clarified as tears started to build in Sy's eyes. He and Le-Le relentlessly witnessed to the family to no prevail. "Yes, I was raped. I was humbled. I was forced to ask myself questions that I've been dodging. I wanted to give up on life, love, faith. Everything. The only way God could show me that He loves me, that He exists, and that He's never left my side wasn't by rescuing me. I got myself in that situation. I was too busy trying to fix our lives to listen to Him in the first place. Had He rescued me from that, honestly, I can't say I would've given Him the props He so rightly deserves. God had to show up and physically move me into faith and action. He lifted me when I surrendered. When I was depleted of self. I was searching for an out, and He stepped in and literally opened a window. He physically lifted me from the ground like I was a piece of paper. I felt weightless and small." Sy dropped to his knees and pressed his face into Rah's lap. I supposed he knew how she felt because he was overwhelmed with gladness. "The Throne Room was dim, but I swear it lit up," she continued. "God gave me an ultimatum; either I follow Him or stay stuck in my mess. I felt a cold wind blow against my body, that's when I truly opened my eyes, and there he stood. The only person God could send besides Big Mama that would make me believe one-hundred percent that He's my God too…you'll never guess who it was."

"Who?" we all asked, except Poo. She'd heard the story and smiled at the recurring light that brightened her daughter's face.

"It was Sal," Rah shrieked, to some of our confusion.

Le-Le gasped. "No!" She held her mouth in shock.

Beaming like she found love twice that night, Rah went on to explain and re-familiarize us with the Bayou boy turned cop that held her heart. Peep this—those two guys that José said betrayed him and was working with Jeri turned out to be undercover cops. The "Indian looking mofo" that Jeri hated was Rah's childhood friend that she used to write letters to, Salmone Abrams, a.k.a. Solo, short for his alias, Solomon Webber, and his partner was Kyle 'Ky' Banneker, real name Kaleb. They were undercover cops for the NYPD drug trafficking unit. That morning when Rah did all of that ranting, raving, and fighting with Jeri, nearly giving me a heart attack, it was because she was wired and trying to get the cops the incriminating information they needed to bring the drug ring that Jeri led down. There was a lot that we didn't know about him, and Rah was tired of it all. Are you shocked? I was. The police were outside of the building the entire time.

I saw the Indian looking mofo that night before I left the club. He was speaking with Jazmine, and they looked like they were about to hook up. Apparently, he recognized Rah as his childhood friend during her Voodoo Doll performance. He used Jazmine, the top Video Vixen, to gain access to the most popular rooms upstairs where he knew that Rah and Doc had to be. Sal didn't get there in time enough to save Rah from being raped, but as she said, he showed up right on time—when she was depleted of self. He and his partner, Kaleb, reached her when Doc was leaving. They went into the Throne Room, where she lay wrapped in red satin sheets and weakened from fighting. Sal scooped her into his arms as Kaleb relayed an order into his wired suit jacket to shut all the lights out on 147th Street. The trio escaped the building in the chaos of a blackout. From the window to the fire escape, up to the roof. Finally, into an awaiting van parked near an adjoining vacant building. I missed all the action waiting to have wack sex with Jeri.

After reviewing Rah's surveillance tape, the cops advised her to listen to Jeri and stay put, so as not to arouse his suspicion. Other arrangements would be made to ensure our safety while they proceeded with the investigation. According to what they heard Jeri state during his argument with Rah, they suspected something big was about to happen. I must admit I was feeling some kind of way. Everyone was speaking of Jeri going to jail for a long time, and oddly enough, I felt like I was betraying him. Rah's emotions were wavering, but ultimately she was ready to move on and put Jeri in the past. She said he had laid his hands on her for the last time. I couldn't fault her. He had made his bed, now it was time to sleep in it. The law was involved. I agreed with the family that waiting in the apartment was the best decision. It was either Jeri or risk all our safety, and he had already shown me how he really felt. Most of us trusted in the Lord, and all of us supported one another no matter how hard life hit us. We ate and planned to move.

C.R.E.A.M.

That night, Jeri came by the basement apartment, acting as nothing happened, and we had to play along with his bipolar mood swings to keep the peace. Rah and I were lying across the twin beds in the girl's room, talking in the dark. We had just awakened from a much needed eight-hour nap when we both heard his voice coming from the bathroom door. He was talking to Cookie and Baby Girl. The girls were bathing in the tub. This may seem strange to you, but out of all of us, Jeri was most taken by Cookie. She reminded him of his older sister, who died; she too had special needs. Cookie spent a lot of time with Jeri and Rah upstairs at the penthouse. He bought her things like he used to do for me. Jeri never rejected Cookie's tight hugs around his waist; they didn't require his involvement. Cookie laid them on thick and quickly retreated. She spoke her feelings through song and dance and only requested snacks in return. Jeri stood at the bathroom door, laughing and teasing with the girls. Then, we heard him questioning.

"Krystal. Where's ya auntie?"

"She's in our room, sleep," Baby Girl shyly answered.

"Y'all almost done?" Poo yelled from the living room, annoyed.

"No!" The girls answered together, giggling.

"Bye. Y'all about to get in trouble," Jeri declared, walking away.

"Jeri, you got cake?" Cookie yelled after him.

"Nah, I forgot. I'll tell Rah-Rah to get you some," he yelled back as he opened the bedroom door where we were and turned on the light. Sucking his teeth, he jokingly told me, "Get ya tired raggedy bum-bum out of here."

"Excuse you!" I rolled my eyes, already getting up. I didn't want to see him either. Sometimes dreams are best when they're left dreamt. You know what I mean?

"Yeah, you're excused," Jeri snapped, pretending to hit at me as I walked past. His disposition was lighter than it was earlier, but something was different about him. I felt his eyes on my butt as I exited the room. *Nope, he's still the same.*

"Leave her alone, Jeri." Rah insisted, wincing as I closed the door. She said that her body felt like a *Mack Truck* hit it.

I went into the kitchen and made myself a big bowl of cereal. I didn't have much of an appetite. After all those years of wanting Jeri and the lifestyle he represented. Suddenly, I felt God was saying, "I will give you what you want, so much so, you'll be begging to go home." He was right. I wanted to call Zee, but I couldn't imagine what to tell him—*I slept with ya boy and he spat in my face. Is it too late for a fresh start?* I sat on the couch near Le-Le with my cereal. She, along with Poo and Pops, was watching television. Le-Le looked down at my bowl and made a face. She had made us a big dinner.

"Maybe, later...my stomach," I explained, before gulping down a big spoon of *Frosted Flakes* with sliced bananas. Le-Le smiled, trying to fix my hair. At that time, I kept it braided under different weaves, but for the big performance, I got a Dominican blowout. After what went down at Jeri's, my thick black wavy natural locks crowned my head and swept my shoulders like bundles of cotton.

Jeri came out of the room first. He was noticeably different. Sweat rolled from his brow like it was a summer day but it was the middle of December. He seemed unsettled but looked good dressed in casual urban gear, *Karl Kani* from top to bottom. *They're gonna love him in jail.* Rah came out after him, still dressed in Poo's raggedy old pink housecoat. She leaned against the arched entryway watching Jeri as he playfully taunted us with smart remarks. He must have sensed her vacant gaze because he turned around.

"Come sit with ya peeps. I want all you clowns to hear me out."

"You got five minutes. You holding up my show," Poo voiced. She should have been concerned about Baby Girl and Cookie pruning in the bathtub. Jeri coldly eyed her, then walked over and shut the television off. Pops grabbed Poo's hand. No one messes with her TV.

"I know you've all grown fond of me and consider me an extension of this…unit." Jeri paced the room, demanding attention. "However, Rah and I are calling it quits." *Who the heck does he think he is?* Poo's face read. Pops nudged her arm. My spirit didn't jump hooray either. *I guess I am over him.* Jeri continued to speak amidst our growing dislike of him. "Because I'm not the beast you all think I am, I have hooked *MOST* of you up in a nice building down—"

''Pfft!'' Poo mouthed in disbelief.

Jeri stared her down, getting annoyed. "Like I was saying…the new apartment is paid in full for six months. Le-Le, you're a businesswoman. You and Sy can manage on ya own. Go-Go, stank, you know what's up." He pretended to make it rain to my rolling eyes and neck.

"Hold up," Rah interrupted, standing. "You mean to tell me we're split up, but you still get to choose where I live? Do I hear you correctly?"

Jeri didn't answer. It was his way of taking care of us. He removed a wrapped gift out of his Army coat pocket and handed it to Rah. Then, he sat with his legs gaped and leaned in on his elbows, watching for our reaction.

"What's this, a parting gift?" Rah asked, loosely holding the present. Poo chuckled.

"Open it! Please," he demanded anxiously.

Rah unwrapped the neatly wrapped box, and a broad malicious smile spread across Jeri's face. He licked his lips in anticipation. "Ahh!" she screamed, dropping everything and jumping on the sofa where Le-Le and I were. We jumped into each other's arms. My nerves were shot.

Jeri laughed hysterically. What looked like two small balls fell splat and clumsily rolled across the hardwood floor, stopping at Pop's feet. Poo jumped into his lap.

In the blustering chaos, Sy ran out of the bedroom. He was in the back calling out on his job. He also made an important call to Pastor Paul for prayer. Everyone anxiously looked over at him, hoping he wouldn't start any trouble.

Jeri stood up. "Oh, you're home tonight, good. Now, I only have to say this once."

Rah got down from the sofa and studied the bloody clumps. "Are those eyeballs?"

"Yeah, do they look familiar?" Jeri asked, looking crazy. He grabbed Rah's waist and pulled her into his arms. She hesitated but was careful not to upset him nor Sy. "They're the last thing I saw…wide and staring. Icy blue." Sweat rolled down his temple, he quickly wiped it away.

"Are they actually from someone's eye sockets?" Poo asked, examining them from Pop's lap.

"Nothing gets past you, huh? Yuh nuh memba dem?" Jeri probed. "He remembered you and your mother."

"Jeri, is that T-John?" Rah yelled, and our mouths fell open. I really wanted to go home. I wanted to hug Zee one last time because I felt there was no coming back from this. Jeri had lost it. "No, Jeri." Rah looked concerned.

"Now, there are no hard feelings between us," Jeri cupped her face. He softly kissed her swollen lip, and Rah rested her hands delicately against his chest. They briefly stared into each other's eyes. Hers were full of tears. His looked conflicted and finally showed signs of life. Jeri let her go and turned to us. "I want all of yous out of my building by two o'clock tomorrow. I hired a moving company. They'll be here by noon." he continued, surveying the room and enjoying seeing the shock on our faces. "They'll be equipped with whatever you need, and you can take whatever you want from here."

"Are you serious?" Rah asked. He ignored her.

"It's been my extreme pleasure, peasants," he rudely added, smiling devilishly. He turned on his beef and broccoli colored *Timbs* to leave but stopped short. "Sy, don't forget about that furniture delivery we talked about last week. They should be here tomorrow around the same time as the moving truck. Unlock the back gate and direct them to the elevator. Key them in, they know the rest."

"Yup," Sy dryly answered, most likely feeling uninclined to help him. Sy helped from time to time with stuff in the building that Pops couldn't handle from his wheelchair. But Pops could have dealt with that. We all suspiciously looked at each other, wondering if this had something to do with the big drug deal.

"Cool." Jeri strode out of the apartment, allowing the door to slam behind him. I could hear his anthem *"C.R.E.A.M."* by *Wu-Tang Clan* trailing behind him. The scent of his *CK One* lingered in the air and made me sick to my stomach. Chills ran up my arms. My spirit said, *say goodbye.*

Redeeming Love

That night, I barely slept. I laid across my old bed, listening to Rah and her cop friend, Sal's, dull phone conversation from in the living room. One minute she was laughing, the next she was crying, but it was obvious that she was in love. She said she was going to tell him about our suspicions over the moving and furniture trucks that were coming. I'm sure she did because we were all convinced that a large drug deal was taking place in the building the next day. It seemed all Rah's problems would soon be over, and she would finally be able to move on with her true love. If only life were that easy for me. Don't get me wrong. I was happy for her. If any of us deserved happiness, it was Rah. I made a mess of my life. That night before bed, as we prepared for the moving truck, the family discussed their plans to move and start new experiences, but what about me? All I could think about was Zee and how I stupidly ruined our relationship. Where was I going? This wanderer wanted to go home, but I didn't have the courage to ask. I did make one call, though, and it broke the ice for me to speak with Zee. I called Blu.

"I'm going back to my husband...if he'll have me," I proclaimed at the top of the conversation before other things that didn't matter were discussed. "I'm sorry, Blu, but I miss him...and our kids. I messed up and I want to be home."

"Zeen." That meant okay. "Mi can undastan dat," he responded rather dryly, but it sounded like he understood my circumstances.

However, if I were there, he probably would have busted my butt completely in two. "Yuh ah madda," he continued. "Yuh belong yaad wid yuh pickney."

Hmm, maybe he does understand? Since the conversation was going well, I figured I'd let him know about his boy too.

"Listen...I did something that I'm ashamed of.—"

"Wha'? Yuh slept wid Jeri?" He said in a smart-aleck manner like he knew it was coming.

"Yeah, I did."

"Blurtnawt!" Which pretty much means, what the hell.

"I didn't plan it...it just happened." I lied, not wanting him to sneak up on me with a gat.

"Yuh lie! Yuh been planning dat." It was true, but I was silent. I was learning that less is more. Blu mumbled something under his breath in hardcore patois, not meant for me to know, then, said, "Pfft! Him is di pot calling di kekkle black." Jeri had gotten on him about leaving me alone. I was too much trouble, he claimed. "Nah, Go-Go, dat ain't all you. Dat him too. Mi so called bredda." Jeri was burning bridges all the way around. "Bless up. Walk good." He hung up before I could speak, but I felt chains breaking.

At five in the morning, after a night of tossing and turning, I finally found the courage to call home. I knew that Zee would be waking soon to get ready for work. I figured I'd call and give him something to consider during his day.

"Hey, it's me." I sat on the toilet, whispering in the bathroom.

He answered, groggy, "Hey, me. Whassup?"

"I need to talk..."

He cleared his throat. "Yeah, well listen, it's early...and I just now got Lorah to sleep. She was up all night with she teething. Can this wait?" He didn't sound his usual engaging self.

"Oh, okay...yeah. We'll..." Zee hung up before I could finish, and I cried like a baby. I got up from the toilet and ran the water in the sink so that no one could hear me. *It's over. Zee doesn't want me anymore, and I can't blame him.* Then, the phone rang.

"What is it, Go? I'm tired. Yuh wastin' mih time, or wha? Ah don't wanna hear no nonsense."

213

He called me back!

"I know! Zee, listen...I love you." That was the first time I officially said it out loud. I always confirmed his love with ditto or the same here. I was beside myself and blubbering as in a drunken confession. "I've loved you from the first day I saw you standing behind that yellow moving truck... and from the moment you opened that marble notebook and told me that you prayed for a best friend, and believed God sent me. I've been afraid of that love. Zee, I'm trash! I knew from the start that I couldn't give you what you deserve...and I've lied, cheated, and hurt you, and I'm sorry." I could hear him sniffling in the background and it made me cry even harder. His tears should never be wasted over me. "I'm sorry...mostly because I know that sorry isn't enough...not now. I don't deserve you...or the kids, I'm unfit. I'm reckless. Zee, I—"

"Solo, please—"

"No! Let me get this out." I turned the water off. It was so hot the bathroom was fogging. I sat on the edge of the cold porcelain tub and thought about my life with Zee. From the very beginning. I lied to him—from the littlest of lies to the greatest. "Remember that time when we were kids, I told you that Brandy Montgomery lifted my dress in the stairwell, and when you confronted him, he punched you in the eye?"

"Yeah," he snickered.

"I lied..." Heavy, uncontrollable tears ran from my eyes, thinking of the numerous times I betrayed him. "I lifted my own dress and showed him the goods because I wanted you to be jealous.

"Solo—"

"No, no, Zee—there's more!" My legs nervously shook like a junkie wanting a fix. "Zee, I never lived with José—I slept with him...many times, but I never lived with him. When you went away to school, I got this notion in my head that I could be this big-time stripper. That I could make something of myself because everyone around me was making moves...no, no let me keep this one hundred. I just wanted the money...and things. I wanted to be glamorous enough to take Rah's place...so that I..." I deeply inhaled. "So that I could be with Jeri," I said in an exhale. "I became a stripper, and I met this wonderful man, who was just as jacked-up as I am. He helped me to become an escort and took me under his wing. He protected me. Tam was a druggie, but even he knew that street life wasn't living. He left me. He told me to go home, and I didn't." I cleared my throat. "I slept with him too. I slept with man, after man, after man. Then, I started using drugs to forget what I was doing. After we got married and had the kids I went back to that life because...because I wanted...drugs, money, and still...Jeri! Zee, I've been living in Brooklyn. I dance at Jeri's clubs now. I live with Blu...I'm sleeping with him too." I stopped because I knew that I had to go all the way and I was scared.

I was saying things that I knew hurt Zee's feelings. *Am I purposely destroying what little hope I have at regaining my marriage?* I closed my eyes and squinted my face. "I slept with Jeri yesterday, and I've been intentionally seducing him for years." I couldn't hear Zee's sniffling anymore. I didn't hear anything. I wouldn't have blamed him if he hung up, but I continued anyway. "A lot went down Saturday night, and I used the opportunity to lure Jeri into bed...Rah caught us. Things got crazy...and I finally saw his true colors. Rah barely made it out alive." I broke down sobbing. "Zee...he beat my sister into a pulp...and there I was—big, bad, and bold Go-Go. I couldn't do anything but cower in a corner. Zee, the more you've called me, the further I have gone from you. You've led me with nothing *but cords of kindness...with ties of love*...and like a fool, I haven't returned. All I do is *multipy lies and violence...* and I know that God...and you, have constantly tried to save me. Now you both *have a charge to bring up against me according to all of my wrong deeds*. I don't even want me anymore. I've been hiding behind a whole lot of nonsense." I went on rambling about how I was useless.

"Solo!" Zee finally yelled, and I stopped. I could hear the baby whining like she was waking up. Zee shushed her lightly, then whispered, "Solo..." He sort of chuckled. "Yo, you had me at I love you."

Did he hear all that I said? I wasn't about to repeat it.

"I'm not a fool. I know who I married. Ah look fuh dat. I knew what I was getting into, and I loved you anyway. I'm not saying I'm not mad. Ah vex! Yuh bol' face and yuh need a real cut-ass—eh! I mean come on, Go, really? Some of dat...ah cyah say ah not hut...but, in truth, I still love you. You're still...my forever. Come home, please."

My heartbeat raced and fluttered. "Zee, I'ma, I'm a wanderer." I stuttered because I knew that my feet didn't always listen to my heart. "I wanna come home, but, but something's wrong with me. Maybe there's something wrong with my head? I don't have it all together. I want to do right; I swear I do! I don't know how, and that scares me. I don't wanna hurt you and the kids anymore."

"And somehow yuh think being away from us doesn't hut? Solo, the Word says, *if you are wandering from God return to Him with repentance.* He will receive you with open arms. He will draw you to himself and will rejoice. So will I. Because like God, *my compassion and love for you are far greater than your sins.*"

"Zee...?"

"Nah! Let me finish. God is saying—even now, **"I have swept away your offenses like a cloud, your sins like the morning mist. Return to me..."** His tone broke. **"...for I have redeemed you."**

"Zee, even me?" I wanted to go home. I wanted to be the long dress-wearing, bible toting, baby having, Seventh-day wife he desired. I wanted to feel 'this love of the Lord' that he was always preaching about. I wanted to have, however, many more kids we could have together as long as I could be perfectly imperfect with him.

"Even you, Solo...if you believe. God isn't looking for empty words...and neither am I. He's looking for a genuine expression of repentance and praise. Come home. If you really want to change, and really want my help. There is nothing that I wouldn't do for you. Let's get through this together, meh chookaloonks."

There it was—the warm and numbing feeling of the Holy Spirit being in the midst of a conversation.

"Yes, I'm coming home." My cheeks tightened with a smile as big as Zee's heart. Then, I thought about the mess that the family was in. "I just have a few things that I need to address here, and then I'll be there...hopefully by the time you're home tonight."

"Tonight? What's going on? Are you okay?" I could tell he really wanted to believe me, but I am who I am...Gomer. I wished that I could tell him everything, but I was being mindful not to mention anything about the cops, Jeri's dealings, or the possible drug bust. Sal advised not to communicate pertinent information to anyone. He also cautioned about using the landline and Rah's cell because of Jeri's access to them.

"Yes, I'm okay...just pray for the family and me. I'll tell you everything later, but we most definitely need your prayer...Jeri wants us out of the apartment this afternoon."

"Whey! You need my help—I can take off—"

"No! Please don't come here. Just pray—please." He was silent. Knowing Zee, he was already praying. That's my Hosea.

"Okay. I love you."

"Damn..." I whispered. "I love you too."

We hung up, and I inhaled and exhaled as deeply as I could, looking at myself in the defogging mirror. I looked like a wounded beast. I shook my head, about to start feeling sorry for myself. About to start telling myself that I didn't deserve Zee and the kids. About to talk myself out of taking my life back. I felt numb. I leaned over the sink, gagged, and vomited. My heart was still skipping beats. I knew that something had to be done. *Enough is enough. You're going to die in this beast.* I looked back into the mirror. I wasn't as cute as I used to be. My chinky eyes had lost their smile, my skin its luster. I looked hardened—like a once vibrant person put through the wringer. I shook my head again—this time triumphantly. *I'm not giving up!* Zee wanted me back.

As I climbed up out of the beast, I could see life coming back into my eyes. It was time for me to face those demons that Tim was talking about. He said that God helped him to do it, so I prayed.

"God...I know I don't deserve your love either, but if you love me as much as Zee claims that you do—please protect my family. I don't care what happens to me anymore. Please, get Rah from under Jeri's hold and free her to be loved as much as Zee loves me. I'm sorry, Lord—for everything. There's so much. If I get the chance—help me to do better. Amen."

Bacon and Café Con Leche

The conversation with Zee lifted my spirits. I felt unshakeable, finally firmly planted in a life choice. Thinking of Zee, I hummed *Aaliyah's "At Your Best (You Are Love),"* as I hopped into the shower. He was the positive, motivating force in my life. The sooner this was all over, the better. I could reclaim my marriage and start acting like I had some sense. God had given me life and love bountifully, and like an idiot, it wasn't enough for me. The grass always looks greener on the other side, in reality, it's growing on top of a whole lot of crap. My lawn was brown, and it was going to take a lot of work to get the grass up to par.

Coming out of the shower, I smelled bacon and coffee already brewing in the air. *Rah must be up. She probably couldn't sleep last night, either.* With a bounce in my step, I threw on Pop's robe that was hanging behind the door and followed my nose into the kitchen. I walked in on Rah and Poo, arguing.

"Poo, you're losing sight of what's important. This is about our safety. Yes, everything else will fall into place." I started to turn around and give them their privacy, but I had that one bowl of cereal last night. A sistah was hungry. Besides, victory was in the air. Why were they arguing anyway? "I have money saved up from selling Big Mama's oils, and don't forget her money—"

"That you can't touch until next year around this time, Rah!" Poo interrupted. She was always fussing about money. I guess that's who I get it from.

"Good morning," I happily sang, adding cheer to the conversation as I entered the kitchen. "Guess who's going home today?"

"At least you got a home to go to," Poo snapped, rolling her neck. She sucked her tongue and started to leave the kitchen, then, stopped and kissed me on the cheek. "You girls are going to be the death of me." She gave Rah "the look." *Finally, someone other than me.* "But! I'll love you both to my grave because that's what mommas do." She emphasized the last words then slowly walked away, suggesting that we let that soak in.

"Okaay? What was that about?" I poured myself a cup of café con leche.

"Never mind her, what's this about going home?" My smiling face glowed with good news.

"I just got off the phone with Zee, and don't worry; I didn't mention anything about the cops or the deal. But I did spill my guts, Rah-Rah," I revealed, popping bread into the toaster. "I came clean about everything—the drugs, the prostitution, the lies, everything, even about Jeri," I added, looking back at my sister. I was shame-faced. Rah's mouth fell open. I realized that I had never said any of those things out loud to her before either. I'm sure she didn't believe me, because of my habit. I wasn't honest with her in the past. Most of the time, I lied through my teeth while *honey dripped off my lips.* I had a lot of proving to do. "I finally told Zee how I really feel about him, but I think he knows my heart better than I do at this point," I continued, pulling out a chair to join Rah at the table. "I don't know what happened, but yesterday when you were sharing your story, something clicked. I've felt conviction before, Lord knows I get preached to enough, but this was different." I took Rah's hand. She looked shocked but squeezed mine anyway. "It was like me seeing myself through your pain. You weren't preaching at me; you probably didn't even know you were sermonizing my soul. I'm not all bad."

"Sweetie, I know you're not." Rah cupped my hand. "I know who you are; we did share a bed together, remember?" We chuckled, but the statement was true. Rah had seen me fight myself through nightmares.

"When I'm acting out...that's me punishing myself for being...me. Unworthy. Unworthy of Zee. Unworthy of the kids. Spoiled and manipulative Princess Go-Go. Yesterday, you helped me to see that what I'm doing isn't running, or self-medicating, or payback. It's hurtful, and it's time that I start facing my demons." I shook my head encouraging myself. "I also learned that despite myself, this God that everyone is always talking about still loves me, and He'll see me through. I don't have to live this wounded life anymore. I don't want to. I can freely love Zee and not feel unworthy." Despite my exterior, my voice cracked. I tried to hold back the tears. "I love him, Rah." Tears blinked from my eyes. "I hurt him so badly, and I'm sorry. I wanna go home and hold my husband and kids and start over."

"What did Zee say?" Rah anxiously asked, engaged in my story.

"He cried. I cried. Then, he told me to come home. He said I'm his forever. I don't understand why this man loves me so?" I sang, standing to get my toast.

"He's an example of God's love, I guess," Rah related from her spirit. I kissed her forehead in agreement.

"Thank you...and I'm so sorry I—"

"Don't, it's over. I love you."

"I love you too," I said it! All that love business was causing the shells from around my heart to shed. I sat down and embraced Rah's hand again. "That's why I need to officially apologize. You're everything to me, my beautiful big sister. I've been jealous, unruly, harsh...big meany." We snickered. "But seriously, from day one, you've never changed. Your love has been consistent, and I've been a consistent brat. You don't deserve what I've said or done to you over the years. I'm sorry."

"Thanks, Go. That means the world to me." Rah's cheeks turned red as she teared up. We embraced. She smelled like homemade memories of Charlotte Street. Sweet and familiar all at once. "So, you mentioned you're leaving today?" she said, quickly coming from our hug and trying not to make the moment too mushy for my sake. But I was softening up. We wiped away our tears.

"Well, I'm not about to leave you guys in this mess. I'm staying until we're all safe. Is the plan the same as last night?"

"Yeah," Rah answered, standing to refresh her cup. "We'll let the movers in and delay them as long as possible, let them pack *ALL* this stuff. Hopefully, before the actual move takes place, we'll know something. Sal is dead-set against us moving to another Jeri location. He got us a safe haven and a storage company. Whatever we need, he says."

"Cool. You like this Sal guy, huh?" I nudged her arm.

"He's a really good friend," she blushed.

"Mhmm, I know about those really good friends. I remember the stuff I used to do to Zee when we were kids." We laughed in remembrance.

"No, you were just nasty. Sal and I were innocent kids. I may wanna do a few of those things now, though," Rah admitted, looking embarrassed.

"I knew it! It's in the DNA," I hollered, laughing. "You want him, don't you?"

Rah covered her red face. "I do, and I feel horrible about it."

"Why? If it's who I think it is, he's fine as all get out," I was tickled by Rah's bashfulness. The Indian looking mofo was indeed fine! His reddish-brown skin looked like it was kissed long by the sun. His features were chiseled, and he had a strong muscular physique. He looked like a bodyguard, but he was too pretty for that, with his long black hair that he kept gathered into a sleek ponytail. He and Rah were made for each other.

Rah sighed, uncovering her face. "I just feel like a floozie. I mean, in spite of all that's happening...I just feel stupid, like I should be a little more focused on our next step. Like Poo said, where are we going to live? What are we going to do? Sal makes me feel...warm and fuzzy inside."

"Mhmm!" We laughed.

"Not like that...entirely. I mean safe. Loved."

"He sounds like my Zee." Rah nodded, agreeing. "Rah, I'm no life coach, but it seems to me you're entitled to this. You've spent too many years trying to love Jeri and trying to make him love you in return. Then, there's us hooligans. Look at the years you've invested. That mental vacation is whassup! In the words of my Hosea, *'God is the only one who can make the valley of trouble a door of hope.'*"

Rah tilted her head in amazement. "When did you get so smart?"

"A few minutes ago." We laughed again. "Seriously, there's nothing like being with someone who loves you completely, and I can't remember you ever having that, Rah. You're twenty-four! Live a little."

"You're right." She looked like she was pondering over her life. Then she abruptly said, "Hey, I've been debating over something, but I think I'm ready now. Can you help me?"

"Anything, sis. What is it?"

"You feel like playing with my hair like you used to? I wanna cut it and let my natural hair color grow out."

Rah said that she was hurt when Sal mentioned that she didn't look like herself. She thought of him searching for her all those years. Voodoo Doll was right there in the public eye, and he didn't recognize her as his friend. The more Rah thought about it, the more she understood. Just like me, she hardly knew who she was anymore. We had a lot in common. We talked and laughed as I washed and cut my sister's hair. I gave her a dope *Halle Berry, Anita Baker* doo, and instead of hot curling it, I moussed her natural wave and curl pattern. She resembled Poo more with the short cut framing her face.

"What were you and Poo arguing about?" I asked while Rah was admiring herself in the mirror.

"Girl, what else? Money!" she answered, turning to me briefly and twisting her lips. She finger-raked her curls until they were to her liking.

"What she worried about? You got that twenty-G, right? She'll be aiight. We'll all work together." Rah smiled and turned from the mirror again, this time walking over to me. I was reclined in Pop's chair, thinking about taking a nap.

"That's nice, Go. We can all chip in, and I'm glad to hear you say that because the truth is all I have is hidden in Big Mama's chest in Poo's closet. It ain't much…but it's mine. It's honest money that I worked for making and selling beauty products over the years to the girls." She stooped down beside me. "Go—that money…" She looked over at the twenty-G, now placed in an envelope on the coffee table. "It's counterfeit." My mouth fell open as my eyes grew. "Yeah, the real money that Canaan gave me is in police custody…and I want it to stay there. That money ain't me. I don't want anything to do with it." Surprisingly, I understood. For Rah, the money held memories of her rape.

That morning while Rah was being wired, she turned in the cash that she received from Canaan, and the cops replaced it with the counterfeit. Rah knew that Jeri would be looking for it, so she had the fake money taped to her thigh hidden underneath the high boots she wore. She said that when I was out in the hall, Jeri charged her and ripped the money from her leg. He almost came across the wiretap, but thank God he didn't.

We all needed a fresh start. Poo would be okay. She disliked Jeri, but like me, she was comfortable with his expensive gifts. Hear me when I say, Poo intended to take everything she owned from that basement apartment, plus some things she didn't.

Doomsday

The moving truck arrived right on time. The family and I were anxious to start packing but agreed to take it slow. According to Sal, what we didn't want was to end up in another location owned by Jeri, and that was alright by us. I only enjoyed horror films. I didn't want to be a part of one. Sal also relayed to Rah that Jeri called an important meeting in the building set for the same day and time as the truck's arrival. He said he couldn't discuss the details but assured her that the NYPD was prepared to take drastic measures.

Sy let both the furniture and moving trucks into the courtyard that afternoon. When he had the chance, he privately told us that three shady looking Mexicans unloaded two huge sofas completely secured in bubble wrap from the furniture truck. Then carefully transported them both up to the penthouse floor. While in the lobby, Sy noted that he also observed a few other random looking men coming into the building. One fit Rah's description of Sal. When Sy came back into the basement apartment, he had two movers with him. I recognized one as Rowan Strong, the guy who met with Jeri and Blu at the club. It wasn't unusual for Jeri to use his henchman as movers. Blu, along with another guy, moved us into the basement apartment.

The men were friendly and came in greeting us. Sy knew them both from his days of working security. They all kidded around and caught up on old acquaintances. The fellas asked if we knew of the large gathering that was taking place on our block. We didn't, but around six o'clock that morning, Rah and I thought we heard a trumpet. We couldn't see anything because all the basement windows faced the sunken courtyard—where the two moving trucks now sat. The trumpet moved on but returned every hour, then grew louder with the help of a bullhorn. We couldn't leave the apartment to see what was happening because overnight, Jeri posted two men at our door, and they warned everyone not to leave. O'Neil, the other mover, informed us that the gathering was a large religious organization that was repeatedly circling the block. We later found out that it was Pastor Paul and some of his parishioners, followed by local community advocates. They were fed up with the direction that the neighborhood was heading under people like Jeri who brought drugs into the communities. Sy called Pastor Paul, asking for prayer. He didn't say what was happening, but he put concern into the pastor's heart. That same night, Pastor Paul got another call from a pastor of a sister church in Louisiana; Pastor Josh, Sal's father. Sal told Pastor Josh that he finally found Rah and was concerned about her safety. Sal didn't get into details either, but he alerted his father enough that he took a plane to NYC and got in touch with Pastor Paul about assembling a prayer march.

Amongst the madness, we started moving. The men brought in empty boxes and we packed them as slowly as we could as they wrapped and carried larger items out of the house. During their first-round out, I noticed Blu exiting the truck. He was the driver. He opened the vehicles, swinging doors, and lowered a ramp to let the men in with Poo's lacquer entertainment set. I hurried and moved away from the window, hoping he didn't see me. He spoke with the men briefly before going back to the driver's seat. He was on his cellphone. All I could think about was how he looked at me that night at the club. I prayed that he would stay in the truck because even though we made our peace, you never know with men like him and Jeri. They all have bipolar tendencies. I continued to pack but made sure to stay away from the window.

Something crashed in the kitchen, startling me. Poo yelled, "Now take ya little narrow behinds and get in that bed, straightaway!" Cookie and Baby Girl had broken some dishes. They were all over the place, running and laughing. Le-Le confirmed Poo's order and led the girls into her bedroom to take a nap. All our nerves were shot. It had been way over an hour, and we still hadn't heard anything from the cops. Annoyed with our slow-paced packing, Blu rushed into the apartment, fussing and barking orders.

"Wah di hell tek suh long, man?" he asked O'Neil. "It so-so ah three-bedroom, yuh acting lak it ah full house!" In the middle of his reprimanding, he caught sight of me sitting on the floor with my back turned, carefully packing Poo's records between crumpled up newspapers. "Hurry up," he finished ordering, then, walked my way. The movers left with the twin mattresses. Hearing Blu yell, I started nervously playing with my hair that was now plaited into two thick braids hanging over my shoulders. Blu stooped down near me and used a hand to tilt my face toward him. "Yuh look nice today," he said in a perverted manner, licking his lips. I saw the gun tucked into his tracksuit pants when he leaned over to kiss me on the lips. The family stopped what they were doing to watch him.

"What's up, Blu?" Sy asked, walking into the living room where we were.

Blu stood and acknowledged him with a hood handshake. "Ayee, long time, bro," he smiled, but stopped the greeting short because a page was coming through.

My heart raced. I could feel danger. It felt like a tingling sensation crawling up my spine. The assembly outside completed their seventh trip around the block and were back in front of the building. This time the horn blew long and loud, and someone yelled, "Shout! For the Lord has given you the city." The assembly cried out in a roar.

Blu looked concerned; something wasn't right about the page he received. He pulled out his cell phone and quickly walked to the front door, opening it. The men who were posted there were gone. Frustrated, Blu slammed and locked the door. At the same time, we all heard sirens. Police sirens loudly sounded over the man with the trumpet and his assembly. Blu cursed under his breath, tossing his cellphone into his pocket. He quickly strutted back into the living room, heading for the window. Cops in matching black uniforms with bulletproof vests crowded the courtyard and detained Strong and O'Neil as they were loading our boxes.

"Yo, what's going on?" Sy yelled as he stood at the window with Blu.

"Mi goin' need fi yuh to take a seat, yahso, and hush yuh mout." Blu issued, taking out that gun that I saw in his pants and waving it toward the couch. We stood in shock, no one dared to move an inch. "Now!" he reiterated as we scampered to the sofa. His cellphone rang. It must have been Jeri because he spoke quietly, but we could still hear his deep carried voice. "Five-O inna di building," Blu warned. "Dem have O'Neil and Strong...Is jus mi here...Yeh, dem man yuh put at di door run gone wen dem hear di police a come...Yeh...mi have yuh woman an har fambily inna di house, wi laying low...Yo, mi nah go a jail. Yuh haffi come down here," he issued before ending the conversation.

About three minutes later, there was a loud bang at the door, like someone kicking against it. Blu checked through the peephole, then unlocked and cracked the door open. Jeri forcefully pushed it in, stepping through backward, holding Mark Canaan by the neck with a gun held to his head. We gasped, someone screamed.

"I have hostages. You surrender," Jeri yelled into the hall. I couldn't see anyone, but there must have been cops there. He pushed Canaan back out into the hallway and, without warning, shot him in the back of the head before moving away from the closing door. Canaan never saw it coming; neither did I.

I couldn't even scream. My voice was lost in my throat. I heard rumors of Jeri killing people, and I most certainly had seen him threaten to do it, but I never witnessed it myself. I had never even heard a gun go off up close like that. What happened with Paw-Paw randomly came to mind, and I looked over at Rah. This would be a reoccurring nightmare for me. *How the hell did she keep it together all these years?* Rah looked shocked but was holding up. Jeri, on the other hand, was sweating like a mad man. He huddled in the corner with Blu, angry and anxious, mumbling on about a setup. We all knew what it was about.

When he started pacing, Rah found the courage to come out from amongst us. "Jeri, what's happening?" She attempted to rest her hand on his arm and my heart stopped beating. Jeri was homicidal. He quickly grabbed and twisted her arm before even noticing that it was her speaking to him. She whimpered as he stared straight through her, as though she was there and not there at the same time.

227

"Go sit with ya family," he coldly instructed before releasing her wrist and pacing again. He seemed confused and was mumbling something about Rah's friend Sal. Jeri couldn't figure out how his seamless plan failed. "I know Solo is a cop. I can feel it," he said, sorta talking to Blu but not really. "But he helped me, that's what doesn't make sense."

"Wah wi gwine do, Jeri?" Blu interrupted, caring less about what happened upstairs. His only concern was what they were going to do then. "Ain't no way wi walking outta here. Wi might as well give up before it too late, cop a plea," Blu stated, acting nervous. I had never seen him nervous. Between Jeri's pacing, he repeated the same request five times in a ten-minute time frame. His pestering was beginning to annoy Jeri.

"Give up? Shut up, I'm the one giving orders here," Jeri declared, pointing the gun at Blu. Blu froze as Jeri stared him squarely in the eyes then, for some reason, he looked over at me like he remembered that Blu and I betrayed him. I nervously looked away; everything was pissing him off. "We jump when I say jump," he scolded Blu.

"Yo, watch weh yuh point dat, pawdie! Sum'ady might get hurt," Blu warned, his nerves were coming back under the pressure, but he was mindful not to aim back at his superior.

"What? Hurt like this?" Jeri fired a shot into Blu's chest that took us all by surprise. Blu's limp body instantly jolted backward as the close-range bullet exploded and exited his chest, entering the wall behind him.

I felt faint. Le-Le threw up into a packed box. Other than her gagging and the echo from the blast still rumbling in my ear, the room was silent for a few seconds longer.

"Ain't no way you're walking outta here today, homie," Jeri stated, staring down at his longtime friend. He momentarily second-guessed his harsh split-second reaction and started to get down on a knee near Blu's trembling body but jumped up, wiping his brow. "Anybody else want some?" he asked, turning toward the family. We all instinctively leaned in to cover Sy. Everyone knew he was a target. Jeri laughed and pointed his gun at each of us, mimicking a gunshot. "One by one, I'ma knock you out," he threatened in a calm yet hostile tone. "Until you…" He aimed at Rah "…have no other choice but to lean on me."

"Cole!" someone with a bullhorn shouted from outside of the front door. "We're prepared to negotiate."

Jeri broadly smiled as though his situation had just changed. He walked toward the door with his eyes on us.

"It's about time!" Jeri shouted back.

"Is everyone okay, we heard a gunshot?" the negotiator asked.

"If you call dead okay, I guess we're good," Jeri laughed, looking at Blu's body laying against the wall. I wanted to mourn over him, his blood was still running warm from his corpse, but I was too scared to take my eyes off Jeri.

"Listen, I'm Officer Smith. I'm going to try my best to accommodate you. Our goal is a peaceful conclusion. Please, we don't want any more incidents. All that matters is the safety of those innocent people."

"Innocent. Ha!" Jeri glanced over our faces. "You don't know these folks like I do."

I couldn't help it. I started to cry. Rah, sitting nearest to me, tried to shush my crying by lightly patting my back. Jeri shifted his attention from the man at the door to us as we focused on him and the gun. I tried to stop crying but whimpered instead. Rah and I both saw the brief, sudden shift in Jeri's eyes. We were the closest thing he had to a family. Then again, so was Blu. For a second, his heart increased in size as it looked like he was considering what he was doing. Observing the split-second change in his demeanor, Rah took advantage, and against our pleading, she slowly got up from the couch again. Jeri gestured with his gun for her to sit down.

"Please, Jeri. Whatever it is, it's nothing that can't be worked out," Rah softly reassured, continuing to walk toward him with her arms open in a warm welcoming manner. Jeri allowed her to move closer. He gawked at her like something was different; maybe he noticed her new cut. He lowered his gun as she approached. Her aura wasn't sensual; it was peaceful. He palmed her bruised face, and Rah enclosed his hand between her cheek and shoulder. His eyes began to swell with tears, and my heart broke. It shouldn't have, but it did. I could feel Rah's agony and dilemma. "Baby, what's happening with you?" she asked, taking his hand in hers. Jeri instantly choked up. After all of that bullying he did the other day, he broke under pressure. He kissed Rah's hand and held it at his mouth, sobbing over it.

"So, do you want a helicopter or not?" Officer Smith interrupted, waiting on Jeri to finish his list of requests.

Jeri quickly wiped his eyes, sucking in his tears. He cleared his throat and redirected his attention. "Yeah. I want a chopper to LaGuardia for me…and my girl," he requested as though spontaneously deciding. We gasped, Sy lowered his head and bit his lip. It was getting harder for him to sit still. Le-Le held his hand firmly and kept whispering into his ear. "Then, a private jet," Jeri continued. "Destination…will be disclosed later. And a million dollars in small unmarked bills." He intently stared into Rah's eyes. I think he knew that he was playing the game of negotiations. This was about as far as it was going to get.

"Okay, and what about the other hostages?" Smith continued. Jeri glanced over at us and then back at Rah. He leaned in to kiss her. She looked frightened. "They're yours." He kissed her despite Poo's grunts. She didn't see nor did she care about any games of negotiations.

Poo abruptly declared, "Oh, hells no! Over my dead body." She stood, preparing to march over, but Pops grabbed her arm and yanked her down with a force that caught her off guard.

"Sit down," he demanded, glaring directly into her eyes. "You'll only make our situation worse."

"Let go of me, James," Poo muttered through curled lips.

"Yeah. I suggest you handle ya woman, Pops," Jeri stated, moving from the door. Poo was acting unruly, and he was already feeling trigger happy. Rah jumped in front of him, knowing he's easily irritated.

Poo gripped the bridge of her nose and breathed out a woosah. "You know, Jeri…just because your life is jacked up doesn't give you the right to drag ours through it." She was tired of quietly sitting by. It wasn't her style.

Oh, dear Lord, I prayed.

"Shut up, Poo," Sy grunted. We all knew once Poo got started, there was no stopping her.

Jeri burst into maniacal laughter. "You just can't leave well enough alone, can you?" he directed toward Poo, waving his gun in the air.

"You ain't taking my child," Poo issued, pointing her erect finger and rolling her neck in attitude. "You chose your lifestyle; Rah didn't. If you REALLY love her, you'd let her go!" She folded her arms. "You know you going to jail, right? YOUR major drug deal JUST got busted, and that's not OUR problem." A unified heave of paralyzed fear could be heard over Poo's sudden silence. As soon as she said it, she knew she went too far, and it read on her face. "And it's not Rah's fault…it's yours." she mumbled, turning her head.

Jeri froze in place, recycling the information. I could hear Pops cursing under his breath, and my heart stopped again. I just knew that Jeri was going to start bustin' caps. He turned to look at Rah, trying to put the puzzle pieces together. *She's guilty*, read on his face. Rah was flushed. She doesn't have a poker face.

"Damn it," he finally mumbled. What little heart of his we saw instantly broke, and his maniacal laughter turned into sobbing. "Noo, Rah!" he yelled in a singing tone of voice as he danced around the room in anger and hurt pride, swinging the gun. Suddenly, he grabbed Rah and pulled her into a hug. We gasped again, praying in our minds. I know I was. "Why would you do this to us? You know I can't do jail," Jeri yelled.

"I…I didn't do anything," Rah attempted to convince him, but I could tell that she was aware that the jig was up.

"Shut up," Jeri shouted, spinning her around to face us. With one arm wrapped around her neck, he placed the muzzle of the gun on her temple. Smelling death in the air, we all stood. "Why, Rah? Why?" There was nothing she could say that could undo what was already said. Jeri released a breath of despair. "I love you," he stated as though a confession and then planted a sloppy kiss on Rah's forehead. "If this is it…it's gonna be you and me forever. Bonnie and Clyde style," he concluded, drawing her nearer as though trying to consume her. His hand, gripping the gun pressed against her temple, trembled.

Click. Jeri cocked the pistol, ignoring our pleas for him to stop. Poo fell to her knees, begging.

Then a tiny voice uttered, "Hi, Jeri," taking everyone by surprise. Cookie walked into the living room, humming a tune and rubbing her eyes like nothing was happening. She wrapped her arms around Jeri's waist from behind. His body physically went limp. Crying isn't Jeri's thing, but it seemed he couldn't stop.

"Move, Cutie Pie," he softly urged, nudging her away from him. We all forgot about the girls napping.

"Come here, Cookie," Poo calmly requested as not to startle her.

Cookie ignored our gestures for her to come over, and instead, she started softly singing into Jeri's situation. Every word she sang spoke directly to him, and involuntarily he crumbled over the beginning verses of "*Heal the World.*"

"Did you bring me cake?" Cookie asked, retreating from their hug. Jeri didn't answer, she annihilated him.

At that very moment, the atmosphere shifted, just like it did when he first walked into my life. I could see something coming and grabbed my heart. I looked into Jeri's once cold dark eyes as they took on a submissive stance. He was in another place. A place where I've thought of visiting but was too afraid to go. The place where life here on earth doesn't matter and your only desire is to be there where there's no tears or sorrows—like in the song that Cookie sung that bulldozed his heart. Jeri's eyes, frozen upon Rah, lost their intensity. The long and bitter war between good and evil that usually played on his face was gone. Rah closed her eyes. She saw it too.

BANG! The gun fired, and I held my breath as everything around me moved in slow motion.

Sy broke away from Le-Le and Pop's grip. He screamed like I've never heard a man scream before, as Rah and Jeri's bodies fell into Cookie's outstretched arms. Cookie attempted to carry their weight, but the pressure forced her to release them. Rah fell over on top of Jeri and laid there motionless as a massive puddle of blood swiftly ran from under them. We froze.

Making the first move, Cookie kneeled over them, maybe not as oblivious as we all thought she was. She closed Jeri's eyes, and the rest of us slowly migrated toward them. Rah's eyes were open too. They dotted around the room, but she said nothing. The room was still and sad. Scared and tense. Consumed and empty.

At Cookie's touch, Rah slowly turned her head. "Am I dead?" she loudly asked, like she was unable to hear herself speaking. She frantically frisked her body, and I started to breathe again. Cookie shook her head no. Rah closed her eyes and sighed in relief then quickly opened them as though she forgot something. She must have thought of Jeri. I did. I touched his warm, still, hand as the tears brimming my eyes flooded over.

232

You can't love someone as long as I did and turn it off just like that. Breathing heavily, Rah sat up and nervously turned to look at him too.

The front door crashed in as Sal, along with the cops, and paramedics rushed into the apartment.

Rah piercingly cried, "Jeri. Jeri!"

Unplowed Ground

Somewhere stuck right in between feelings of sanity and insanity, is a place of normalcy called home. I knew that I was welcomed, and I no longer felt that I didn't deserve to be there. Zee accepted me, not in a manner which we kissed and made up, but in a way that made me feel like I belonged. He made me take responsibility for my wrongdoings. Love isn't how Poo described; then again, I guess it's different for everyone. Poo said that love is two people acting stupid together; for many, that might be true. But I was the "stupid" party. Zee says that *love is patient, love is kind. It does not envy, it does not boast, it is not proud. It does not dishonor others, it is not self-seeking, it is not easily angered, it keeps no record of wrongs. Love does not delight in evil but rejoices with the truth. It always protects, always trusts, always hopes, always perseveres. Love never fails.* I failed at love, and it was my time to make amends.

I would like to say that after the ordeal with Jeri, there was no more drama, and things were perfect between Zee and me. I would like to say that we picked up where we left off, but not this time. Zee welcomed me back under terms and conditions. I was appreciative and humbled. I wanted to continue being as honest with him as I possibly could. This meant airing all my fears, including my doubts about him being Lorah's father. "She mine," was all he had to say about that, in a very calm and factual manner. She could be his, at least I hope so, but I'm not one hundred percent sure. I do know that they are completely in love with each other, and somehow, she looks like him. They're the same person only in different wrappers.

Whatever I admitted to Zee didn't take him by surprise. He deeply inhaled as though soaking it all in then slowly exhaled, letting it all out, saying, "No matter what you tell me, this is what the Lord says, 'Go, show your love to your wife again, though she is an adulteress.' Then, he told me, "Let's start over on a trial basis." We both agreed that there should also be a period of abstinence and testing, mostly on my part. I wasn't to be intimate with Zee or any man, and he would do the same toward me until we both felt that we could come back together as husband and wife in the marriage bed. I agreed because it was time for me to *sow for myself righteousness.* I needed to *break up the unplowed ground* that I never took the time to work. I was too busy shipwrecking my life to notice the beauty that it possessed. It was time for me to seek the Lord, to acknowledge him lurking in the background. "*Your sins have been your downfall,* Solo," Zee proclaimed. "And you need to change for yourself, not for me." Turns out, I had to get lost to be found.

I started acknowledging the Lord first by thanking him for all the many things that he had done, even in my absence from Him. I dove further into gratitude and acknowledged and apologized to those whom He sent to keep me. Besides Zee, Jem was the first person on my list. What woman do you know would raise your children and never look down on you, other than a mother? Jemimah Felix raised mine, and I apologized for my behavior over the years. I didn't want her to leave, but we all knew she had to go for me to become a real mother to the kids. It was hard because her spirit was etched into the essence of the apartment, making it a home. Jez cried every day, all day, for at least a month. He wanted nothing to do with me. To make matters worse, Zee moved Lorah from Jez's room to her own. We even painted and decorated their rooms to their liking. Still, Jez wouldn't sleep at night, nor would he eat properly. I'll admit, my cooking wasn't the best at the time, especially since Jem fed them Trinidadian home-cooked meals every night. My go-to was fast foods like nuggets, burgers, winglets, fries...oh, and spaghetti. I can make a mean pot of spaghetti. Jez wasn't trying to hear that, though. He and I both longed for Jem, but I agreed with Zee that it was best to go cold turkey. Jem suffered too. She had fallen in love with our children. We started talking regularly, helping each other manage through the rough time, and subsequently, we became the best of friends.

Jez finally broke. It took a meltdown, on my part, and a *Barney: In Concert* tape that Pops gave the kids to finally break the ice. I was feeling strange that morning like I was coming down with something. Jez's crying was testing my patience, and honestly, many days, I felt like walking out the door. He cried, and he cried, and he made Lorah cry too. That morning, hoping to possibly get a moment and a cup of coffee, I put the VHS tape in. As soon as the *Barney* theme song came on, all eyes and ears were on him. Jez whined at first, insisting on being intolerable. Lorah walked over to him and gave him her bo-bo; she wanted some peace and quiet too. Then, the unimaginable happened, Jez got up from the floor, walked over to me, and crawled up onto my lap. Lorah, never wanting to be left out, joined him. We all watched *Barney*, laughing, clapping, singing, dancing, and crying—well, I cried because I was so happy. We watched the entire show three times in a row, and learned every song from, "*You Are Special*" to "*John Jacob Jingleheimer Schmidt.*" I became their mommy that day. I wish I could say that was it. That we instantly became a family, but from that moment on, I grew sicker and sicker until Zee asked, "Do you know who the father is?" I hadn't seen my period in two months.

It was Lorah's first birthday. We planned a big party because I missed Jez turning one. When Zee asked me that question, I ran into the bathroom to throw up. We both knew that I was pregnant. God couldn't let me off the hook that easily. I took a pregnancy test before the party, and it came back positive. It was Jeri's baby. This is where the real test began, mine, Zee's, and Jeri's. Oh, did I mention? He was still alive.

That unforgettable day when Jeri shot himself, the bullet entered his chest, puncturing his lung but missing all other major arteries. The paramedics quickly placed an endotracheal tube into his lungs to help with breathing. They started an IV and immediately transported him to the hospital. Jeri was then seen by a trauma surgeon to repair the damaged lung and whatever else was injured. He endured several other complications and was left permanently disabled. We all expected him to die, and from what I heard, mentally, he wasn't willing to heal either. The state had him on suicide watch. Rah mentioned that he was extremely claustrophobic and preferred death over jail. No matter what, God wasn't done with us yet. Jeri stayed in ICU for nearly a month before being transferred over to the Prison Ward in Bellevue Hospital, where he was a prisoner of the state with around the clock protection. None of us were allowed to visit because of our connection with his case. Rah wasn't even permitted to leave the state. Jeri's only visitors were his lawyer and the older man that he used to play cards with when visiting Pelham Parkway Nursing Home. That man was Jeri's real father and the keeper of all his assets, William Jeremy Daughtrey.

Zee and I kept our distance during Lorah's party. We put on fake smiles and uncomfortably avoided each other's stares. I was sure he had enough. It was bad enough that because of me, he lost his position as co-pastor at the family church in Brooklyn. They said that his home life didn't meet the standards of his walk with God. We were asked to move from the front pew elsewhere in the church. I was the harlot whose family's connection with Jeremy Cole was all over the news. Parading my marriage to Zee was considered a disgrace to the church and congregation. But I had personal amends to make with the Lord. Despite their dirty looks, I went to church every Saturday with my family and bible study on Wednesdays. This time, I went with a purpose. Zee showed me a bible verse that changed my perspective and gave me hope to change. The apostle said, *"Nothing good lives in me, that is, in my sinful nature. I want to do what is right, but I can't. I want to do what is good, but I don't. I don't want to do what is wrong, but I do it anyway. But if I do what I don't want to do, I am not really the one doing wrong; it is sin living in me that does it...Oh, what a miserable person I am! Who will free me from this life that is dominated by sin and death? Thank God! The answer is in Jesus Christ, our Lord."*

I can't explain it, but that passage summed it up for me. Hearing that even an apostle battled with his nature somehow made me feel less abnormal. As Zee explained, "Sin lives in everyone. We were born into sin. If you want to kill what's nagging you, Solo, you need to stop minimizing your wrongdoings—and hate them! Stop feeding it—starve it. Focus on centering all of your energy on pursuing a relationship with God other than the streets."

I can proudly say that in all that I went through during that time, I kept my faith.

Zee and I stayed together throughout the entire pregnancy. I knew he

237

wasn't happy that I was pregnant from another man, especially one whom he grew fond of, neither was I. We slept in separate rooms. I started out on the sofa bed, but as my stomach grew, Zee moved to the sofa and gave me the bed. Which eventually turned into us sleeping in one bed. I can't express how much I love him. He continually denies himself for others and without anger or bitterness. Zee kissed me every morning, and every night before bed, telling me that he loved me. He asked me how I was doing and even attended my prenatal appointments. It was all a struggle for him, but Zee never showed it; he was a perfect gentleman. "You are positively glowing, Mrs. Felix," he would say. We talked a lot and we even dated. I was determined to stay committed to him and not leave like in the past.

I went through the full pregnancy without bed rest or premature delivery. Rah entertained me for the first few months before she was free to move on with her life and love. She and Sal reunited in New Orleans. They quickly married and became pregnant right away. In my later months, when caring for toddlers got out of my hands, Poo helped. Our strained relationship healed as she became more of a mother to me than she'd ever been. We still got on each other's nerves, but I gave her the respect that she earned and deserved. Poo was still sober and drug-free for over two years. She, Pops, and Cookie moved into the five-bedroom Victorian in Yonkers that Le-Le and Sy bought. Sy pastored his own church on Charlotte Street, and Le-Le's small shop on Fordham Road grew into an empire; her brand, Purple Palace, is now the *Danskin* to divas. She dresses showgirls nationally and ministers to the lost amongst them.

Against the doctor's belief, Jeri was still living. His lawyer pulled some strings and got Zee and me into the North Infirmary Command of Rikers Island to see him. Jeri had a trach tube down his throat, so we communicated using a notepad along with his father's help. Ashamed, he embraced and cried over Zee like he was a lost puppy when he saw him. Zee, always sensitive to the feelings of others, returned his emotions. Jeri reached for my hand and smiled. He was proud to see Zee and me back together. I nervously walked over, trying not to cry, but that was hard to do. I was seven months pregnant and very emotional. Jeri took my hand into his and rubbed my stomach with his other hand, boyishly smiling as if to say, *Dang! Y'all didn't waste no time.*

His father, William, who sat near him meticulously caring for his needs, interpreted his emotions, "He's glad to see you both." Jeri nodded in agreement. "He's told me nothing but good things about you all...we see you fixin' to have a baby soon, huh?" Jeri nodded again, looking anxious to hear more. I was nervous. Zee felt that Jeri should know that he fathered a child. I wanted to write to him, but of course, Zee thought it best to tell him in person. I didn't know how Jeri was going to take it, but I knew that Zee was by my side. "Children are always a blessing," William affirmed, looking at Jeri with wet eyes and making it easier for me to confess. Undoubtedly, he and Jeri had a complicated relationship. William was in jail for murder most of his life. When he was released, he went straight into a nursing home where he and Jeri picked up their relationship.

"Yeah, well, that's why I'm here," I said, squeezing Jeri's hand. I didn't know how else to say it but to say it. I looked over at Zee for encouragement, and he nodded his head in support. I looked down at Jeri—my dark chocolate addiction was now a disabled prisoner. I cleared my throat. "Jeri, this is your baby," I admitted, choking up in more tears. It seemed they never stopped.

I could see the shock in Jeri's wide eyes and expression. He instantly looked over at Zee, humiliated. Zee nodded again, this time letting Jeri know that it was okay. To break the tension, he jokingly said, "Yuh lucky yuh in dat bed, cuz meh would have put yuh der, dred."

More tears ran down Jeri's face. Trembling, he reached for his pad to write, but he was roused and began coughing. William jumped up to soothe him. I stepped back, but Jeri reached out for me. He rested his jittering hands on my belly and closed his eyes, attempting to soothe himself.

"That's it, boy! You can do it." William sternly attested, pouring him a glass of water.

Jeri opened his eyes and tried to speak. His speech was limited and his voice different. "My baby?" I understood between the mumbling and stuttering.

"We can have a DNA test done if you like...but it's yours. I—" He stopped me, waving his hand and sort of chuckled as he looked over at his father glassy-eyed.

"Shoot!" William exclaimed, giving Jeri water. "This is the best news we've heard in months! Right, son?" Jeri nodded, trying to laugh.

I openly sighed in relief, taking Zee's hand.

"Here, here, take my seat, sweetheart." William offered. "When you due?"

"September fifth." I took a seat and watched as Zee and Jeri communicated with each other like blood brothers, touching hands and faces. I almost tore apart their friendship.

Zee's primary purpose from the beginning with Jeri was to reach him for Christ. I don't know if he accomplished that, but before our visiting time was over, with every eye closed and heads bowed, Zee led us in prayer. I always peek during prayer. Apparently, Jeri did too. We unashamedly gazed into each other's eyes caught up somewhere between the room and our past. Surprisingly, he mouthed, *I love you.* I reached for my chest and patted my heart, trying to soothe myself from having an outburst. *I love you too,* I mouthed back as the tears escaped. We had a connection, and forever we would carry love in our hearts for each other.

Jeri and I met for the first time on Labor Day 1988, and I gave birth to his son on September 4, 1995, in Bellevue Hospital, also on Labor Day that year. Of course, Zee was with me during the delivery, and he was just as strong, patient, and kind as usual. When the baby came, Zee cheered and cried as he had done with Jez and Lorah. He cradled him, claiming him as his own son and handed out blue cigars to all the men in the maternity ward.

Before leaving the hospital, we sent a Polaroid picture of the baby's face into Jeri's room by William. By this time, Jeri was in critical condition and back in ICU. Poppa Will, as he later became, told us that Jeri acknowledged the picture with tears. He died later that night, and Liam, short for William, Jeri's dad's name and my maiden name, Cole Felix, was our remembrance of him. He was a chubby, chocolate, handsome baby with deep dimples, curly jet-black hair, and deep chestnut shaped eyes. Definitely a heartbreaker.

After a month of healing, I returned to the church, along with baby Liam. Unfortunately, the church family hadn't changed. That day, the pastor preached a message geared directly toward Zee. He boldly and publicly professed that Zee's walk with the Lord was sinful because the Lord was punishing him like Job. He went on to say, "You *see, God will not reject a blameless person nor take the hand of evildoers."* Zee was the most faithful and loyal person I knew. I shifted in my seat, watching Zee's cheeks tighten with embarrassment and anger. I wanted to revert into street Go-Go and run up on the pastor and smack him across the head. Instead, I exhaled and asked God for forgiveness. He was a man of the cloth. Ten minutes into the appalling sermon, he turned his direction toward me. "The promiscuous woman that trapped the naive man of God into her web," he said. With that, Zee stood up in the aisle. He straightened his suit and cleared his throat before taking Lorah into his arms and extending me his hand to leave. Amidst the silence of the room, I quickly gathered our things into the baby's diaper bag and handed it to Zee. I cradled Liam in one arm, whispered to Jez to get up, and took my husband's hand. We proudly walked out as a family, and the pastor went on to preach with even more conviction. So much so, that Zee and I had to stop and turn around. To our surprise, Anna, Barry, Jem, Cousin Shelton, and Tanty Bev were all walking out with us. I tell you my heart melted. Barry ushered for us to continue walking as Anna smiled and winked toward me, taking up Jez, who was bidding everyone in the aisle seats goodbye.

Zee now co-pastors under Sy in his church on Charlotte Street, where we all grew up together. They have the community on fire for Christ, especially the youth. We christened all three of our children there. Zee waited because he wanted me to be a part of it. Mother and father together. My best friends stood as their godparents, Tim and Jem. I would tell you about the sparks between those two, but I don't want to jinx it.

Life is funny. We think we are doing something, but God has bigger plans. What scares you one day makes you laugh another. My life has its ups and downs, yet I can proudly say that now my ups and downs are with Hosea Felix. I'm not perfect, I still make mistakes, but I haven't given up on my family nor my walk with God.

I finally completed cosmetology school, and I now operate a day spa featuring Rah's famous beauty line, simply named Lotti, after Big Mama. Jeri did have intentions to leave Rah, as Canaan suggested, but he didn't want to leave her high and dry. Along with the apartment he rented downtown for her and the family, he also secured us a salon. Jeri knew about Rah's beauty products and my notion to do hair. He believed in us even when we didn't, he just had a lousy way of showing it. I guess that's the life of a gangster. They wear their hearts on the sole of their shoes and are always on the run. Sometimes we lose our way. But in the wise words of Poppa Will, "You can't understand where you're going if you don't understand where you've been."

As for me...my name is Gomer...and I am fearfully and wonderfully made.

Epilogue

The Biblical Story of Gomer

No one wants to claim Gomer. She led a messy life. The truth is, she was an ordinary woman just like you and me. She was a mother, wife, sister, friend, and daughter...who also happened to be a prostitute. Life isn't always pretty, especially when you're considered to be from the wrong side of the tracks. Your character, and judgment thereof, become a reflection of that life. From my perspective of Gomer, you'll find a young woman plagued by emotional trauma, generational curses, bad influences, and neglect. Gomer was unruly, disrespectful, immoral and at times—downright nasty. She was convinced that she didn't deserve happiness and was determined to follow the slippery slope of discontentment. Love was an interruption, a thorn in her side, an experience that sideswiped Gomer into caring about herself and the impact she made on others. In the existence of Gomer, we discover the intricate world of a soul lost and then found; and in it, an illustration of God's love for mankind.

The story of Hosea and Gomer is not your typical love story. It's not told with all the bells and whistles of a fairytale romance; rather, this story can be discerned as either a marriage gone completely wrong or a true love that endures over time. If you enjoy a good love story, this one is the real deal. God uses the relationship between Hosea and Gomer as a metaphorical picture of Himself loving mankind despite our sinful ways.

The prophet Hosea was called by God to speak on His behalf to the people of Israel during a period of great spiritual and moral misconduct. The people of Israel were readily adopting the ways of the neighboring lands and worshiping pagan gods instead of the God of their forefathers. Hosea, often referred to as the prophet of doom, paid a high price for understanding God's heart.

When the Lord began to speak through Hosea, he said to him, "**Go, take to yourself an adulterous wife, and children of unfaithfulness…**" because the land, in which they lived, was *guilty of the vilest adultery in departing from the Lord*. So, Hosea obeyed God's instruction and married Gomer.

Gomer was a promiscuous woman, a harlot, a whore. She married the prophet Hosea and *conceived and bore him a son* named Jezreel, meaning *God sows*. This name may have been given to Jezreel to signify the replanting of Israel back on its soil. The Bible only refers to Jezreel as being conceived by Hosea, but Gomer conceived again and gave birth to a daughter named Lo-Ruhamah, meaning *the unpitied one*. After she had weaned Lo-Ruhamah, Gomer had another son named Lo-Ammi, meaning *not my people*, to mark God's rejection of Israel because of their unfaithfulness. Since Gomer was unfaithful herself, it is possible that Lo-Ruhamah, and perhaps her brother, Lo-Ammi, were illegitimate children.

We can only imagine the drama that the prophet Hosea sustained, but he remained faithful to God throughout his suffering. Hosea, so eloquently, compares the actions of Israel to those of his loose wife. Like the Israelites, Gomer went after her lovers, those who gave her beautiful clothing, jewels, and sumptuous food and drink for her favors. There was no *faithfulness, no love, no acknowledgment of God in the land*. There was only *cursing, lying and murder, stealing, and adultery*. The Israelites, just like Gomer, had forgotten who gave them their past blessings. Gomer would soon sell herself into slavery...possibly as a temple prostitute.

It is hard to conceive that Hosea would even want to take Gomer back after she ran from him and their children, but throughout his dilemma, the people were watching. Hosea's task was to show them God's heart. *The prophet was considered a fool— the inspired man a maniac.* The people's spirit of prostitution led them astray, but Hosea does as the Lord instructs and repurchases Gomer at a bounty of thirty pieces of silver.

The Lord said to Hosea, **"Go, show your love to your wife again, though she is loved by another and is an adulteress. Love her as the Lord loves the Israelites, though they turn to other gods."**

Hosea bought Gomer back with fifteen shekels of silver and about a homer and a lethek of barley. Since Hosea paid half of the asking price in silver and the other half in grain, it can be determined that he did not have enough silver to pay for his wife. Here we learn that love is rarely free; it comes at a price. Remember the cross? And let's not overlook that Hosea paid for Gomer what Judas was paid to betray Christ.

Hosea took back his wife. He possibly held her tightly while lovingly gazing into her desolate eyes and proclaimed, "Thou shalt abide for me many days; thou shalt not play the harlot, and thou shalt not be for *another* man: so *will* I also *be* for thee." Through slavery, Gomer undoubtedly learned how good life was with Hosea. Through Gomer, we too can learn that no matter how low we get, God's love never ceases, and in Him, there's always a home.

Today, we have the same corruptible spirit toward unfaithfulness. Anytime we turn to culture for gratification or comfort, instead of turning to God, we exhibit that same dangerous spirit of waywardness. Many who read the story of Hosea and Gomer, want to hate Gomer, but the truth is we can't do that without hating ourselves as well. Sin resides in all of us. God purchased us out of slavery through the precious blood of His son Jesus Christ, and he who believes with his heart, and confesses with his mouth that Jesus Christ is Lord, shall be saved.

Gomer wasn't what you would consider a perfect woman. She was flawed in many ways, but like the lost sheep, the good shepherd found her worthy enough to leave ninety-nine others in search of one. He found her worthy enough to place on his shoulders and rejoice. *I tell you that in the same way there will be more rejoicing in heaven over one sinner who repents than over ninety-nine righteous persons who do not need to repent.*

Character Glossary

Gomer	Wife of the prophet Hosea, referred to her as a "promiscuous woman."	**Book of Hosea**
Hosea	Married to Gomer. Son of Beeri, 8th-century BC prophet in Israel. He authored the book of Hosea. One of twelve prophets in the Jewish Hebrew Bible. Known as a Minor Prophet in the Christian Old Testament. The name Hosea means, salvation, he who saves. Hosea's wife was Gomer and their children were Jezreel, Lo-Ruhamah and Lo-Ammi. Hosea was also called, "'The Prophet Of Doom'."	**Hosea**
Timothy	Timothy was from the city of Lystra in Asia Minor. Born of a Jewish mother, who had become a Christian, and a Greek father. He became Paul's companion and co-worker in ministry along with Silas.	**1st & 2nd Timothy, Acts, Thessalonians, Hebrews, and Philippians**

Rahab	A harlot in Jericho. Believed in the Lord. Hid the Hebrew spies and was saved when the walls of Jericho came tumbling down. Great-great-grandmother of King David.	**Joshua, Matthew, Hebrews, James**
Puah	One of two midwives who attended the births of the Hebrew women. They were ordered by Pharaoh to kill the baby boys but let the girls live.	**Exodus 1**
Silas	Leading member of the early Christian church. Accompanied the Apostle Paul on his missionary journeys.	**Acts, Thessalonians, 2nd Corinthians, 1st Peter**
Paul	An Apostle. First mentioned in Acts as Saul. Penned Author of thirteen of the Epistles.	**Acts, Thessalonians, Titus, Galatians, Romans, Corinthians, Philippians, Philemon, Timothy and, Colossians**
Joshua	Succeeded Moses as leader of the Israelites.	**Joshua, Exodus, Numbers, Acts, Hebrews, Deuteronomy**
Jeremiah	The oldest of Jobs' three beautiful daughters was given to him in the later part of his life, after God made Job prosperous again.	**Job**

Lydia	First documented convert to Christianity in Europe. A seller of purple.	**Acts**
Mary Magdalene	Traveled with Jesus as one of his followers.	**Gospel of Matthew, Mark, Luke, and John**
Salmon	Married to Rahab. Father of Boaz. Great-great-grandfather of King David.	**1 Chronicles, Ruth, Matthew, and Luke**

THE END

God, help your children...those silently crying out to you and those screaming with rage. Like Rahab and Gomer.

Dear Reader,

Thank you for reading, They Call Me Gomer. I would greatly appreciate it if you would share this book and review it on Amazon. In return for your kindness, please subscribe to my website www.authorjcmiller.com and receive a free PDF version of my favorite cake recipes, from the motivational cookbook, Finding God in The Kitchen: Christ and Cake. Thank you for your continued support.

— JC Miller

The following sample passage is another eagerly anticipated spin-off of JC Miller's the I AM RAHAB: A NOVEL series, Introducing—MARY MAGDALENE. Coming soon. Enjoy.

Chapter 1

"Mrs. Owens! Mrs. Owens, it's time for your medicine." A portly, age-spotted, nurse, announced in a deep dry nasal tone, hovering over Mags while forcefully shaking her from slumber. Without care, nor courtesy, she yanked the bedding aside from Mags' thin, poorly-dressed body.

Although it was the early nineties, the staff at that particular psychiatric wade didn't show any empathy toward insane black women. An inmate doped with expensive drugs was a free ride for the state.

Irritated and still dazed from the previous day's medication, Mags slowly opened her eyes, attempting to focus. In her disorientation, there appeared to be three blurry nurses. The long needles they each held in their hands caused Mags to shake her head so violently it cleared her vision. "**Mags...focus**," the reasonable voice inside her cluttered mind related, as the other sinister thoughts chanted, "Die!" She wanted to respond, but her mouth, dry and twisted with chapped lips, didn't cooperate with her thoughts. Her speech, limited and slurred, sounded like that of a babbling fool. Wanting to hold the nurse back, Mags flinched and realized her arms were harnessed to the bed. Feeling exasperated, she quickly studied her situation then focused on the nurse who was tapping the syringe.

"No," Mags managed to mumble. "Tink, tink, tink, tink," she continued, trying to encourage herself to come up with a plan.

"Come on now, Mrs. Owens. Let's not fight today." The nurse suggested but still ushered over two male orderlies. "Doctor's orders, don't ya know," she added, in an intolerable Irish accent, preparing an entry for the needle.

Mags violently thrust her body up and down on the thin mattress where she laid and back and forth against the cold metal bed railings, causing the harness to grow tighter across her chest. She shook her head in disagreement while kicking the bedding to the floor. "Tink, tink, tink," she continued to mutter until thinking wasn't an option. In her white tent-sized uniform, the heavyset nurse appeared to quadruple in number as she laughed and documented her victory.

"Now, don't you feel better?" She asked, observing Mags' dilated pupils, with her face hanging inches between Mags' own.

"Uglass, bitch," Mags managed to slur with the utmost contempt expressed upon her drawn face before closing her eyes. The cold medication that rushed through her veins took its effect.

Appalled, the nurse huffed and collected her troop of orderlies and stormed away.

"Ain't nut'n good ever gon' come by ya. You too much lak ya diddy—no good fuh sho' and damn right good fuh nothing," Mags heard her grandmother say as she drifted off. The same lies that she used to speak over her, holding her spirit hostage from the very beginning.